The Horse from the Sea

VICTORIA HOLMES

The Horse from the Sea

AN EPIC
HORSE STORY

HARPERCOLLINS*PUBLISHERS*

Library of Congress Cataloging-in-Publication Data
Holmes, Victoria.
    The horse from the sea : an epic horse story / by Victoria
Holmes.— 1st ed.
        p.   cm.
    Summary: In 1588 in western Ireland, fourteen-year-old Nora
risks her own life to rescue a boy and a stallion from a Spanish
vessel shipwrecked on the beach.
    ISBN 0-06-052028-0 — ISBN 0-06-052029-9 (lib. bdg.)
    [1. Horses—Fiction. 2. Ireland—History—1558-1603—
Fiction.] I. Title.
PZ7.H7377Ho 2005   2004016977
[Fic]—dc22

Typography by Henrietta Stern
1 2 3 4 5 6 7 8 9 10
❖
First Edition

FOR JOE—ALWAYS,

IF NOT MOST

ACKNOWLEDGMENTS

I WAS HELPED IN my research by the following people, who have been infinitely generous with their time and knowledge. Any historical inaccuracies are entirely my own.

Joseph and Norah McNicholas, Enfield, County Meath; Joe Boyce, Aughnanure Castle, County Galway; Professor Katharine Simms, University of Galway; Carmel Geoghan, Railway Lodge, Oughterard, County Galway; the staff of the Lower Radcliffe Camera at the Bodleian Library, Oxford; the staff at Errislannan Riding Stables, who helped me find where Nora lived; and Matt Haslum, who told me about the myth of Manannan mac Lir and the Spanish word for "oranges."

I have borrowed the names of Murray ne Doe O'Flaherty and Sir Richard Bingham from genuine historical figures, but their personalities and all the other characters in this book are fictitious. Any similarity to any persons alive or dead is entirely coincidental. Errislannan, Sraith Salach, and the spectacular tower house of Aughnanure are all real places in Connemara. I have also mentioned the Lynches, for many years the most powerful family in the city of Galway. During this time they banned members of the O'Flaherty clan from entering the town walls, as a protest against their raids on other clans in the surrounding countryside; popular myth claims there was a sign above the city gate that read, "From the ferocious O'Flahertys, may the good Lord protect us."

According to tradition, the modern Connemara pony is descended from Andalusian stallions that swam ashore from the shipwrecked Spanish Armada in 1588.

1

IAR-CONNACHT
(MODERN-DAY COUNTY GALWAY),
WESTERN IRELAND, 1588

"ARE YOU NOT COMING to dance, Honora Donovan?"

The voice came out of the shadows, making Nora jump and clutch her long woolen brat more closely around her shoulders. "Who's there?" she called, narrowing her eyes to peer past the rumps of the ponies in the byre. As she spoke, the sound of music—a high-pitched fiddle over the steady hollow beat of the bodhran—struck up in the great hall on the other side of the courtyard, filtering through Aughnanure Castle's thick stone walls and the quiet twilight. The pony beside Nora shifted uneasily, her ears flicking at the unfamiliar noise, and Nora rested one hand on the pony's warm damp shoulder to calm her.

"Easy, Ballach," she soothed. The mare's name meant "freckled," a fair description of the dark gray flecks that spotted her almost white coat. Ballach tossed her head and rubbed her nose against the sleeve of Nora's dress, streaking it with a trail of foam. Nora pulled her arm away, and the man by the doorway laughed.

"Is that you, Con Foyle?" she demanded, recognizing the tall, long-limbed figure when he shifted briefly into the gray light seeping through the open door. There were no torches in the byre, though, later on, a burning branch or two might be spared so that the chieftain's guests could safely retrieve their animals for the journey home. "What are you doing, hiding there fit to scare the wits out of the horses?"

"I'm waiting for you, of course." Con Foyle stepped forward, ducking his head to avoid the low wooden beam that stretched across the roof. Nora's older brother Sean was married to Con's sister, Rua. Their families lived side by side on the Errislannan Peninsula, two days' ride from Aughnanure. Since his sixteenth birthday a year ago, Con had joined the rank of soldier known as a kern in the private army of Murray ne Doe O'Flaherty, the lord of Aughnanure Castle. For tonight's feast Con proudly carried a short iron sword, but Nora knew he was just as likely to wield a stout wooden cattle prod; he and the other kerns tended their chieftain's huge and much-envied herds when they weren't defending the tower house from quarrelsome neighbors or English soldiers.

He held out his hand. "Come on, you've had long enough to

settle your mare. I saw Sean and Rua go into the hall ages ago."

Nora hesitated, twisting her hands into the edge of her cloak. Ballach blew warm breath onto her back and for a moment she wished she could stay here in the quiet, steamy byre. "I should just make sure that Ballach has enough hay," she hedged.

Con gestured impatiently to the corner of the byre. "There's a whole field of hay there," he said. "Are you sure you don't have hooves instead of feet, Nora? If you stay here any longer, you'll miss the feast altogether."

Nora shrugged. She was well used to being teased for preferring the company of horses to people—if not gentle Ballach, then the wild ponies that lived in the mountains between here and her home in Errislannan.

The musicians in the great hall paused briefly before launching into another tune, one that she recognized as a swirling, energetic reel. This was only the second time she had been to a feast at Aughnanure, but there were plenty of people in Errislannan who played the fiddle and bodhran, and however much she might shy away from noisy company, Nora loved dancing and singing as much as any of her neighbors. The reel was clearly popular with the rest of the O'Flaherty clan because the noise of feet grew louder, pounding against the rush-strewn floor.

Con grabbed Nora's hand. "Quick," he said. "We're missing

the best of Padraig's playing," and he led her at a run out of the byre and across the courtyard. His long legs carried him easily over the rutted ground, already sticky from the early autumn rains.

Nora was a whole head shorter than Con and hampered by the woolen dress which dragged at her legs. Halfway across the courtyard she wrenched her hand free and stopped. "Enough, Con Foyle!" she exclaimed, using both hands to push her heavy black hair away from her face.

He glanced over his shoulder and grinned at her, his teeth a pale gleam in the half-light, then bent low in an exaggerated bow. "Murray ne Doe O'Flaherty, most feared chieftain of Iar-Connacht, awaits the pleasure of your company, Nora Donovan," he told her. "Will you be keeping him any longer?"

"He'll not be wanting me looking like a bog-wraith!" she retorted, straightening her dress and shaking out the long folds of her brat. Privately, she doubted the chieftain would even know who she was. Nora's was not one of the more important families protected by the O'Flahertys—her father, Tom Donovan, farmed a tiny croft on a strip of land jutting into the sea on the far side of the Connemara mountains—but they provided their fair share of oats and butter to their chief's household, and for tonight's feast Nora's eldest brother Colm had brought a barrel of salted oysters. Murray ne Doe was a generous man and held feasts for his clan throughout the year;

this one was celebrating a good harvest safely in, and not too much of it paid in tithes to the English lords in the town of Galway.

Satisfied that her clothes were straight and that there were no wisps of hay in her hair, Nora followed Con more slowly, listening to the noise of music, dancing, and chatter grow louder. Murray ne Doe had built his single-story banqueting hall outside the wall that surrounded his tower house; guests were permitted as far as the courtyard inside the first bawn, a stone wall taller than the height of two men and thicker than a man's outstretched arms, but no further. As well as the hall for feasting, the outer wall surrounded several little huts, thatched with reeds like the hall but with simple wooden walls, where the animals were kept and Murray ne Doe's huge extended family and servants lived.

Nora paused in the doorway of the hall and waited for her eyes to get used to the flickering yellow torchlight. The room churned with people like salmon in a weir, and the air was thick and stinging with smoke from scores of tallow candles. The great hall was twice as big as her cottage, with a lofty beamed ceiling and rough stone walls with iron nails driven in at the height of a man's upstretched arm. Round wooden shields, short swords, and long-handled axes hung from the nails, although tonight they were being used as hooks to keep the guests' woolen cloaks out of the way of leaping feet. A long table stretched along the far side of the room, made from doors laid on top of a bank of rushes, and stout wooden barrels and packs of straw served as seats. They had been placed on the wall side of the table facing out so that no one's back faced the door; it was not unusual for a neighboring chieftain to take advantage of a feast to launch an attack on his rival's clan.

At fourteen, Nora was the youngest in her family, and she knew that it was a great honor to be allowed to come to the chieftain's feast with Sean and Rua, her sister Anne, and her eldest brother Colm. Their parents had stayed behind with Nora's brother Walt and sister Meg. She had been too excited to sleep last night, and had shivered without her brat for two whole days while she waited for the newly washed cloak to dry on bushes on top of the cliff. But now Nora thought longingly of the empty shore below her cottage, where the wild ponies came to step delicately among the seaweed and drop their heads to lick the salty rocks. The bracken-colored mare Dunlin would be there, her coat turned pinkish gray in the dusk, and maybe Dubh, the jet-black colt she had foaled earlier that year. One of his forelegs had been hot and swollen the last time Nora had seen him, and she had fed him a handful of knapweed to soothe the pain and bring the swelling down.

"Nora! There you are!"

A young woman with hair the color of candlelight spun out of the crowd of dancers and ran over to the doorway, pulling a broad-shouldered man behind her. He was a head taller than most people in the room and his flushed red face was topped with thick black curls that stood on end as if he had been dragged by his heels through the forest of yew trees that surrounded the castle.

The fair-haired girl stopped and frowned critically at Nora. "Honora Donovan, what have you been doing? You look like you've just stepped out of a midden."

"I've been settling Ballach," she replied defensively. Her sister Anne was only three years older but she treated Nora as if she was a troublesome child scarcely out of swaddling clothes. All the same, Nora felt hot and untidy beside her sister's shining hair, as straight as a fall of water, and her gown, which remained spotless in spite of reeling across the floor of sticky rushes.

The black-haired young man behind Anne winked conspiratorially. "Good evening to you, Nora," he said, grinning.

"And to you, Mor," Nora replied, smiling back. The nickname meant "big" and suited her sister's massive-framed suitor, who shared a fishing boat with Nora and Anne's brother Colm; they trawled for oysters close to the shore to trade in the market at Sraith Salach and sometimes even as far away as Galway.

"Only two of Tom Donovan's daughters here tonight?" said a voice from the doorway.

Nora turned to see a thin young man with light brown hair and green eyes the shade of holly. It was Dan Devlin, a horse trader who did not belong to the O'Flaherty clan but turned up at every one of Murray ne Doe's feasts with as many ponies as he could lead behind his cart.

"No doubt you're looking for Meg, Dan Devlin," Anne said archly.

The young man grinned. "And why shouldn't I? 'Tis only a matter of time before she says yes."

"My sister's not thinking of being married for a good while yet," Nora blurted out, and everyone looked at her in surprise. She looked down at the floor, embarrassed and wishing that Meg was here to fend off Dan's attentions herself. It was nearly a quarter-year since he had asked Meg to marry him and Nora couldn't help feeling that her sister should have made it clearer by now that she had no intention of agreeing.

"No matter, I can wait," the horse trader replied, and his eyes gleamed like a cat about to pounce on a weasel. "Is your brother Colm here? I've a pony that he should look at, only six years old, strong as an ox and with more years of work in him than that gray nag of yours."

Nora dug her fingers into her cloak, bracing herself for a sharp reply, when she felt Mor place one hand on her shoulder. "Steady," he whispered in her ear. "He's only trying to rile you. You know what he's like."

Nora took a deep breath and forced herself to meet Dan Devlin's gaze. Sure enough, his green eyes shone with amusement and a smile twitched at the corners of his mouth. "Ballach is in great health," she told him calmly. "We've no need for another horse just yet."

"But I'm sure Colm will be pleased to know that you thought of him," Mor put in.

"In that case, will you tell Meg I was asking for her?" said Dan. As Anne nodded, his eyes slid past them and he waved at someone across the hall. "Will you excuse me?" he added. "There's a man over there who might be willing to look at a mare I've been trying to sell all summer. As long as she manages not to kick him out of the byre before he makes an offer, I might have her off my hands at last." He nodded to Anne and Nora, then hurried away, and disappeared into the throng of people.

Anne stared after him with her lips pursed. "I hope Meg has enough sense not to marry that man, whatever he promises her," she muttered. "He's as slippery as an eel."

Con appeared beside Nora, holding a piece of roast beef folded into some oatbread. "There's plenty of food left," he said.

She shook her head at Con's outstretched hand, too excited to eat. Con opened his mouth to say something but the fiddler struck up another tune, the bodhran leaping in behind, and suddenly it was too noisy to talk. Con dropped the roast beef and oatbread onto the rush-strewn floor—Nora felt one of Murray ne Doe's wolfhounds brush past her skirt as it slipped out of the shadows in pursuit of the tidbit—and led her into the dance. It was a hey, one of Nora's favorites, and she quickly gathered up her skirt in one hand to begin winding in and out of the circle of men. On the far side of the hall, she saw Anne and Rua, easily spotted with her hair the color of beech leaves, join in as well, although her shy brother Sean stayed sitting on a wine barrel, clapping his hands in time with the bodhran. Cupbearers moved around him carrying slim-necked earthenware jugs, keeping their chieftain's guests supplied with ale and mead and creamy buttermilk.

Like a hive full of bees, the banqueting hall thronged with as many people as Nora had ever seen in one place. A few she recognized from Errislannan, and some she thought she had met on her last visit to Aughnanure, but most of the faces were unfamiliar. She knew that they were families like hers who lived under the protection of the O'Flahertys, or else part of Murray ne Doe's own household. The old man had twelve sons and it seemed as if they had generated enough grandchildren for an entire clan from the number of squalling, tousle-haired toddlers who crawled among the rushes and tugged at the wolfhounds' tails and ears. While Nora twirled and sidestepped, she tried to store as many of the faces in her mind as she could. She had promised Meg that she would tell her every last detail about the feast, and as she danced past the still-laden table she wondered if she could hide a few slices of roast beef or a honey-sweetened oatcake under her brat to take home to her sister.

"Hungry, Nora?" laughed a familiar voice, and she looked up to see Mor grinning down at her. He took hold of her hands and spun her away from the table into the circle of dancers, so fast that his face became a blur.

Nora stumbled as her shoe got stuck under a knot of rushes. "Look out!" she gasped, clutching at his sleeve.

Mor grabbed her firmly around the waist and hoisted her into the air until her foot was tugged clear, then set her down on the outside of the circle.

There was a loud cheer from behind them, and the sound of wooden beakers being drummed on the table. Nora glanced over her shoulder and saw five or six men with long hair and tangled beards sitting on the other side of the table. A handful of dice lay scattered in front of them. They cheered again when they saw Nora looking at them and she felt her cheeks burn.

"Will you come and sit down with us, lass?" one of them shouted, raising his beaker in one hand and patting the straw seat beside him with the other. His hair and beard were the exact color of fox fur, matching the fox pelt that was draped about his shoulders. Nora watched, fascinated, as the tiny paws scratched on the tabletop when the man leaned forward to grab at a joint of meat. He looked up and winked, and she noticed that his eyes were the same russet-brown as his hair.

Mor drew her away. "Pay no heed to them," he shouted in her ear. "Especially not that fox-haired one. He's been causing trouble all night with the other gallowglasses."

"He looked a bold one, for sure," Nora agreed. Gallowglasses were fierce men who came across the sea from Scotland and who would fight to their deaths for a price. From the look of these wild-eyed, broad-shouldered men, Murray ne Doe paid handsomely for his army, and they would never be spared from guarding the castle walls to herd cattle like Con and the other kerns.

The dance swept Nora around the room past several scarlet-faced, smiling strangers and she was on the far side of the hall, close to the door, when there was an uproar from the corner where the gallowglasses had been sitting. Everyone stopped to see what was going on, and even the fiddler lowered his bow and tapped his companion on the shoulder so that the bodhran fell silent as well.

Nora stood on tiptoe, craning her neck, but all she could see were huge shadows stretching against the ceiling in the far corner. There were shouts, then a crash as if a wine barrel had been knocked over.

"I'll show you what happens when you cheat!" someone

roared, and Nora recognized the voice of the fox-haired man.

"Who are you calling a cheat, Alaric Campbell?" came the reply.

Nora's sister-in-law Rua slipped through the crowd to stand next to her. "Sounds like there's a game of dice turned sour," she whispered, her green eyes wide with alarm.

There was a strange creaking sound followed by a startled yell, then a loud splash that echoed through the banqueting hall. As they faded away, the watery sounds were drowned by a deafening bellow from the far end of the table.

"Who dares disturb my feast like this?"

THE CROWD SHIFTED UNEASILY, and Nora caught sight of a man pushing himself up from the single chair in the hall, a sturdy wooden seat with high, carved arms and draped with furs. The man was no taller than those around him—a brave observer might have dared to say that he was a handspan shorter—but he carried his stocky frame with such an air of power that everyone else in the hall seemed to shrink. Long gray hair fanned out around his shoulders and tangled with his thick beard, still mostly black but streaked with silver like a badger, and his heavy woolen cloak was lined with dark brown fur that gleamed almost red in the candlelight. These marten pelts alone would have told Nora that this was a powerful and wealthy man, if she had not already known this was none other than Murray ne Doe O'Flaherty, mighty chieftain of Iar-Connacht and lord of Aughnanure Castle.

His eyes black with fury, Murray ne Doe pushed his way past his stunned guests. Nora couldn't help noticing that the hem of his long cloak gathered up a chunk of oatbread and a gnawed bone as it swept over the well-trodden rushes.

"Where's Alaric Campbell?" the chieftain demanded, and Nora frowned. How could the fox-haired man have disappeared so suddenly?

One of the gallowglasses mumbled something she couldn't hear, and a shocked ripple spread through the guests standing nearest to him.

"Who did this?" bellowed Murray ne Doe. "I'll have him punished, by God!"

Nora was about to ask Rua if she knew what had happened when Con appeared beside her, his hair standing on end and his face glistening from the heat.

"Come quick!" he whispered. He took her hand and led her along the wall past the arched windows, decorated with patterns of grapes to boast of Murray ne Doe's trade with Spanish wine merchants, and of the wealth that enabled him to hire the finest stonemasons. Nora followed Con willingly, relieved for once that she was small enough to squeeze past the other guests who were pushing curiously toward the corner.

They reached the far end of the hall and Con pushed Nora ahead of him until she could see the end of the table where the gallowglasses had been sitting. The wooden board had been wrenched off the banked-up rushes, toppling beakers, meat, and flagons of ale onto the floor. Murray ne Doe had his back to Nora and Con and was facing a slender, dark-haired man who seemed reluctant to meet his chieftain's gaze. The fox-haired gallowglass, Alaric Campbell, was nowhere to be seen.

Con tugged at Nora's sleeve and pointed to a black square on the floor. "Do you know what that is?" he hissed into her ear.

With a start, Nora realized that the black shape was actually a hole yawning treacherously among the flagstones. She knew that the river, which flowed on two sides of the castle, came right underneath part of the banqueting hall. Had the floor given way and sent the gallowglass crashing into the icy black water?

"'Tis Murray ne Doe's own device," Con explained quietly as if he could follow her thoughts. "A handy way of getting rid of unwanted guests, is it not?"

Nora whirled around to face him, shocked. "Surely no man would survive a fall like that?"

"D'you think that would be a concern to Murray ne Doe?" Con replied, raising his eyebrows. "The river is only a man's length below us, but if his senses were confused with drink, he'd not stand much chance against the current and be washed out to Lough Corrib for sure."

But Alaric Campbell was no enemy, and Nora could understand Murray ne Doe's anger if the gallowglass had been tipped into the river by one of his own men. She became aware of a new, but quieter, commotion by the trapdoor and stood on tiptoe to see a cupbearer on his knees, lowering a thick rope into the gaping darkness.

"Make haste, will you?" Murray ne Doe ordered, impatient to save his expensive soldier.

There was a splash as the end of the rope hit the water and a faint cry from the darkness that echoed into the warm and brightly lit hall. Several men hurried forward to take the strain on the rope and Nora heard the sound of splashing followed by feet scraping against stone.

A few moments later, Alaric Campbell's head appeared, his hair plastered darkly around his shoulders and the fox pelt black and dripping like a strip of seaweed. A trickle of blood ran down his cheek, but to Nora's relief and surprise, the gallowglass was smiling.

"I'll have you for this, Rhidian," he swore as he hauled himself out of the hole.

The dark-haired man, shorter than the gallowglass by a whole head, laughed. "You'll not scare me if you're so easily taken by surprise," he replied.

"Enough!" roared Murray ne Doe. "You, bard—" he pointed to the dark-haired man—"you're here to play your harp, not drown my best men. And you," he went on, turning to Alaric Campbell, who was now standing on the flagstones with water streaming off him, "can sober up in the east watchtower."

Con winced. "That's the watchtower next to the long drop," he explained to Nora under his breath. "The midden-pit's not been cleared out for a while and the stench keeps even the rats away."

Nora felt laughter bubble inside her and she frowned to keep her expression serious.

Alaric Campbell said something to the chieftain in a language that Nora couldn't understand. The low-pitched rhythms were similar to Irish, but the words were unfamiliar. She could speak a few words of English, as could most of her neighbors since the arrival of the English soldiers, and she had learned some Spanish from the fishermen who came ashore in spring and summer to salt and pack the herring they had caught far out at sea. They had gone now, leaving their open-sided wooden huts empty through the winter storms until the shoals of fish returned. But Campbell had spoken in neither of these languages and Nora guessed he had used his native tongue, the language of the Scottish Picts.

Murray ne Doe replied in the same tongue, his brows so tightly drawn together that his eyes almost disappeared. His hands were clenched by his side, and Nora thought his lined face looked old and tired, as if he had enough to worry about without losing his best men down holes in the floor.

The gallowglass met his chieftain's eyes for a long moment, then nodded, and stalked toward the door. The fox pelt's drenched tail swung back and forth with each stride, flicking drops of water over the guests who parted like scythed rushes in front of him. Alaric Campbell was tall enough for Nora to watch him all the way to the door until it slammed behind him, making the candles gutter and spew out oily smoke at the far end of the table.

In the corner by the trapdoor, Rhidian the bard picked up his wooden harp and started plucking at the strings, humming to himself with his head bowed low.

Murray ne Doe scuffed at the edge of the hole with his boot. "Get that stone into place," he ordered before walking back to his seat.

Two servants ran forward to haul the flagstone back level with the floor. The edges fitted so neatly against its neighbors that it was almost impossible to guess it could tilt away and send someone plunging into the river below. A tuft of flax was sticking up from one side and Nora realized that the rope had been left behind, dangling into the blackness. She wondered if she should tell Con or one of the servants—Murray ne Doe would not want any of his enemies using it to climb into his great hall—but before she could say anything the door at the other end of the hall burst open and everyone stopped talking and twisted around to look.

A shout went up from near the door. "Brenan Odoyne is here!"

"Welcome, peddler," declared Murray ne Doe from his chair. He waved his beaker to beckon the new arrival into the hall.

Nora stood on tiptoe to see the visitor. Brenan Odoyne was one of the men known as gray merchants, who traveled around with a mule laden with salt, pepper, iron for spades, and occasionally a bolt of fine cloth that was much softer than the cottage-spun linen. Once he was inside the hall, Brenan dumped his pack on the floor and pushed back the hood of his cloak to reveal a thin, beaked face scoured red by the wind. Nora wasn't surprised to see her sister Anne pushing her way forward with the other women to examine what the merchant had brought with him this time. Their fingers looked like pale hungry birds pecking at the oilcloth wrappings, and Nora stayed where she was, happy to let Anne decide if any precious coins could be spared on spice or cloth.

There would be no more music until the peddler had finished the first round of bargaining, and she was tempted to slip outside to see Ballach. The mare would be warm, dry, and well fed in the comfortable byre, but without the dancing to distract her, Nora felt shy and clumsy among the gossiping women and laughing, wine-flushed men.

The chieftain stood up and shooed the women away from the gray merchant. "There'll be time enough for that later," he said. "Sit down with me, Brenan Odoyne, and say what news there is from Galway. Cupbearer, more wine!"

The twelve powerful merchant families who ruled Galway had recently banned the O'Flahertys from entering the city, in protest against the warmongering chieftain who caused trouble among all the clans around the town walls. As members of Murray ne Doe's clan, the ban extended to Nora and her family; her brothers could take their barrels of oysters and mussels as far as the fishing village of Claddagh on the edge of the town, but no further. Colm and Sean had taken Nora with them once three years ago, before the ban was imposed, and she had a fading memory of being dragged by the hand along crowded streets between towering, gray stone buildings.

Not being able to pass under the city gates left Murray ne Doe hungry for news, and this was as valuable to Brenan Odoyne as any of the wares in his well-stocked bundle. The peddler obediently left his pack on the floor and went over to balance his bony rump on a wooden churn next to the chieftain's chair. This time it was the men who crowded around him, candlelight gleaming in their eyes and making huge, craggy shadows of their noses and chins.

"He might have word of the Armada," Con remarked quietly to Nora, and she nodded. Like everyone else at the feast, she had heard about the great fleet sent by the king of Spain to force Queen Elizabeth of England to recognize the pope as the true head of the holy Catholic Church. Elizabeth's father, Henry VIII, had turned his back on Rome and declared himself the head of the Church of England, and Elizabeth seemed determine to persist with this blasphemy.

"Have the Spanish ships reached England yet?" demanded a fair-haired gallowglass, setting down the knife he had been using to carve thick, dripping slices from a haunch of beef.

"From the score of English soldiers I passed today, you'd

think the ships were anchored in Galway Bay," complained an old man with cheeks the hue and texture of old leather.

"The English are cowards!" the gallowglass roared. "They'd send fourscore of their men to capture a midden-pit." He snatched up his knife and slammed it point-first into the wooden tabletop where it stuck, quivering.

"But surely the Armada isn't coming here?" someone put in. Nora couldn't see who was speaking, but around him people nodded in agreement. The English might have ransacked every church and abbey in Ireland, but there was no question that the Irish people still held to the Catholic faith. There was no need for King Philip of Spain to send his armies here.

"Quiet, and let the man speak," Murray ne Doe ordered.

The room fell silent and Brenan Odoyne straightened up, his heavy gray cloak hanging from his shoulders like loosely folded wings. "An invasion of Spaniards is exactly what the English fear," he announced hoarsely. There were a few puzzled exclamations, quickly silenced by Murray ne Doe's raised hand.

"The whole of Galway talks of nothing else," the peddler went on. "Five weeks ago, the Armada was defeated off the southern coast of England. The ships fled north, around the land of the Scots, and they have been spotted off our shores not three days' ride from here."

Nora stared up at Con, her heart pounding. "Is this true?

Are we going to be invaded?"

"Hush, listen," said Con. He put his hands on her shoulders and turned her back to face the gray merchant.

At the far end of the hall, Murray ne Doe echoed Nora's question.

Brenan Odoyne shrugged. "No one knows for sure," he admitted. "It looks like Sir Richard Bingham is expecting the worst, for he has ordered more soldiers to be sent from Dublin." He was speaking about the English governor of Iar-Connacht, and Nora saw the chieftain's shoulders tense. It was Sir Richard Bingham who had allowed him to take over this castle some twenty years ago, when English soldiers had defeated Murray ne Doe's cousin Donal Crone.

The fair-haired gallowglass seized his knife from the table-top and clasped it in his massive fist. "Catholic or not, we'll let no Spaniards take this castle," he vowed.

He was joined by a chorus of agreement, and daggers were brandished in the air. One man even snatched an axe from the wall and thrust it above his head. "O'Flahertys will not fall to Spain or England!" he shouted.

For one wild moment, Nora expected the men to rush out there and defend their homes from invading Spanish sailors, but Murray ne Doe called the hall to silence and glowered at them, his eyes black and furious. "This is a serious matter," he said, "and we need to discuss it further, but not here. Come, men of the O'Flaherty clan, and you, too, Brenan." He swept his cloak around him—this time nearly bowling an unsteady toddler into a heap of soiled rushes—and strode out of the door with the gray merchant beside him. The gallowglasses and some of the guests followed, amid discontented muttering from the women who had hoped to empty some of Brenan's pack of wares.

Nora turned to Con. "Will you go too?"

Con shook his head. "No, I'll be given my orders afterward, whatever Murray ne Doe decides. 'Tis hard to know what threat there is. The Spanish are no enemies of ours, but not friends either. More likely Murray ne Doe will want to make good our walls against the English, if there's going to be more of them about."

He stepped aside to let a servant go past with an armful of clean rushes. "Look, they're making up beds for the night," he said, as the servant began spreading the rushes thickly on the floor. "There'll be no more dancing after Brenan's news, that's for sure. Will you be all right if I leave you now? I'll be needed on watch if so many are in council with Murray ne Doe."

"Of course, go," said Nora.

Con touched her arm in farewell and threaded his way through the excited, chattering crowd to the door. Rua came over to Nora, her beech-leaf-colored hair escaping from the pins that had held it neatly at the start of the evening. Like all married women, Rua wore her hair coiled around her head and covered it with a folded sheet of linen whenever she went outside.

"'Tis worrying news that Brenan brought tonight," she declared, her cheeks flushed and her eyes bright with alarm.

Nora's brother Sean came up behind her. "And what would those Spaniards want with us?" he said gently.

"They might think we'd help them fight against Queen Elizabeth," Nora suggested.

Sean shook his head. "Maybe, but they'd be wrong. Murray ne Doe's not likely to spare any of his men to help another country's quarrel. More likely the ships will sail straight past and not spare a moment's thought on us."

Nora hoped he was right. Pushing all thoughts of invaders and foreign ships from her mind, she went to help Rua and Anne set out blankets on the rushes that would be their beds for the night.

As the people in the hall settled down to sleep, a woman began singing a ballad about Manannan mac Lir, the sea god who lived in a palace beneath the waves and rode a horse the color of storm-whipped foam. Nora shut her eyes and pictured the underwater world, littered with broken ships and the bones of drowned men. For now, the fate of the Spanish sailors lay in the hands of Manannan mac Lir, not English soldiers or Irish chieftains.

3

NORA WOKE AS THE FIRST SHAFTS of light seeped around the hides that hung at the windows, dimly illuminating the sleeping bodies lining the hall. She pushed off the heavy blanket and sat up, being careful not to disturb Anne and Rua who were curled on either side of her. All the women slept at one end of the hall, while the men were at the other end by the door. Last night Nora had been grateful to be so far from the draft that whistled under the door, but now she wondered how she was going to make her way out without disturbing the other guests.

As she started to unfold her brat, which she had bundled up to put under her head, the rushes crackled like musket fire. Nora held her breath, then someone at the far end let out a deafening snore and a wolfhound started barking outside. A cockerel crowed, splitting the air like the wail of a banshee, and suddenly it seemed as if the whole hall had sprung awake from an enchanted sleep, with people on all sides struggling upright and pushing their hair out of their eyes.

Nora jumped to her feet, shaking out her cloak with a snap and wrapping it around her shoulders. "I'm going to see to

Ballach," she told Anne and Rua.

"If you find Colm, tell him we want to see Brenan Odoyne before we leave," said Anne.

Nora nodded and made her way as quickly as she could toward the door, stepping over a few bodies that stubbornly slept on, their brats clasped over their heads. Outside, the courtyard was deserted aside from a few servants carrying hay and water to the animals. A baby shrieked in one of the thatched huts and was quickly shushed by its mother. For a moment, the only sounds were the chickens muttering shrilly to one another and the brisk slap of water from the far side of the courtyard, where the River Drimneen flowed through a gap in the wall to form a narrow harbor. Ships from Spain and France could sail all the way from Galway, along Lough Corrib to Aughnanure, which was why Murray ne Doe was able to offer his guests the finest wine and rare treats such as almonds and spices. Today the harbor was empty except for a single cur-rach, a small round boat made from tarred hides stretched over a wicker frame, which bobbed like a water bird as the waves slapped against it.

Picking up an armful of hay, Nora followed the servants into the byre and counted her way along the row of warm flanks until she came to Ballach. The speckled mare was dozing with her nose resting against the stone wall and one hind leg crooked beneath her belly.

"Hallo, my beautiful girl," Nora whispered, squeezing past to put the hay in front of her. "Did you sleep well?"

The mare opened one eye and blinked at her, then tossed her head and began to pick at the hay. Nora ran her hands down each of Ballach's legs, checking they weren't hot and swollen after the hard journey the day before. Ballach was nearly as old as Nora, past her prime for a working horse, and they had a long way to go back to Errislannan.

"Honora Donovan, are you in here?" came a voice from the doorway.

Nora stood up and waved. "I'm over here, Colm!" she called.

Her eldest brother ducked his head as he entered the byre and walked over to Ballach's corner. Nora hadn't seen him at the feast, and she guessed from his dark-circled eyes and rumpled clothes that he had spent all night playing dice with Murray ne Doe's kerns in one of the huts around the edge of the courtyard.

"Are you ready to leave?" he asked. "I've sent Mor to bring the cart, and Sean's fetching the empty barrel."

"I think Anne and Rua wanted to see Brenan Odoyne first," Nora replied, picking a wisp of hay out of Ballach's mane.

Colm nodded. "I saw him going into the hall just now. I'll go and help Mor with the cart." He turned and walked out, sparing no more words than he had to, as usual.

Nora fished in the rushes and picked up the rope halter she

had buried there the evening before. She slipped it over Ballach's head, then led the mare out of the byre. Mor and Colm were hauling a small, wooden-wheeled cart into the courtyard. There wasn't room for all the carts inside the outer wall, so visitors had to leave them among the yew trees outside the west gate. By the time Nora backed the mare into the shafts and made sure the rope harness was firmly tied, Anne and Rua had emerged from the great hall with a small leather bag of pepper and a coil of saffron-colored ribbon. Close behind them, Sean rolled the empty oyster barrel across the courtyard and hoisted it onto the cart.

All around, the other families were preparing to leave as well, and the gray dawn was filled with shouts of farewell and light-hearted warnings to keep watch for Spanish sailors. Anne and Rua hung over the sides of the cart, calling to friends and laughing. The feast seemed to have spilled over into the morning, the excited mood lasting in spite of Brenan's news. Nora stood quietly at Ballach's head, feeling cold under her brat and wishing they could set off so that the walk would warm her up.

"Ready?" said Colm. Nora nodded and clicked her tongue to make the mare walk on. The solid wooden wheels of the cart stuck for a moment in the soft ground, then lurched forward when Sean and Mor put their shoulders against it. On the back of the cart, Anne shrieked as she nearly tumbled over, and Mor reached out with one hand to steady her.

The cart rolled through the main gate in a line of similar carts, mostly pulled by sturdy ponies like Ballach but one or two by oxen, their huge horns and flared scarlet nostrils making them look like monstrous fairy creatures as they passed into the green half-light under the yew trees. A shout from the nearest watchtower made Nora look up, and she saw Con waving at her, a thick woolen brat drawn all the way up to his chin. She waved back, then tightened her grip on Ballach's leading rope to steer her between the deepest ruts on the forest track. In spite of the throng of people around them, she wanted to be out of the forest as quickly as she could. The dawn light had barely pierced the tangled branches, and it was all too easy for Nora to imagine the yellow eyes of wolves watching her from among the shadows.

By THE TIME THEY LEFT the yew trees behind them, the sun had risen, linen-colored behind the clouds that stretched across the sky like dirty fleece. One by one, the other carts turned off to follow narrower paths home, until Nora's family was traveling with barely half a dozen others. Ahead of them, the Maam Tuirc mountains loomed against the horizon, their gently sloping sides streaked with the scars of winter streams. Beyond the flattened peaks lay the mountains of Connemara, and Nora felt her heart lift.

She pressed her face against Ballach's cheek when they

paused to rest and drink from the pail of buttermilk that Rua had brought from Aughnanure. "We'll soon be home," she promised the tired mare. Her own feet ached from trudging along the uneven track; the worst of the holes had been patched with stones, but in between, the ground was slick and treacherous, the mud often giving way to a boggy scoop of dark brown peat that sucked at boots and cart wheels. Nora could feel a blister blooming on one heel, and she kept an eye out for some moss to pad her boot where it rubbed.

They were still two or three leagues from the Maam Tuircs when they saw a company of English soldiers cantering toward them, the horses' metal-shod hooves clattering like musket fire over the stones. The line of carts drew to the side of the track and Nora kept her gaze fixed on the ground while she waited for them to pass. Colm, Sean, and Mor stood beside the cart with their arms folded, watching the soldiers through nar-rowed eyes. English troops rarely came as far west as Errislannan, and curiosity got the better of Nora as the first soldier went past. She glanced up to see a tall, square-jawed man with tufts of sandy hair sticking out from under his high, beehive-shaped helmet. His long boots and leather jerkin were spattered with mud and his sword swung wildly as he spurred his horse forward. Nora drew back against Ballach's shoulder to avoid the pounding hooves. The soldiers were mounted on huge war horses, bright bay geldings bred further east in

Munster. They were several hands taller than Ballach and the mountain ponies and were able to gallop for a whole day under the weight of a rider in full armor.

"Captain Money, should we stop and ask them about the Spanish fleet?" one of the soldiers shouted, raising his voice above the deafening creak of bridles, bits, and saddles. Nora was amazed the horses could move at all with so much leather on their backs; like the rest of her clan, she only ever rode with a rope halter and a loosely girthed cloth to sit on, and she wouldn't dream of trapping her feet in heavy metal stirrups.

"No need," replied the sandy-haired man, bunching the reins in one hand and twisting around to address his companion. "I doubt these filthy peasants have even heard of Spain! Just make sure they don't have any venison in those carts. They don't seem to understand that the deer in these forests belong to the queen now." He clapped his heels against the gelding's sides so that the horse stretched out its neck and galloped even faster.

Nora glanced sideways at her brothers but their expressions didn't change, even though she knew they understood as much English as she did. They stood as still as stones while the soldiers kicked their horses close to the carts and peered into each one. Ballach's cart was empty aside from the oyster barrel, and Anne and Rua tucked their skirts under their legs so that the soldiers could see there were no deer carcasses stowed underneath.

When the noise of the soldiers had faded away, Colm and Sean turned and walked on without saying a word. The other carts moved off too, and Nora clicked her tongue to Ballach through chattering teeth. She reminded herself that she had nothing to fear from the English soldiers, as long as she wasn't caught practicing the Catholic faith. Her family and neighbors had long ago started to celebrate Mass in one of the caves at the far end of the beach, with a lookout posted further along the cliff in case any troops chanced by.

They stopped for the night in Sraith Salach, a cluster of houses tucked between the Maam Tuircs and Connemara. A long, narrow lake stretched out beside the houses, the water still and flat except for a tiny thumbprint where a fish had surfaced. As Nora halted Ballach in front of one of the cottages—squat and stone-built like the others, with a thatched roof of reeds—a stocky, fair-haired man came out of a hut at the side of the house. A hoop of wood was slung over his shoulder and he carried a hammer loosely in one hand.

From her seat on the cart, Anne spotted him too. "Good day to you, Fionn mac Gowan," she called.

"Welcome to you all!" he said, his face creasing into a broad smile. Fionn was married to Nora's eldest sister, Mainie. They had not come to the feast at Aughnanure because their newest babe, Fergal, was barely one month old and too young for such a long journey. "You've made good time if you've come from

Aughnanure today," Fionn added as he came over to greet them.

"We have indeed," said Sean. "The road's in fair shape all the way to the castle."

"Murray ne Doe must have had his kerns rebuilding it," Mor commented as he helped Anne jump down from the cart.

"He'll not spare any of his men for road mending much longer if what they say about those Spaniards is true," said Sean, and Fionn looked at him with interest flaring in his eyes.

Nora didn't want to hear the unsettling rumors again. "Shall I take Ballach to the pasture?" she asked, untying the ropes that held the shafts in place.

Fionn nodded. "Aye, but there's no need for you to sleep out there too. There's plenty of room inside for a skinny thing like you!" He laughed, and Nora forced herself to smile.

As she led Ballach around the side of the cottage, she heard Anne and Rua ask how Mainie and the children were. Nora's family seemed to multiply around her like eels in a pot, although it was a hard task to find enough to feed the mouths they already had. She slipped off Ballach's halter, and the mare put her head down at once to pull at the dry, bristly grass. A soft *humph* from the shadows told Nora where Fionn's cow lay, tucked against the stone wall for shelter. When there weren't so many guests, the animals would be brought in at night to share the fire and help warm the cottage with their steamy breath, but now Nora envied the cow and the mare for being able to stay outside in the quiet dusk.

When she went inside she was relieved to find that Una and Alis, Mainie's two little girls, were fast asleep in the rushes. They were swaddled in blankets so that only their noses and a wisp of hair, fair like their father's, showed. Anne and Rua were kneeling beside Mainie to show her the ribbon they had bought from Brenan Odoyne. Mainie's face was pale and her eyes black-circled with exhaustion, but she asked eagerly about the feast, which other families they had met, and what dancing there had been. The men were sitting on the other side of the fire, cloaks bunched against the cold stone behind their backs and their voices low and serious as they discussed the news of the Spanish fleet.

Nora helped herself to a beaker of broth from the metal pot over the fire and lay down on the rushes next to Una and Alis. The whispers of their breathing lulled her, and the quiet mountains that loomed behind the cottage made her feel safe, a long, long distance from the noise and bustle of Aughnanure.

4

⟶⟨⟩⟨⟩⟨⟩⟶

THEY SET OUT AT FIRST LIGHT the next morning; Una and
Alis clung to Nora's skirt so that she had to unhook them like
tiny burrs before she could take hold of Ballach's lead rope.
Today the sky was dark granite-gray and the wind was stronger,
carrying with it a spatter of rain. They would be lucky to make
it back without a soaking. Nora used some of the moss she had
found yesterday to pad Ballach's halter behind her ears, where
the rope would rub if it got wet.

They were traveling alone now, and the heavy silence was
broken only by the creak of the wheels and the sound of mud
sucking at Ballach's hooves. Nora looked up at the mountain
that reared up beside the path and felt a familiar sense of
excitement stir inside her. Somewhere on those barren, treeless slopes, the wild ponies lived, scrambling surefooted over
the stones and grazing in the narrow, bog-lined valleys. She
could see one of the herds on a distant peak, moving slowly
across the rocky ground in search of grass, but there were too
many dun and dark brown rumps for it to be Dunlin's herd.

Mor came up alongside Nora and followed her gaze. "Are

you looking for those ponies of yours?" he asked.

Nora turned to him, her cheeks reddening. Her family couldn't understand why she was so drawn to the mountain ponies, since they were considered to be impossible to tame and too bad-tempered to do anything useful like pull a plow or a cart. But Nora knew differently. Even Dunlin, whose walleye betrayed her uncertain temper, came cantering down from the hillside like a well-fed cottager's pony in answer to Nora's whistle.

She knew Dunlin's herd better than all the others because their territory stretched from the mountains to the beach in Errislannan. The dozen or so mares were led by a stallion that she had named Fiach, meaning "raven." He had been black as night when she first saw him several years ago, but as he grew older his coat had faded to gray until now only his legs and belly were dark, as if he had just waded through a bog. Nora had been too cautious to approach the wild stallion, who guarded his herd with teeth and hooves like flint, but after a few months of watching them, one of his mares, bracken-coated with a cloudy, blue eye, had seemed willing to take sea-weed from her hands. This was Dunlin, named after the tiny birds that pecked among the waves at low tide.

Mor's eyes were unexpectedly kind as he smiled at Nora. "It's an easy journey from here," he said. "I'm sure Colm and Sean wouldn't mind sparing you to find a different way home."

Nora grinned. "Thank you, Mor." She turned back to look at Colm and Sean, who were trudging behind the cart with their brats pulled up around their ears and their eyes half-shut against the wind.

"I'll see you at home!" she called, and they nodded, too cold and tired to argue.

Nora paused only to rub Ballach's ears and promise that she'd fetch her a meal of hot oats that evening before she gathered up her skirts and jumped off the side of the track. The narrow strip of stones gave way at once to bogland, which bubbled with watery popping sounds as it waited for unwary travelers, or a slow-witted sheep, to step into the bottomless broth of peat.

Suddenly Nora's legs felt full of energy and she sprang from tussock to tussock with the wind tearing at her hair and stinging her eyes. The clumps of grass wobbled like wool spindles set on end, but she was running too fast to lose her footing and soon she reached the firm granite slopes at the bottom of the mountain. She paused, gasping, but the wind snatched her breath away as soon as she opened her mouth. Her hair was wrenched out of the long plait that hung down her back and whipped against her cheeks like brambles. Nora held it back impatiently with one hand while she lifted her head and whistled as loud as she could.

For one blissful moment, the wind dropped and she heard

an answering whinny from high up the mountain. Nora tipped back her head and spotted a familiar tawny shape cantering down the slope, sending pieces of scree clattering ahead of her. The rest of Fiach's herd were just visible below the summit, watching the dun-colored mare with their ears pricked forward. A smaller, long-legged shadow appeared at the edge of the herd, and Nora recognized Dunlin's foal, Dubh. Nora was too far away to tell if he was walking evenly, but she could ride up to him and judge for herself if the knapweed poultice had worked. She had quickly discovered that she could go much nearer to the wild ponies when she was riding Dunlin, as if the herd regarded her as one of them when she approached with hooves and a tangled mane and tail instead of a pair of unsteady, slow-footed legs.

The mare skidded to a halt at the bottom of the mountain, her flanks heaving and her nostrils flaring in welcome. Nora waited for Dunlin to come right up and blow warmly on her hair before she reached up to pat the mare's thick-furred, damp neck. A sharp gust of wind made the mare step sideways with her ears flat back, and quick as lightning, Nora grabbed a handful of mane and leaped onto Dunlin's back. There was no need for halter and saddlecloth now, since Nora rarely tried to tell Dunlin where she should go, or how fast. It was much more exciting to join in with the life of the wild ponies as they moved restlessly through the mountains, searching for the sweetest grass and the most sheltered windbreaks.

Nora gently closed her legs against the mare's sides, as much to hold on as to tell the mare she was ready to go, and thrust her hands deep into the wiry, light brown mane. With a snort, the pony wheeled around and set off up the mountain, her back hunched under the weight of her rider. Nora sat as still as she could, bent low over Dunlin's neck so that she didn't unbalance her. Through her wind-blurred eyes, she was aware of the land stretching out beneath them: the tussocked, peaty bog split by gleaming, silver lakes and smooth, gray mountains rising into the sky on every side. The track that ran from Errislannan to Aughnanure, and further on to Galway, was just visible as a fragile line of stones, but there was no sign of Ballach and the cart.

Dunlin slowed down when she reached the rest of her herd and the ponies lifted their heads to stare at Nora with huge, curious eyes. She smiled, keeping still and quiet so as not to alarm them, then turned very carefully to look at Dubh. The foal picked his way toward them over the rocky ground. He was still limping but his head wasn't nodding as much, which told Nora that he was able to carry more weight on his injured leg. As far as she could tell, the swelling had gone down, and the foal's eyes were bright and clear so there was no infection in his blood.

A proud, dark gray head shot up on the far side of the herd, followed swiftly by a regal-sounding whinny, and Nora smiled. The stallion seemed insulted that Dunlin hadn't brought the two-legged visitor to see him first.

"She wanted to show me how well Dubh was getting on, I think," Nora told him softly.

The stallion trotted around the edge of his herd and came to a halt a few strides away from Dunlin. He studied her for a long moment, his long mane rising and falling in the wind, then tossed his head, and wheeled away to lead his mares at a fast-paced trot over the summit of Binn Ghleann Uisce and down the far side to the gentler slopes of Barr na Oran. As the ground flattened out, the ponies broke into a gallop. Nora crouched low over Dunlin's neck, feeling her hair whip loose from its plait and stream behind her. The other ponies pressed close around her, sometimes brushing against her legs before swerving away to leap over a tussock or a shallow, peaty runnel. Dubh cantered next to his mother's flank, and Nora was thrilled to see that he kept up easily, favoring his sore leg only when the ground was very stony.

The herd streamed into the valley, blindly heading wherever Fiach led them. Nora laughed out loud when they hurtled past a crofter cutting peat. His head jerked up in surprise when he saw her, and she risked letting go of Dunlin's mane with one hand to wave as they galloped on. It was no matter if he recognized her. Tom Donovan's youngest girl was well known for chasing about with the wild ponies instead of churning butter or spinning linen like his more obedient daughters. Nora wished people weren't so disapproving—she never did less than her share, and she reasoned that with so many hands to help in the family, she could be spared for a few hours each day. At least she wasn't idle and bad tempered like Con Foyle's youngest sister; Nora had heard Meg say more than once that Clara couldn't be trusted to churn milk because the scowl on her face turned it sour. Some people even said that Clara Foyle was a changeling, a fairy child that had been swapped for a mortal baby, but Nora thought that was nonsense. Not because she didn't believe in fairies, but because nobody could look at lumpish, whey-faced Clara and mistake her for a visitor from the land of Tir na nÓg, the Land of the Young.

Fiach slowed to a trot and the mares bunched up behind him before steadying their pace to match his. Nora sat up straighter and pushed her hair out of her eyes. There was a solitary figure trudging along one of the invisible paths that wound through the bog. He was dressed like a journeyman shepherd, one of the laborers who traveled around accepting food and shelter in return for helping to shear sheep or mend walls. His woolen brat was so old that it was worn almost to a shine across his narrow shoulders. His trews were tied at the knee with twine and his boots looked in even more need of padding with moss than Nora's. It was impossible to tell how old he was because although his hair was gray, his blue eyes were alive with warmth and kindness, and his face was hardly lined at all except when he smiled.

Now that the herd was walking, and even stopping occasionally to snatch at the grass that grew around the yellowed, bristling tussocks, Dunlin seemed to notice where Nora's attention had strayed. She swerved away from the herd toward the unseen path, until Nora was within calling distance of the man.

"Father Francis!" she exclaimed. "We weren't expecting you back so soon."

The man's face broke into a warm smile and he waved. He wasn't a journeyman shepherd at all but a priest, forced into hiding by the English soldiers that came to Ireland to stamp out the Catholic religion on the orders of Henry VIII and his daughter Elizabeth after him. Nora couldn't understand why this should matter so much; after all, Catholics and Reformists worshipped the same God, didn't they? But Father Francis had looked so sad the one time he had talked about the ransacked monasteries and the churches robbed of all their treasure that she hadn't wanted to ask him about it again.

Dunlin halted a few paces away from the priest, her head high and her nostrils flared.

"It's all right, sweet girl," Nora murmured as she slipped from the mare's back. "He's a friend."

Dunlin snorted in disbelief and turned to trot back to her herd, where Dubh waited at the edge with his ears pricked forward curiously.

"Ah, Nora, I wouldn't be surprised if you grew a tail and hooves one day!" chuckled Father Francis, leaning on his hazel staff.

Nora joined him on the narrow path, shaking the prickly horse hairs out of her skirt. For once she didn't mind being teased because Father Francis had told her that he often preferred the company of animals to humans. As if echoing her thoughts, there was a sharp cry from above and a soft black shadow swooped down to land on Francis's shoulder.

The priest reached up to stroke the bird's wings. "Where have you been today, Alex?" he murmured. "He flew off at first light this morning, when we were leaving Roscrea," he explained to Nora. "'There must be bad weather coming. He always flies for longer when the wind's up."

Nora reached out and smoothed Alex's cold feathers. Father Francis had traveled with a tame squall-crow for as long as she could remember, although she suspected this might not be the same bird she had known seven or eight years ago.

"You should get home before the storm breaks," Father Francis advised. "Let the mare take you, if she will. Alex and I will not be far behind."

Nora frowned. "'Tis not the first storm we've had this

autumn. You've not come back to warn us about the weather, surely?" The priest had only visited Errislannan the day before she left for Aughnanure, and it was unusual for him to celebrate Mass in the cave below the Donovans' cottage more than twice a month.

Father Francis shook his head. "No, Honora, I've not come because of weather. I met some men at Roscrea who had come from the north and seen the Spanish fleet sailing close to the shore less than a day's journey from here. I fear the storm will bring something more than the usual flotsam to Errislannan tonight."

Nora felt her stomach turn over. "Do you think the ships might try to land?"

The priest's eyes were dark and serious. "Whether they want to land or not, my child, this wind will drive them onto our shores."

DUSK WAS FALLING BY THE TIME Fiach's herd picked their way through the dense forest of oak, holly, and hazel that stretched between the Connemara mountains and Errislannan. For once, Nora used her heels to make Dunlin gallop faster, half-afraid that she would get home to find Spanish sailors already swarming up the beach. As they neared the edge of the trees, the branches clashed angrily overhead, and she realized that the storm was nearly upon them. In the bay, a savage wind hurled the waves against the shore so that the air seemed to be filled with thunder, and the clouds were an ominous pale saffron in the darkening sky. The stallion halted at the edge of the trees, stiff-legged with alarm.

"It's all right, Fiach," said Nora, scrambling off Dunlin's back and twisting her wet, tangled hair into a knot at the base of her neck. " 'Tis no weather to be grazing on the beach. And you—" she turned to Dunlin, and smiled as Dubh stepped hesitantly forward on sapling legs, stretching out his nose to puff curiously at Nora's sleeve—"you two stay here as well. I'll see you tomorrow, I promise." She gritted her teeth, ignoring the tiny, scared voice inside her that said, *but what if the sailors come?* and ran out of the trees.

Head down, Nora stumbled over rocks and clumps of grass toward a tiny speck of light that flickered in the shelter of a ridge, halfway along the peninsula. On her right, the sea bellowed like a hundred wolves. The sea god Manannan mac Lir would have good hunting tonight.

Nora ran along the highest part of the ridge so that when she drew level with her cottage, panting and clasping her side, she was looking down at the thatched roof through a copse of hazel trees. Out here, the rain was mingled with windblown seafoam, sharp and salty, and Nora screwed up her eyes as she tried to see beyond the cottage to the beach. A line of white breakers pounded against the sand, the sea dark and heaving behind them.

Suddenly a voice carried above the wind, piercing the air like the cry of a gull. "Nora Donovan, is that you?"

A figure appeared at the edge of the hazel trees, one hand holding back a rapidly unraveling plait of light brown hair.

"Yes, Meg, it's me." Nora ran down the hill toward her sister, suddenly feeling so tired that by the time she reached the trees she could hardly stand, let alone speak.

"Look at you, you're wet through!" scolded Meg. She took Nora's arm and led her toward the cottage. The shutters on the windows were flapping wildly, slamming against the stone like a crazed bodhran. Walt and Colm were trying to nail them shut but as soon as Walt forced a shutter into place, the wind wrenched it out of his hands again so that Colm had to duck to avoid having his head clipped.

Meg hurried Nora past their brothers and pushed her into the cottage. She heaved the door shut behind them and leaned back against the wood, gasping for breath. As if a fairy had cast a spell for deafness, the noise of the storm was cut off. Nora stood still for a moment, letting the quiet wash over her. The only sound was rainwater dripping from the hem of her brat and the soft crackle of the fire at the far end of the room. The speckled mare and a small black cow stood nose to tail in one corner, their eyes half-closed as they dozed companionably. Anne was sitting on a three-legged stool beside the hearth with a bunch of watercress on her lap, carefully discarding any blackened, rotten leaves. She didn't look up when Nora came in, but kept her head bowed over the watercress so that her hair shielded her face in a shining gold curtain.

A black cooking pot hung over the flames, tended by a woman with the same black hair as Nora, held in two carefully pinned coils on either side of her head. She straightened up and turned to Nora with her blue eyes blazing. "What were you thinking of, staying out this late, you foolish girl?"

Nora took a step toward her, holding out her hands. "Mother, I —"

"Enough!" snapped Maria Donovan, brandishing a wooden ladle at her youngest daughter. "'Tis bad enough that Colm and Walt had to see to the animals on their own, without your feeble excuses. Sean offered to stay and help, but I told him to take Rua home before the storm took hold." She slapped Ballach on the rump to give weight to her words, and the gray mare threw up her head, startled.

"There's no need to take it out on Ballach!" Nora protested, stepping quickly over the rushes to run her hand down the mare's nose.

"And you can keep off those rushes, too," ordered her mother. "Meg's only just put them down, though the good Lord only knows how we'll sleep tonight with that racket out there."

Nora was tempted to tell her mother that it was a great deal noisier outside the cottage's thick stone walls, but she thought better of it and concentrated instead on smoothing her hand down Ballach's broad, gray face until the mare's eyes closed again.

"Now that you're here, you can make yourself useful by fetching some butter," Mrs. Donovan went on, pointing with the ladle toward a wooden pail. "We'll eat as soon as your father gets back."

Nora looked up at her mother in alarm, Father Francis's dire warning echoing in her ears. "He's not gone far, has he?"

Mrs. Donovan shook her head. "Only as far as Donal Foyle's house. Apparently Clara let loose their mare when she was trying to bring her in this evening. Donal wanted an extra hand to help round her up, the witless animal."

It was not clear if her scorn was directed at the storm-shy horse or Con's hapless sister Clara. Nora caught Meg's eye and watched her sister's shoulders shake with silent laughter as she unfolded thick, woolen blankets and laid them on the rushes, ready for the night. Nora went over to scoop out a handful of butter that they would spread on oatbread to make the scratchy dough easier to swallow. When she pushed her fingers into the slimy, yellow butter, the bucket wobbled on the lump of coal that was stored underneath to keep greedy fairies away. Nora scraped the butter off her fingers onto a wooden trencher and carried it over to the fire to soften.

Maria Donovan reached out and rested her hand on Nora's arm. Her eyes were softer now, twin points of flame reflected in the clear blue. "I was worried about you, child," she said, and Nora knew that her mother was apologizing for her outburst.

"I'm sorry I've been out so long," she said. "I would have been home sooner if I'd known the storm would rise so quickly." She wondered if her mother knew about the Spanish fleet that was somewhere out there in the darkness, that might even be heading toward their bay now, ready to disgorge hundreds of wild-eyed, shouting sailors armed with swords and muskets.

Nora reminded herself that the Spanish sailors had no quarrel with the Irish people, that their enemies were the English, which gave them something in common. But the thought of any strangers landing so near to her cottage was alarming, especially desperate, shipwrecked men ready for battle.

At that moment, the door crashed open behind her. Nora spun around and snatched up one of the heavy fire-irons, feeling her hair stand on end with fear.

"By our Lady, Nora! What on earth's got into you?" exclaimed the man standing in the doorway. Water streamed off him, turning his light brown hair darker than seaweed. His trews were stiff with mud and his jacket hung open to reveal his soaked undershirt.

Nora let the fire-iron clatter onto the floor. "Pa!"

"Did you catch the mare?" asked Anne.

Thomas Donovan ducked his head under the lintel and came into the room, tugging off his jacket. "Yes, thank the Lord. We would have lost the daft creature over the cliff if Father Francis hadn't turned up to help."

"Father Francis?" Meg echoed as she went over to help her father wrench his arms out of the sleeves.

"But he went to Roscrea, didn't he?" said Mrs. Donovan, glancing up from the cooking pot and frowning.

Tom Donovan nodded. "Aye, but important news has brought him back."

Nora held out two wooden bowls and her mother started ladling the steaming broth into them. The door opened again and Colm and Walt were swept in on a blast of cold, wet air.

"Has Pa told you about the news from Father Francis?" demanded Walt. At twenty-two, he was the youngest of Nora's brothers, with black hair like his mother's and hazel eyes.

"He was just about to," Anne said, putting the watercress onto the trencher with the butter and standing up. She took the bowls of broth from Nora and handed one each to her brothers.

Nora's father hung his dripping jacket on a nail beside the door and came over to the fire to collect a bowl as well. Then he sat cross-legged on the rushes beside Colm and Walt and waited for his wife and daughters to join them. Nora blew on her broth, cupping her hands around the bowl to warm them, and listened to the storm whistling around the house. She knew why the priest had come back to Errislannan and she didn't want to hear her father repeat his terrifying warning inside these four sturdy walls.

Usually on the first evening home after one of Murray ne Doe's feasts the family stayed up late, those who had gone to Aughnanure recalling every last detail for the ones who had stayed behind. Last time it had been Meg who came back with tales of handsome gallowglasses and more roasted meat on the table than the Donovans would eat in a year. But it seemed that the feast had been forgotten in favor of Father Francis's warning that the storm might blow the Spanish ships into Ardbear Bay, beside their cottage.

When she had finished her broth, Nora drew a blanket over her legs and settled down, bundling her brat under her head to keep her ear from being scratched by the rushes, or worse, nibbled by mice. Her brothers and sisters had teased her when she was little, saying that if she wasn't careful a mouse would bite her ear clean off while she was asleep. Even now, Nora wasn't brave enough to risk sleeping on bare rushes, although the lack of injuries suffered by anyone else sometimes made her wonder if mice weren't that interested in human ears.

She shut her eyes and listened to her father talking quietly about the sightings of the Spanish fleet. Anne and Meg gasped in alarm, but Colm pointed out that if the fleet had been seen as far north as Achill Island, they'd have needed to make good speed to have got this far since then. More likely, once the wind picked up, the captains would have ordered the ships to lie at anchor and ride out the storm some distance from the rocky shore.

Nora told herself that Colm was right, that no sailor would be foolish enough to try to land in this weather. She heard Meg lie down beside her and shuffled over to let her older sister tuck herself under the same blanket.

"Promise you'll tell me all about the feast tomorrow," Meg

murmured sleepily in Nora's ear. "Anne said Dan Devlin was wanting to know where I was." She sounded bored, but Nora suspected this was the piece of news her sister had wanted to hear most, even if she had no intention of marrying the horse trader.

"All right, tomorrow," Nora whispered back. She felt Ballach sniff her hair and stretched one hand out from under the blanket to shoo the mare back into the corner. There was enough peat stacked in the hearth to keep the fire going for most of the night, so the cottage would never be so dark that the animals might tread on the sleeping people, although more than once Nora had woken with her cheek pressed against a soft, furry flank where the cow had lain down beside her.

The rest of her family settled down, Colm and Walt nearest the door, Mr. and Mrs. Donovan in the middle of the room, and the three girls beside the hearth. The wind howled in anger as it rattled the shutters and the waves tore relentlessly at the bottom of the cliff. Nora thought she would never be able to sleep, but she must have dozed off because at first she was confused by the sound of someone hammering against the door. Had Donal Foyle's mare got loose again? she wondered, pushing back the blanket and struggling to sit up. The fire had all but gone out but it was long before dawn because no light seeped out from the edge of the shutters. Nora could barely make out the shapes of her father and brothers who were already on their feet, reaching for the fighting sticks that were propped against the wall.

"Who is it?" shouted Nora's father, raising his voice above the wind.

"Donal Foyle," came the reply. "Open up, for God's sake, man!"

There was the sound of the wooden bar being drawn across the door, then it was flung open, letting in a squall of rain that blew half the rushes across the floor and made Ballach snort in alarm.

Their neighbor stood in the doorway, his long hair wild around his bony face and a wooden cudgel gripped in one fist. "Come down to the shore, quick! There's a Spanish ship being wrecked!"

OUTSIDE, ALL WAS NOISE and wind and raging sea. Nora stood on the clifftop with her fingers dug into her brat to keep it from being ripped off her shoulders. The horizon beyond the mountains was streaked a milky gray, but to the west the sea was black and heaving, broken only by flashes of white foam that curled for a moment before vanishing again. On the beach, the tide was so high there was barely room for a man to stand at the bottom of the cliff. Nora peered through the half-light, straining to see if any men were emerging from the surf. But the waves hurled down nothing more than broken pieces of wood, shreds of canvas that might have once been sails, and occasionally a barrel, miraculously whole in spite of the battering it must have received on the rocks at the mouth of the bay.

Nora shivered. Ships had been wrecked in the bay before, but nothing more than a herring boat or a pucain, a small masted boat like the one her brothers used to collect oysters close to the shore. Usually she had known nothing about it until the next morning, when the tide left splintered planks strewn on the beach. It was a hundred times more shocking to stand here and watch the waves throw pieces of deck, mast, and sails onto the shore. Manannan mac Lir had spared little to suggest that this had once been a mighty warship, and it was impossible to think that any of the sailors could have survived.

Donal Foyle was already at the top of the path that led down to the beach. He had discarded his brat, and his undershirt clung to his wiry body, making him look like one of the merfolk with his wild eyes and wind-flailed hair. "Come on!" he shouted to Nora's father and brothers, who were struggling to follow him, bent double against the gale.

There was a faint noise behind Nora and she turned to see her mother and Anne trudging toward her, their brats over their heads and tendrils of hair whipping against their cheeks.

"Can you see anything?" Anne called.

"Only pieces of wood and barrels," she replied

Nora's mother stopped beside her and made a hasty sign of the cross, murmuring, "God save those sailors' souls." Her eyes grew wide as she stared down at the flotsam that was tossed in the foaming waves.

"What does Donal Foyle want with going down there?" asked Nora, following the men's unsteady progress down the side of the cliff. She clenched her fingers even tighter into her cloak as a sudden gust of wind sent Walt staggering close to the edge of the path. "Do they think the Spanish sailors will try to attack us?" she added, staring at her mother in dismay.

Maria Donovan shook her head and risked letting go of her brat to lay one hand on Nora's arm. "No, my love, we have no quarrel with Spain. The fate of those men lies with Manannan mac Lir tonight. But there could be something washed up that would be useful to us, for firewood if nothing else."

Anne leaned forward so that Nora could hear her above the wind and the bellowing surf. "Just think how well stocked those ships must have been, with food and wine for hundreds of men."

"But what if there are any survivors washed up as well?" Nora persisted.

" 'Tis the English they have to fear, not us," said her mother. Her eyes narrowed as she watched the four men reach the foot of the cliff. "Though I couldn't say what Donal Foyle might do. This storm's stirred him up for a fight, there's no doubt of that."

A giant wave, tossed by the unseen hand of the angry sea god, crashed over the men and sent Colm sprawling to the sand. Tom Donovan reached out and grabbed him as the undertow swirled around his legs and tried to suck him back into the sea. Nora's mother muttered a prayer under her breath, then said, "Anne, go inside and help Meg to build up the fire. If those men have a grain of sense between them, they'll come back and wait until morning."

Anne ran back toward the cottage, and Nora and her mother watched in dismay as the four drenched figures carried on along the foot of the cliff. There was a heap of barrels roped together halfway along the beach. They were stuck fast against a rock, but with every wave it seemed as if Manannan mac Lir was trying to wrench them free.

"They must be trying to reach those barrels," Nora said, pointing.

"Then they're bigger fools than I thought," Maria retorted. "Stay on the cliff, Nora, while I fetch them back." She shook her head and set off toward the path that led to the shore, her brat snapping behind her in the wind like a sail. She began calling down to her husband and sons, but her words were lost in the storm and the men kept going.

Left alone, Nora turned into the wind and forced her way along the top of the cliff. Further from the cottage, the land dipped down closer to the shore, and she thought she might be able to shout to the men and make them turn back without going down to the shore herself. At the end of the beach, the cliff rose sharply again and jutted out in a headland that fell straight and sheer into the sea, and on the other side of this was a smooth, white ribbon known as Carraig Sands. The beach stretched all the way to the tip of the peninsula, where Sean and Rua lived in one of a handful of cottages clustered around a tiny harbor. Mor and his family lived here, too.

On the near side of the headland there was a cave, almost as large as Murray ne Doe's banqueting hall, where Father Francis came to celebrate Mass. There was a smaller cave further around the headland, where the waves crashed in from the open sea. It could only be reached at low tide, though the sandy floor sloped up at the back of the cave so that nets could be stored here safely in winter. As a child, Nora had played in the cave with her brothers and sisters, until she got stranded one high tide and had to swim out, which made her mother so angry that they were forbidden from going near the little cave again.

Now she could hardly see the headland through the white-crested surf, let alone the gaping black mouth of the Mass cave. Suddenly, a flash of silvery gray at the edge of the water caught her eye, and Nora stopped dead, staring in disbelief. There was a horse in the sea! A wave reared up and the creature thrust its way out of the wall of water, its powerful legs churning against the current and its noble head held up so that its mane streamed back and mingled with the foam. Nora felt her heart pound. This must be the mighty horse of Manannan mac Lir, reaping his grim harvest of Spanish sailors.

The wave crashed down and the horse vanished, dissolving once more into surf and stirred-up sand. Nora blinked, wondering if the men on the beach had seen it too. But when she looked down she saw that they were too busy clinging to the base of the cliff, stubbornly making their way toward the heap of barrels. Donal Foyle was almost upon them now, and there was enough light for Nora to see him draw a knife from his belt to cut the ropes around the barrels. With his long hair whipping about and his mouth wide open in a hard square, shouting words that Nora couldn't hear, he looked like a banshee about to pounce on an unsuspecting traveler.

Nora knew there was no use trying to tell the men to turn back. Donal Foyle would have those barrels, and the Donovans seemed eager to help him for their share of the flotsam, shuffling along grim-faced and drenched. She walked further along the cliff until the drop to the beach was little more than the height of a tall man and stared into the waves for another glimpse of the sea-horse. There was no sign of the creature now, no pounding hooves or flowing mane half visible among the foam.

But there was something else. A pale face bobbed for the blink of an eye just beyond the line of breakers, then disappeared under the surface. The water rolled onto the beach and Nora saw the figure of a man clawing at the surf as it lifted him high above the sand before plunging him down into the roiling undertow.

For a moment, she wondered if it was Manannan mac Lir himself, his horse invisible under the surface, its flared nostrils breathing water as easily as air. But the next wave brought the figure closer to where Nora stood and she saw that this was no sea god but a drowning boy, his eyes wide with terror and his hands flailing. Nora started murmuring a prayer under her breath, not one that Father Francis would recognize but words as old as the mountains themselves, pleading with Manannan mac Lir to spare this man's suffering and harvest his soul quickly. It was not for ordinary folk to decide that a man should be saved from the sea god's grasp; the people of Iar-Connacht believed that Manannan would claim the rescuer's own soul or one of his family in return, like for like.

Nora glanced back at the men at the foot of the cliff. Donal Foyle was sawing at the rope around the barrels with his knife, its blade glinting in the gray dawn. Nora's father and brothers stood in a line, ready to haul the barrels one by one above the reach of the waves. They had not noticed the boy being washed up at the far end of the beach. Below her, the face appeared in the waves again, looking straight at Nora with pleading eyes, and this time he shouted. His words were tossed in the wind like the mew of a sea gull, but Nora had learned enough Spanish from the herring fishermen to know that he was begging her to help, to save him in the name of God and everything holy.

Nora twisted her hands in the hem of her brat, feeling tears well in her eyes. How could she explain that if Manannan mac Lir wanted to have his soul there was nothing she could do, unless she wanted to risk losing her own life to the jealous sea god?

Almost without realizing it, she had walked closer to the edge of the cliff, where a steep path led down to the beach. It was much rockier at this end, the sand hidden beneath huge boulders covered in seaweed and sharp-edged limpets.

Stumbling forward, her mother's warning to stay off the shore forgotten, Nora was halfway down the path when the man was thrown almost to the foot of the cliffs by a crashing wave. She met his terrified gaze and realized with a jolt that he was barely older than her, his face smooth and beardless beneath the sheen of seawater.

The boy grabbed hold of a rock with both hands and clung to it as the undertow washed noisily back into the sea. "Help me, please!" he begged.

Nora stared at him in disbelief. He had spoken to her in Irish, the meaning clear in spite of his strong accent. The boy spoke to her again, and his eyes grew huge with fear, as if he knew that he could not hold on when the next wave struck. In that moment, Nora knew that she could not stand there and watch him die, however much Manannan mac Lir wanted his soul.

"Hold on!" she shouted, hoping he would hear her above the roar of the sea. She looked wildly around for a piece of driftwood long enough to reach him. Along the beach, the men were still busy with the barrels, though there were only two or three left on the heap, and Nora was suddenly struck with fear that one of them would notice her. They might be angry with her for risking her life to save one of Manannan's souls. Worse than that, Nora remembered the gleam of Donal's knife and her mother's remark that the storm had stirred him to near madness, and she was afraid of what he might do to the half-drowned boy. If she was going to help him, it would have to be done quickly.

There was a salt-bleached branch wedged among the rocks, like the thigh bone of a long-dead giant. Nora tugged it free and carried it as close as she could to where the boy was lying. The surf churned and foamed around him, washing right over his head every time a wave came up the beach and making him choke and curse in his own language. Nora held out the branch but she was too far away to reach him. Gathering up her skirt in one hand, she scrambled over a low rock and stepped into the icy water. The undertow sucked the sand from under her feet and she nearly toppled backward, but she steadied herself with a gasp and jumped onto another rock as the next wave struck.

Now she was only a man's length away from the boy, and the tip of the driftwood touched the edge of his shirt.

"Catch hold of the branch!" she shouted, hoping that her voice would not carry behind her to the men beside the heap of barrels.

For a moment the boy did not move but lay on the sand with his head down, water streaming from every part of his body and running pink down his leg where something had sliced deeply into his thigh to leave a gaping wound. Nora's heart started pounding so hard, she thought she would slip off the rock. Had Manannan mac Lir taken his soul after all? Or had the boy not understood her words?

"Here!" she cried, jabbing the end of the branch into his ribs. To her relief, the boy twitched and looked up. She prodded him again, and the boy slowly let go of the rock with one hand. The piece of driftwood suddenly went heavy as he grasped the end, and Nora scrabbled with her stiff, drenched shoes for a better foothold. She started to pull the branch toward her, hand over hand, terrified of losing her grip. The boy was a dead weight at the other end, like a huge fish, and Nora screamed, "You'll have to help me! I can't pull you out on my own!"

Whether he understood the words or not, the Spanish sailor dug his toes into the sand and started to haul himself forward, out of the surf. He cried out in pain when he straightened his injured leg, but Nora saw him clench his teeth and try again. Another wave crashed down on him, rolling his body right over and twisting the branch so violently in Nora's hands that she stumbled and fell onto her knees. A pointed limpet dug painfully into her shin, and suddenly she was more angry than scared.

"Let me have him, Manannan mac Lir!" she shouted at the churning sea. The sky was light all the way to the west now and the rain had stopped, the wind ripping the clouds to shreds. Beyond the headland, the water heaved and swelled as if Manannan mac Lir had summoned armies of merfolk to push their way up to the surface, but Nora was not giving up now.

She scrambled to her feet and heaved on the branch again, and this time the Spanish sailor half-slithered, half-crawled up the beach toward her until he was lying on the rock at her feet. "*Gracias*," he murmured through cracked and swollen lips. "Thank you."

Shaking with fear, although she couldn't say whether she was more scared of being seen by Donal Foyle or the wrath of Manannan mac Lir, Nora threw down the branch and grabbed hold of the boy's arm. "Come on!" she panted. "You can't stay here."

The sailor's head rolled to one side, his eyes shut, and Nora realized that he had passed out. He was out of reach of the strongest waves here, but she didn't want to leave him stranded on the rocks like a dead salmon. She jumped down onto the sand and tried to drag the sailor off the boulder. His skin was bare where his shirt had been ripped open, and it scraped against the limpets until a thin trickle of blood started to run across his ribs. His face was deathly white, and only the faintest rise and fall of his chest showed that he was breathing.

Nora stopped, looking down at him in dismay.

Suddenly there was a shout behind her. "Nora! What have you found there?"

NORA WHIRLED AROUND AND STARED at her brother Colm. His hair was plastered to his shoulders and his drenched shirt flapped against his body as he clambered over the rocks toward her. He didn't seem to have noticed the boy lying at Nora's feet, and she knew she couldn't let him come any closer.

"Nothing, there's nothing here!" she exclaimed wildly, gathering her skirt in one hand and jumping down from the boulder. "Where's Donal? Did you get all the barrels?" She didn't think for a moment that Colm would want to hurt the Spaniard, but now that she had saved him in spite of Manannan mac Lir, she wanted to keep him away from Donal Foyle or anyone else who might take a fancy to the clothes of a half-dead sailor, or think that the boy had a pocket stuffed with Spanish gold.

Colm stopped with one foot propped on a rock. If he climbed onto the top, he would definitely see the boy. "The barrels are safe," he told her. "Donal is with Pa and Walt, taking them up the cliff." He tried to look past Nora. "So you've found nothing worth having?"

"No, nothing," Nora repeated. "Not even firewood." She scrambled onto the rock and held out her hand for him to help her down the other side. As they trudged along the beach, keeping close to the base of the cliff, she forced herself not to look back. She had saved the Spanish sailor from Manannan mac Lir; whatever fate befell him now, it was out of her hands.

"SHALL I WAKEN NORA NOW?"

"No, Anne, let her sleep. Lord knows what she was doing on the beach, the foolish girl, but she looked exhausted when she came in. And she'll only be upset about Walt."

Nora lay curled in the rushes and listened drowsily, the voices muffled as if they came from a long way away. But when her mother finished speaking, a wave crashed inside her mind, bringing with it a surge of pictures: the storm, the half-drowned boy, the horse in the sea . . .

Hurling aside the blanket, Nora sat bolt upright. "Walt?" she burst out. "What's happened to him?" Had Manannan mac Lir already claimed a soul in payment for the Spanish sailor? Cold dread clutched at her limbs, already stiff from where she had fallen asleep in her wet clothes.

Maria Donovan and Anne were bending over the fire. They looked around, startled, as Nora sat up. "You're awake at last, love," said Mrs. Donovan, coming over and laying a cool hand on Nora's forehead. "And by the looks of it you've not caught a chill, thank the Lord. You were like a drowned rat this morning."

Nora ducked away from her mother's hand. "What's happened to Walt?" she repeated.

Anne carried over a cup of buttermilk. A gritty scraping sound coming from the bowl told Nora that there was a hot stone inside to warm the milk. Her stomach growled with hunger, but she was too anxious to eat, so she took the bowl from Anne and held it to warm her hands without drinking from it.

Mrs. Donovan tucked a loose strand of Nora's hair behind her ear. "He slipped on the path carrying those barrels up and broke his arm."

"Oh, thank goodness!" Nora gasped, dizzy with relief to hear that her brother was alive.

Anne raised her eyebrows. "God's bones, Nora! What do you mean? Pa and Colm carried him to Donal Foyle's house for Nuala to see to him. She said he's lucky it's a clean break, but there's nothing to be grateful about that I can see. We've a lot to do just now, with winter coming and everything." She bustled back to the fire, tutting under her breath.

Nora shook her head. "No, of course, I didn't mean that. . . . " She broke off, confused, and her mother stroked her hair.

"There's no need for you to get up yet if you don't want to," she said to Nora's surprise—usually Maria Donovan liked to know that every member of her family was busy doing something useful, which was why she was so impatient with her youngest daughter over the mountain ponies. "Meg's put Ballach out to graze and milked the cow, and Anne's made the bread."

Nora lay back on the rushes and waited for her heart to stop pounding. Walt was going to be all right—Donal's wife Nuala would see to that with her store of healing herbs. The thick tallow candle that stood in the center of the room had not yet been lit, so she guessed it was not much later than the middle of the afternoon. Outside, the storm had eased, although gusts of wind still battered the walls of the cottage and flew down the chimney, sending cloudy belches of smoke into the room. She hoped the wild ponies had made it safely back to the mountains. Fiach would not have let his mares linger in the forest because of wolves, but the storm had hit so fast, there was a chance their usual paths might have been blocked by a fallen tree. If all was well, the herd would come to the beach at dusk, but if there was no sign of them, Nora decided she would go looking for them to put her mind at rest.

She was sitting up drinking the warm buttermilk with a blanket around her shoulders when the door opened and Meg came in, followed closely by her father. They were windblown and flushed but their brats were dry and they looked in good spirits. Nora guessed the barrels had been worth the risk of retrieving them.

"Seven barrels of wine, and three of salt," Tom Donovan

declared, answering Nora's unspoken question.

"Then we should be thankful to Manannan mac Lir for sending them to us," said Nora's mother. "Though I'm not sure Walt will enjoy the taste of that wine after his fall. How is he?"

"Nuala's put a wooden splint on his arm and dressed it with water buttercup," said Meg. "She gave him a drink of chamomile and wants him to rest before coming home."

Nora nodded. That was exactly what she would have done. Nuala Foyle was well known as a medicine woman, and Nora was a willing pupil whenever she had time to spare from helping her mother and looking after the wild ponies. Tom and Maria Donovan were only too happy for their youngest daughter to learn which plants had healing properties and how to cure wounds and ailments; Nora was careful not to let them know that she used her knowledge most often to treat the mountain ponies.

Maria Donovan opened a wooden chest and took out a stack of thickly folded blankets. "We'd best make Walt a bed near the fire," she said, her voice suddenly tight with emotion. "He'll want to keep warm while his arm is mending."

Tom Donovan went over and laid a hand on his wife's shoulder. "It's all right, Maria. The boy will be fine. He's happy enough with the barrels we found. That storm brought us more good fortune than bad, you know."

"Not for the Spaniards, it didn't," said a quiet voice.

Nora looked up. Colm stood in the doorway, a stack of peat at his feet.

Tom Donovan shrugged, as if he had little sympathy to spare for men who were fool enough to put to sea at this time of year. But Nora could tell there was something else troubling her brother. "What do you mean, Colm?" she prompted, unwrapping the blanket from her shoulders and standing up.

"A company of English soldiers came by while Donal and I were fetching the peat."

Maria Donovan gasped and dropped the blanket she was holding. "Soldiers, here?"

"Yes, though they didn't stay long. From the sounds of it, there've been shipwrecks all along the coast, and more expected tonight if this wind doesn't let up."

Meg held out a bowl of hot broth to her brother. "Sit down and tell us all," she urged him.

Colm took the bowl and sat cross-legged on the rushes, staring at the broth as if the role of storyteller made him uncomfortable and he might find help in the rich, lamb-scented liquid. Nora sat down next to him, breathlessly waiting to hear what the soldiers had or had not found on the beach below the cottage.

"They were looking for Spanish sailors," Colm began. "You remember that troop that passed us outside Aughnanure?" he said to Anne and Nora, and they nodded. "Well, 'twas the same men, led by the fair-haired captain. He speaks enough Irish to ask Donal and me if we'd been down to the beach since the storm."

"I hope you said nothing about those barrels!" Tom Donovan interrupted. "They're safe behind Donal's midden, and I won't see them going to feed any English hogs after we went to the trouble of bringing them up."

Colm shook his head impatiently. "Of course we didn't, Pa. They didn't seem interested in what the ships had been carrying, except for men."

"Surely there weren't any survivors last night?" exclaimed Meg, tucking her skirt under her as she sat down on the rushes.

"The soldier said they'd found none so far," Colm reported.

His mother's lips tightened into a thin line. "Manannan mac Lir may have spared us a few barrels of wine, but his palace is fuller by a shipful of souls."

Nora clenched her hands around her empty bowl. If the English soldiers had said there were no survivors, did this mean the Spanish boy had died on the rocks where she had left him? Had she risked the anger of Manannan mac Lir for nothing?

"'Tis as well for those sailors to have stayed in the sea," Colm said darkly. "The English are so afraid the Spanish have come to raise an army against their queen, that they won't let any of them live if they've made it ashore. A swift death at the hands of Manannan mac Lir might be kinder than for a half-drowned man to have his throat slit by a cowardly Englishman."

Nora stared at her brother in dismay, only dimly aware of Anne and Meg gasping out loud and her mother making impatient shushing movements with her hands. "S-surely we should help the sailors, if we find any?" Nora stammered. "The English are our enemies as much as theirs."

Her father shook his head. "'Tis not for us to meddle in, Nora," he said, but his voice was gentle. "The English would slit our throats as well if they caught us. Those Spaniards took it upon themselves to sail this way, and I'll not put my family in danger by helping them." His eyes slid sideways in the direction of Donal Foyle's cottage. "Though I dare say there's some who'd willingly round up any survivors in return for a purse of English crowns."

"Hush now," said Nora's mother, stabbing fiercely at the stack of burning peat with a fire-iron. "I'll have no more talk of soldiers and Spanish sailors. 'Tis lucky enough that the soldiers didn't find those barrels. We must pray that no more ships end up on this shore, and thank God we have no shipwrecked men to worry about."

"Thank God—or Manannan," murmured Anne.

Meg tutted loudly and Nora turned to see her sister frowning down at a wooden pail in her hand. "These oysters are no good," she said. "They've all opened, we can't eat them now."

She gave the pail an impatient shake and the oysters shuffled grittily in the seawater.

Maria Donovan went over and peered into the bucket. "You're right, Meg, those are no use to man nor beast. Nora, will you go down to the beach and fetch some mussels? There's precious little meat left to add to the broth, and we'll all be hungry after last night."

Nora stood up, sending the blanket slithering onto the rushes. Her arms and legs felt as if they were made of stone, and anxiety prickled in the pit of her stomach. What would happen if she saw the Spanish boy again? From what her father said, it looked as if she had only rescued him for a far worse fate. She had risked enough by taking him out of the clutches of Manannan mac Lir; she didn't want to be responsible for what happened to him now.

She wrapped her brat closely around her before taking the bucket of rotten oysters from Meg and heading outside. The wind still howled across the cliff and the sea was the color of dirty sand, whipped into white froth where it met the shore. But the storm seemed less overpowering now that it was daylight, even if the afternoon was fading rapidly to dusk under the thick, black clouds. Nora tipped the useless oysters into the midden, then ran straight past Donal Foyle's cottage and down the rocky path to the beach, slowing down when she remembered Walt's broken arm. The strip of white, boulder-strewn sand was wider now than in the night because the tide was lower, and when she ran along the bottom of the cliffs she was well beyond the reach of the waves. The sand was littered with splinters of wood, the remains of spar and deck occasionally tangled in a piece of flapping canvas that might once have been a sail. There were no more undamaged barrels like the ones her father and brothers had helped Donal Foyle to fetch, but many others had been shattered against the rocks and lay about in pieces like the ribs of sturdy wooden beasts.

Nora came to the furthest end of the beach where the mussels were clustered thickly on the rocks, glossy black with sharp white tips. Wrapping her fingers in the bottom of her cloak to protect them against the razorlike shells, she started to wrench them off and drop them into the pail. When the bucket was full, she hoisted herself onto a rock. The waves had drawn back with the tide, exposing a swath of boulders and seaweed strewn with yet more wood, and here and there a gleam of metal. To Nora's relief, there was no sign of the Spanish sailor. He must have recovered enough to make his way up the cliffs; he might even have reached the shelter of the forest by now.

But there was something else: a pale gray shape lying close to the edge of the water. Nora slithered down the rock, wedged the bucket of mussels in the sand, and walked cautiously along the beach. Her heart started to beat faster as she made out a smooth, arched flank the color of seafoam and a long mane tangled with seaweed and sand. In a flash, she remembered the horse she had seen in the waves the night before, the storm-swept stallion of Manannan mac Lir as he gathered his harvest of Spanish souls.

Then the horse on the sand lifted his head and snorted, and Nora realized that it was as real as her Spanish sailor—and alive.

THE HORSE SNORTED AGAIN and propped one front hoof on the sand, trying to push itself up. Instinctively Nora held out one hand toward it. "Easy there," she murmured. She was close enough to see a wound on the horse's shoulder, swollen and rubbed raw by the rocks.

At the sound of her voice, the horse twitched and looked around with its ears pricked. Nora stared at it in amazement. This was no wild mountain pony, but a noble creature fit for a king, with its wide forehead and large oval eyes. From the breadth of its back as it lay on the sand, she guessed it would be several hands taller than Dunlin—taller even than the Munster-bred war horses ridden by the English soldiers.

The horse dug its front leg into the sand and heaved itself up. It shook itself vigorously, sending sand and grit flying from its smooth, gray coat. Then it stood stiff-legged and looked at Nora, its head set high on a long neck the shape of a swan's and its tail so long and thick that it brushed the ground. From the rapid rise and fall of its flanks, Nora could tell the horse was scared and exhausted, which was little wonder considering the struggle it must have had to survive the storm. Her mind filled at once with the names of healing plants: tansy to make the heart strong, knapweed for the wounded shoulder, and chamomile to bring soothing sleep. And food and water as well, since it must be at least a day since this horse had had anything to eat or drink.

She glanced around and saw a clump of the bright green seaweed that the mountain ponies came to graze. Bending down, she tore up a handful and held it out to the horse. "Here, eat this," she urged, walking closer.

The horse tensed, its ears flicking back and its nostrils flaring with each hurried breath. Nora's head was barely level with its withers and for the first time she felt a flicker of alarm. This was a stallion, just like Fiach, and however used to people he had been in the past, she should treat him as cautiously as she would one of the wild ponies.

She held the seaweed at arm's length and stood very still, forcing her breathing to stay quiet and measured. Very slowly, with his eyes open so wide that the whites showed, the horse stretched out his head and brushed his lips against the seaweed. His huge sculpted nostrils flared twice, then he snatched the slippery green leaves out of Nora's hand and chewed at them, tossing his head up and down like the mountain ponies did when they ate something unfamiliar.

"Good boy," Nora praised him, and this time the stallion

didn't flinch at the sound of her voice but pricked his ears toward her as if waiting for the next mouthful. There was another clump of the bright green seaweed nearby, and Nora fed the horse handful by handful with excitement building inside her. This exotic, washed-up creature was as fine as anything Manannan mac Lir might ride—or indeed Dan Devlin might have to sell, she added wryly to herself, admiring the stallion's slender legs and powerful hindquarters.

A cold gust of wind made the horse shy sideways, and Nora saw that he was trembling with pain and exhaustion. He needed shelter, but he was too weak to climb up the cliff path. While the stallion dipped his head to eat the last handful of seaweed, she looked over his ears to the headland at the end of the beach. The cave where Father Francis held Mass yawned blackly against the sheer rock. The horse would be sheltered from the wind inside the cave, but too easily seen from the cliff, even if Nora could persuade him to stay there. But the little cave further around the headland was well hidden from passersby, and just as sheltered. It was low tide now which meant that the cave would be empty of water. When high tide came, the horse would have to keep to a small patch of dry sand at the back of the cave where the nets were stored.

Nora bit her lip as she wondered what would happen if the tide came so high that the cave filled up completely—it had happened once before during a storm, and Colm and Mor had found their precious store of nets either ripped to shreds or washed away. But the wind was definitely not as strong as it had been the previous night, and she told herself that it was a risk worth taking. If the worst happened and the cave flooded, the stallion had already proved he could swim.

Her thoughts were interrupted by the horse pushing impatiently at her arm, leaving a smear of seaweed-green foam on her sleeve. Nora laughed and reached up to rub his ears, just as she would with Dunlin, but the stallion shied away in alarm, his hooves skittering on the sand. Nora stayed very still and waited with her heart pounding. The horse stopped a few paces away and looked back at her, the muscles stretched tight along his neck as if he was ready to take flight.

Nora scolded herself for startling him. She would have to be much more careful if she wanted to get him into the cave. Tearing up another handful of seaweed, she held it out to the stallion as a peace offering and felt a jolt of relief when he took a step toward her and reached out to take the leaves. Nora bent down very slowly to gather more seaweed—not just a handful, but as much as she could carry in a fold of her brat. Then she walked a few steps past the stallion, toward the headland, before turning back to him with another offering of seaweed.

"Come on, beautiful," she whispered.

The stallion tossed his head and his long mane was lifted by the wind so that it curled over like a wave, the exact color of storm-whipped foam. An image flashed into Nora's head of the first time she had seen him, plunging through the water like a fairy horse.

"I'll call you Lir," she murmured. It was the name of Manannan's father, the most powerful sea god of all. She said it again, louder, and it was snatched up by the wind like the cry of a gull, a name fit for a horse from the sea.

The stallion came close enough to eat the seaweed and Nora walked on again, threading her way between the boulders. Handful by handful, the horse followed her across the beach; Nora saw with relief that he walked evenly in spite of the scrape on his shoulder, which meant that the wound hadn't damaged muscle or bone. When they reached the Mass cave, Lir balked and stared warily into the shadows, but Nora urged him past with another clump of seaweed. Now came the most difficult part, persuading the stallion to follow her to the other cave. The wind had whipped up the waves so that even though it was low tide, they still washed right up to the foot of the headland. Nora and Lir would have to wade through foaming, knee-deep water to reach the cave, swirling with currents that waited to suck them out to the middle of the bay.

Nora stopped when she felt the first wave wash over her shoes. The water was icy cold and her skirt wrapped itself heavily around her legs like a pair of heavy trews, but she forced herself not to gasp or jump back. Instead, she faced the stallion and held out her hand again. This time when he came up to take the seaweed, she reached up very slowly and ran her free hand down his neck. The horse's ears flickered and he snorted, but he stayed still, watching her closely as he chewed.

"Good boy," said Nora, letting her hand slide all the way down his neck to his broad, well-muscled chest. She knew Lir would refuse to go back into the sea unless she could persuade him to trust her, and that meant he had to let her stroke him. She had watched the mountain ponies for many months before daring to touch Dunlin, who had always been the boldest of them, the most curious about the two-legged creature who came to watch them on the beach. Nora couldn't wait that long with Lir, but she hoped that whoever had looked after him before had treated him kindly and taught him that people could be trusted.

The stallion finished the seaweed and ran his muzzle over Nora's hand. It felt as soft as squirrel fur, and she smiled when his whiskers brushed against her fingers. Another wave washed around her legs, reminding her that there was not much time to get Lir safely into his hiding place. The tide was still going out, but Nora wanted to fetch him an armful of grass and fresh water before nightfall, which would mean another trip to the cave.

She waded forward a little way and turned back to Lir. "Come on," she urged. "You have to follow me." She held out another handful of seaweed and clicked her tongue, realizing that he probably didn't understand a word she was saying.

The horse craned his neck forward, trying to reach Nora's

hand without stepping into the water. A wave washed right up to his hooves, swirling around his fetlocks, and Lir leaped back at once with an alarmed snort.

Nora forced herself to stay calm. "Come on," she repeated. "You'll be safe, I promise."

The wave pulled away again, and as the water grew shallower Lir took a hesitant step forward.

"Good boy!" Nora praised, letting him eat the leaves from her hand.

This time Lir followed her when she walked on, as if he wanted to get as far across the sand as he could before the next wave came. His ears flicked uneasily back and forth and his breath came in rapid, shallow puffs. Nora kept one eye on the sea so that when the wave broke, she was standing close to the stallion, feeding him with one hand and stroking his neck with the other. His coat felt hot and damp and she hoped he wasn't catching a chill. The wild ponies were well used to getting a soaking at this time of year, but Lir obviously came from a much warmer place because his coat was not nearly as thick as Dunlin's or Fiach's.

They had almost reached the furthest point of the headland where the open sea rushed into the bay. The waves were fiercer here and the water sucked hungrily at Nora's legs. She staggered and clutched a handful of Lir's mane as she nearly lost her balance. The stallion flinched but stayed still, seafoam reaching almost to his belly and dragging his tail along the surface of the water like a tangled length of flax.

Now Nora could see the mouth of the smaller cave, a dark shape on the other side of some jutting-out rocks. When the water went down, she kept hold of Lir's mane and tugged him forward, bunching up her skirt with her other hand to stop it from tripping her up. To her relief, Lir broke into a trot beside her and she ran with him, stumbling and splashing through the shallows until they reached the mouth of the cave. Here the beach sloped upward under the hollowed-out cliff. The horse slowed to a walk as they came out of the water and then stood, gazing into the shadowy hole with his ears pricked forward.

Nora stopped breathlessly beside him. "Good boy," she panted. "Come on, you're nearly safe."

She had no more seaweed left so she just had to hope that the stallion trusted her enough to follow her into the dark. Lir tossed his head, flicking the ends of his mane against Nora's cheek, then walked beside her up the beach. The entrance to the cave was a handspan higher than the stallion's ears, but he ducked his head anyway and stood just inside with his muzzle almost touching the floor, blowing uncertainly at the sand. The afternoon light was fading, but Nora could just make out the heap of nets that lay tangled together at the back of the cave, dotted with broken mussel shells and scraps of seaweed.

Lir walked over, stiff-legged with caution, and lipped up a piece of seaweed. Then he lifted his head and looked back at Nora. A scrap of green leaf hung from his muzzle and his long forelock hung over one eye, so that he looked like one of the wild ponies rather than a shipwrecked stallion from some far-flung shore. Suddenly Nora was even more determined to keep him safe and hidden, although what she would do with him once his strength returned, she wasn't quite sure. For now, she had precious little daylight left to gather herbs and enough grass and fresh water to last the horse until morning.

Taking off her brat and bundling it under one arm so that it wouldn't drag in the water, she slipped out of the cave to wade back to the beach. She heard Lir follow her, his hooves thudding softly on the wet sand, and she glanced around for a way to barricade the entrance. The salt-bleached remains of a fir tree were wedged against a rock not far off. The tree's needles had been stripped away by the sea, but there were enough brittle, spiky branches left to make a sort of skeleton hedge when Nora dragged it across the mouth of the cave. Lir looked at her over the top, but he made no attempt to break through, aside from sniffing at one of the branches, then jerking his head away when a twig pricked his muzzle.

"You stay there now," Nora called, raising her voice above the wind and the crashing sea. "I won't be long, I promise."

She wedged her brat more securely under her arm, gathered up her skirt with her other hand, and splashed back into the waves.

NORA RAN ALONG THE BEACH with her head down, hoping there would be no one from her family on the cliff to spot her and wonder why she wasn't taking the pail of mussels straight home. The bucket banged uncomfortably against her legs, making a few of the mussels leap out onto the sand, but Nora kept running. She decided to look for some watercress or shamrock to take back as well, which would at least give her a reason for being out for so long. She avoided the path that led up to the cottages and headed instead for the far end of the shore, where the cliff sloped down until it was no more than a rocky scramble above the sand. The bay was much narrower and more sheltered here, the waves rolling into a strip of water edged with mud flats, where small brown birds pecked about in search of sandworms.

She fastened her cloak around her neck to leave both hands free and wedged the pail under her elbow, then pulled herself up the rocks until she was standing on the edge of the peat-colored moorland that stretched between the sea and the forest. The wind snatched at her hair and her clothes, but Nora was feeling hot after her run, so she hardly noticed it as she started hunting for the tufts of sweet, bright green grass that grew here and there among the dry, bristly tussocks. Most of the grass had been cropped almost to the ground by the wild ponies, but Nora found a few untouched clumps which she uprooted and stored in a fold of her cloak. She spotted knapweed and watercress growing close together at the bottom of a dried-out ditch and slithered down the crumbling, red-brown peat to pick a few careful handfuls. The knapweed would make a start on easing the pain in Lir's shoulder; tansy and chamomile would have to wait until tomorrow because they would be harder to find.

Nora was still crouched in the narrow runnel when she heard soft footsteps behind her. She froze, fearing a return of the English soldiers, or at the very least a curious member of her family who would want her to go straight home. Then she heard a familiar snort and the stamp of a hoof, and turned to see Dunlin looking down at her.

"Hallo there, girl," Nora murmured, smiling with relief. She stood up and scrambled out of the ditch, being careful not to drop any of the precious, sharp-scented leaves.

Dunlin wandered up to let Nora rub her nose. The rest of the herd were a little way off, grazing among the tussocks with their thick coats ruffled by the wind. Nora quickly scanned the gray, chestnut, and dun-colored rumps, relieved that none of them seemed to be missing. The black foal, Dubh, lifted his head to look curiously at her a few moments, then lowered it again, his tiny muzzle searching for the sweetest blades of grass. Fiach was on the far side of the herd, grazing close beside a small dappled mare who had given birth to a stillborn foal that spring.

Dunlin shoved her nose against Nora's arm, reaching for the leaves and grass she held in her cloak.

"Oh no, greedy, they're not for you!" Nora laughed, pushing the mare away. "You can find your own."

The mare blew sharply down her nostrils and ambled along the side of the ditch with her head down, pausing every now and then to run her muzzle over the peaty ground and lip up a mouthful of green shoots. Nora started to walk back along the cliff, wondering how she was going to take fresh water to Lir. She would have to fetch another bucket from the cottage, but she didn't want anyone to see her in case they asked awkward questions.

She waited in the hazel copse for a few moments to make sure there was no one around. Ballach came up and sniffed curiously at her folded cloak but seemed happy to stay in the shelter of the trees when Nora slipped into the open, her pre-cious bundle held close to her chest. She left the pail of mus-sels under the trees; she'd take it indoors later, so she didn't have to explain why she was going straight out again. The

Donovans' small black cow was standing beside the cottage where a wooden bucket stood under the edge of the roof to collect rainwater. Sometimes the animals drank from the bucket, but mostly they went to a broad, shallow stream on the far side of the copse. To Nora's relief, the bucket was just over half full—less than she would have liked to give the exhausted stallion, but probably as much as she could safely carry down the cliff path and through the rising tide.

Squeezing between the cow's warm, furry flank and the rough stone wall, Nora picked up the bucket, then froze as she heard voices. Her father was coming around the corner with Colm, talking in a low, urgent voice.

"We should think ourselves lucky that nothing more than a few barrels washed up here last night," Tom Donovan was saying.

There was a short questioning noise from Colm, and his father explained, "Father Francis told me there've been wrecks all along the north coast for the past week, and the English are turning themselves inside out trying to round up the ship-wrecked men. Whole families have been killed because these English hogs think they've given shelter to the Spanish sailors."

Nora's heart began to thud painfully. By dragging the boy out of the sea, she had come far too close to bringing down the wrath of the English soldiers on her family's heads. Maybe it was just as well that he had vanished.

Mr. Donovan went on, "Whether they're here by accident or purpose, those Spaniards will bring trouble with them. It's best if Maria and the girls stay close to home for a few days."

"You may be right, but they'll not thank you for keeping them like caged birds," Colm remarked.

The footsteps drew nearer. Nora crouched behind the cow, holding her breath and thinking rapidly of what excuse she could offer if they discovered her with a cloak full of grass and a bucket of rainwater. Food for Ballach, perhaps, so that the elderly mare could stay in the copse while the cold wind was still blowing?

Suddenly Nora's mother called from the other side of the cottage. "Tom, Colm! Could you bring more peat? And look out for Nora, too. Lord knows where the foolish girl has wandered off to."

"Some birds are easier to cage than others," Nora heard her father mutter. "Come on, Colm, let's fetch the peat before we find your sister. No doubt she'll be on the beach feeding seaweed to those ponies of hers."

Nora sent a silent prayer of gratitude to her mother as the footsteps changed direction and headed away from the cottage, toward the three-sided hut on the top of the ridge where the people of Errislannan stored the peat they cut from bogs further inland. If Colm and her father planned to go to the beach next in search of her, she barely had time to take the grass and the water to Lir's cave. As soon as the footsteps had faded away, Nora grabbed the bucket and ran in the opposite direction, along the wall of the cottage and across the cliff to the path.

She kept her head down, not daring to look around in case she saw her mother or one of her sisters calling her back. The bucket banged against her shins, slopping precious water over the brim, so she forced herself to walk slowly and keep the bucket level. She picked up speed when she reached the bottom of the cliff path and hurried across the sand, winding in and out of the boulders and shattered pieces of flotsam. The tide had turned and the waves crashed on the shore, each one washing higher up the beach than the last.

The water around the headland had risen so far that Nora had to hold the bucket level with her waist to prevent it from being washed out of her hand. Her shoulder burned with the effort and the cave suddenly seemed a hundred leagues away, through waist-high waves that pulled at her skirt and tried to unfold the cloak that held Lir's grass and herbs. Tears of exhaustion welled in Nora's eyes and she crossly blinked them away.

At last she reached the mouth of the cave and tucked the bundle of grass under her arm while she dragged the fir tree aside. The waves ran right into the entrance now, but the sand sloped up enough to keep most of the cave dry, at least while the tide was not at its highest. Lir was standing by the nets, a pale gray shape in the shadows. Nora waited for a few moments to let her eyes get used to the half-light, then carried the bucket up to the horse and wedged it in the sand to stop it from falling over if he knocked against it in the night.

"See? I told you I would come back," she murmured as she unfolded her cloak and shook the grass onto the floor of the cave, except for the small bundle of watercress. There seemed to be much less than she had thought, but it would do until morning. The knapweed leaves were well mixed in, and with luck the stallion's hunger would make him eat them up along with the grass; the mountain ponies often balked at their bitter taste, which exasperated Nora because she knew how good the herb was for easing pain.

The stallion drank thirstily from the bucket of rainwater, the muscles underneath his long neck convulsing with each swallow.

"I'll bring you some more tomorrow," Nora promised him, running her hand down his shoulder. Lir flinched as her fingers brushed the edge of his wound. "The knapweed will make that feel better," said Nora. It was so dark that she could barely make out the injury, but it didn't feel any hotter or more swollen than when she had first found him. Hopefully the saltwater had kept it clean and stopped any infection from setting in.

A wave boomed outside the cave, and Nora suddenly realized that she was in danger of being stranded by the rising tide.

After a last pat on Lir's neck, she tucked her cloak around her shoulders and ran back into the sea. By now the water was higher than her waist and she was forced to swim when the swirling currents below the surface made it impossible for her to keep her feet. Shivering and with salt stinging her eyes, she made it to the beach and started trudging back along the bottom of the cliffs.

She was almost at the path that led up to the cottages when she saw two figures emerging from the shadows beneath the cliff.

"Nora! What on earth are you doing?" one of them shouted, breaking into a run.

"I . . . I got caught by a wave, Pa," she faltered, offering the only reason she could think of for being soaked from head to foot.

Tom Donovan rolled his eyes. "Honestly, Nora, you've no more sense than a shamrock, sometimes." He put his hand under her arm. "Come on, let's get you home."

Colm walked on the other side of her, his face hidden in shadow as the last of the afternoon light slipped away, and together they steered Nora up the cliff and back to the cottage. She let her father and brother go in first, telling them she needed to visit the midden, then ran to the hazel copse and retrieved the pail of mussels.

Once indoors, Nora braced herself for a scolding from her

mother for soaking her clothes the second time in a day. But Mrs. Donovan was more concerned about Walt, whose broken arm was so sore that he couldn't make himself comfortable on the rushes even with three times his share of blankets. Even Nora's sisters seemed too busy to ask her why it had taken so long to fetch the mussels; Anne took the pail from her and tipped them straight into the broth, while Meg was laying rolled-up hides along the bottom of the door to keep out the worst of the drafts. Feeling clumsy and unhelpful, Nora retreated to a quiet corner beside Ballach and the cow, where she let her mind fill with the shipwrecked horse waiting for her in the sea-swept cave.

NORA HAD TO MILK THE COW and churn half a pail of cream into butter before she could escape to see Lir the next morning. She hoped her mother would not notice that the butter was thin and lumpy, with a few gritty specks of ash in it where she had sat too close to the fire, trying to warm herself after a cold, uncomfortable night. Walt had finally dozed off under nearly all the blankets the family possessed, so Nora had felt chilled to her bones when she woke up.

The storm seemed to have blown itself out and the thick gray clouds were lodged sullenly on the peaks of the mountains. Nora pulled up as much grass as she could from the pasture behind the cottage, watched curiously by Ballach and the cow. She was afraid her mother would start asking questions if another bucket went missing—she had heard Anne remark crossly that the pail of rainwater must have been blown away during the storm—so she decided to use the bucket from the cave to fetch more water.

Her father and Colm had gone to the harbor, and Anne and Meg were safely indoors with Maria, combing out brittle lengths of flax ready to weave into linen, so there was no one to see Nora run across the cliff and down the path to the beach. The tide was out and the waves were calm enough for her to make it nearly all the way to the cave without getting her feet wet, and she felt a surge of excitement when she reached the fir tree and started to haul it away from the entrance.

To Nora's delight, Lir came up and stretched his neck over the fir tree to blow warmly into her hair.

"You recognize me, don't you?" she said to him, slipping past the tree and reaching up to pat him. The stallion whickered softly and tossed his head. Laughing, Nora unwrapped the bundle of grass and tipped it onto the sand. Lir put his head down at once and began to eat.

She stepped away to let him graze in peace, happy to wait until he had finished before she examined the wound on his shoulder. She sang quietly to herself, her voice barely lifting above the wash of the waves. The stallion's ears flicked back as the cave echoed with the old ballad about Manannan mac Lir, riding his foam-gray horse over the sea and summoning a storm wind to reap another harvest of souls. As she sang, Nora's eyes drifted to the back of the cave, where the roof sloped down to meet the sand. The low morning sun had flooded every corner, and she could clearly see the stack of fishing nets.

And not just the nets, but something else as well. The stallion had not been alone in the cave last night. Curled up among the shreds of seaweed and broken pieces of shell, his eyes tightly closed beneath a peat-dark fringe of hair, was the Spanish sailor.

10

NORA STOPPED SINGING AND GASPED. The boy's eyes shot open and he lifted his head, looking wildly about. When he saw Nora, his eyes grew huge in his pale, bony face.

"*Ayúdame!*" he rasped, his throat burned dry from saltwater. "*Por el amor de Dios, ayúdame.*"

Nora stared down at the boy in horror. She knew that he was begging her to help him, but how could she? Her father's dire warning rang in her ears, of what the English soldiers would do to anyone found helping a shipwrecked sailor.

"I . . . I can't," she stammered, backing away. "I'm sorry. You don't understand."

The boy struggled to sit up, propping himself on one elbow with his injured leg crooked uncomfortably beneath him. "*Por favor, ayúdame,*" he repeated, his voice growing weaker.

Nora spun blindly away, trying to force the boy's cries out of her head. She told herself there was nothing she could do for him. Colm's small fishing boat was barely strong enough to make it to Galway along the coast, so there was no chance it could take someone as far as Spain. Nora didn't know exactly where the sailor's country was, but she was sure it was a long way away, on the other side of the ocean.

Hot, frustrated tears blurred her eyes and she stumbled straight into Lir, who let out a surprised snort and shied away. Nora paused for a moment with her cheek pressed against his coarse, tangled mane. "I'm sorry," she whispered, as if she could make the horse understand why she was running away. "It's too dangerous, my family . . ."

The stallion blew gently into her hair, his lips flicking over the loose strands escaping from her plait.

Nora straightened up and forced herself to look back at the heap of nets. The boy was lying very still, half-buried in the tangled mesh, and Nora could see how she hadn't noticed him in the shadows the night before. She had already risked her life—and possibly the life of one of her family, if Manannan mac Lir demanded another soul in payment—by rescuing the boy from the storm. There was nothing else she could do to help him now.

Folding her brat in half and draping it around her shoulders, Nora hurried down the gently sloping sand. She hesitated when she reached the fir tree, then shoved it aside so that it rolled down the beach into the waves. Now there was nothing to keep Lir in the cave. As she splashed back through the shallow water, she told herself that she had left the cave open for the stallion's sake; she couldn't keep him penned in any longer, and he would be better off finding his own food and water like the mountain ponies. She doubted he would stray far from the peninsula while his shoulder was still sore, so she would be able to find him and maybe take him to one of the valleys deep in the mountains, where he would be hidden from the greedy eyes of horse traders and English soldiers.

But deep down, Nora knew she had moved the fir tree because she didn't want to have to go back to the cave again. She forced from her mind an image of the Spanish boy's terror at being left alone, wounded and starving, when it seemed that there might have been someone able to help.

ON TOP OF THE CLIFF, behind Donal Foyle's cottage, a thick-waisted girl with hair the color of dried peat was sitting on a three-legged stool beside a basket of cabbages. She was picking slugs out of a bundle of leaves in her lap, flicking them one by one onto the grass. She looked up as Nora approached, her eyes hard and round in her plump face.

"You're in trouble, Nora Donovan," she announced, waggling a slug between her short, thick fingers.

Nora had run all the way from the cave, and her hands were grazed and sore from slipping on the cliff path. "What are you talking about, Clara?" she demanded, gasping for breath.

Clara Foyle pinched her lips together. "You'd best go in and find out." She tossed the slug onto the ground and lifted up another cabbage leaf. "All I know is, Anne's been sent down to the harbor looking for you after you left that pail of butter half churned. Did you not think your ma and pa would worry about you wandering off, with all the English soldiers?"

"I've not seen hide nor hair of soldiers," Nora started to say angrily. Then she realized she had no intention of defending herself to her neighbor, who was clearly taking delight in giving Nora the bad news. "I'd best get indoors, then," she said, hugging her brat around her and running across the grass.

Ballach lifted her head curiously as she went past, her nostrils flaring, but Nora didn't have time to do more than stop and run her hand down the mare's broad nose. She burst through the door to the cottage and stopped on the threshold, her heart sinking. The cottage was so full of cross-looking people that there was barely room for her. As well as her parents, her sister Meg, and Walt, who was lying on a thick-furred hide with his arm tightly bandaged, Father Francis was standing in the far corner. His face was in shadow, hiding his expression, but the squall-crow on his shoulder flapped his wings disapprovingly.

"Oh Nora, where have you been?" cried her mother, hurrying across the rushes and throwing her arms around her. "We couldn't think what had made you go out without finishing the butter."

Nora wriggled away. "I'm sorry, Ma," she began.

"Maybe you are, but you should have thought more carefully before vanishing like that," said her father. He was sitting on a churn by the fire, his hair on end and his face red as if he had been running about in the wind.

Nora flushed guiltily. "I . . . I didn't know you were looking for me," she lied. "I thought I'd finished the butter and —"

"You call this butter?" said Meg scornfully. She held out the pail of lumpy yellow liquid. "There's not a fairy in Tir na nÓg who'd touch this."

Tom Donovan lifted his hand to calm his angry daughter. "Hush, Meg. What's important is that Nora is safe."

"And what about Anne?" asked Meg, setting down the pail and putting her hands on her hips. "She'll have told Sean and Rua by now that Nora's missing, so that's another household worried half to death."

From her sister's white, strained face, Nora could tell that Meg had been really frightened. She went over and touched her arm. "I'm sorry, Meg. I didn't think." Meg sniffed and looked away.

Nora realized that everyone looked far more troubled than her vanishing for half a morning deserved. A cold pool of fear welled in her stomach. "Has something happened?" she asked.

Father Francis stepped forward, his blue eyes serious. "There were some survivors from the shipwreck, Nora. Eight of them, washed up on the far side of the point. Mor saw them heading inland yesterday afternoon. Your parents were worried you might have crossed their path if you'd gone to look for the wild ponies."

Nora stared at him. More Spanish sailors, here on Errislannan? "H-have the soldiers caught up with them yet?"

"Not as far as I know," said the priest. "If the good Lord has delivered them this far, they may yet find someone who can help them return to their country."

Nora frowned. "But surely it's too dangerous?"

"There's more than one chieftain who'd be willing to give shelter and arms to a Spanish sailor," said Father Francis. He lifted Alex down from his shoulder and smoothed the squall-crow's dusty black feathers. "Even Murray ne Doe O'Flaherty."

Nora's mother let out a disbelieving snort. "Surely not? 'Tis no time at all since he declared himself a loyal subject of Queen Elizabeth." There was a note of scorn in her words; like many who lived under the protection of the O'Flahertys, Nora's parents had not been pleased when their chieftain pledged allegiance to the English queen in return for the castle at Aughnanure.

The priest smiled, though his eyes stayed solemn. "Murray ne Doe is less of a friend to the English than people might think. And what's more, he often has Spanish ships visit his harbor with wine and spices. 'Tis likely the Spaniards have already heard of Aughnanure."

Nora stared at Father Francis, her skin suddenly hot in spite of her soaked clothes. Might there be hope for the boy in the cave after all?

11

———∞∞∞———

"LET US SAY A PRAYER FOR ALL the shipwrecked men." Father Francis broke into Nora's thoughts and opened his hand so that Alex fluttered away to perch on the windowsill. The priest folded his hands together and bowed his head. Nora watched her parents and Meg do the same. In the corner, Walt stirred fitfully, his face twisted with pain.

Nora barely listened as Father Francis began reciting the familiar Latin phrases. Would the Spanish boy be able to make it as far as Aughnanure? She frowned as she realized she was getting too concerned about the fate of the shipwrecked sailor. Maybe it was because she had defied Manannan mac Lir by rescuing him in the first place, but she could not put him out of her mind. Father Francis would say that her fears about Manannan mac Lir were just superstition, but he still let the cottagers keep coal under their butter churns and put out salt to lure the fairies away from newborn babies, which they might be tempted to swap for a changeling.

She shook her head helplessly and her mother said, "Are you all right, Nora?"

Nora opened her eyes. "Yes, I'm fine," she said. Father Francis had finished praying and was crouched beside Walt, holding a bowl of buttermilk to his lips. The squall-crow was pecking in the rushes next to the fire, his wings glowing orange in the flames. Nora's father and Colm were fastening their brats around their shoulders.

"I'll go to fetch Anne," said Tom Donovan. "And make sure that Sean and Mor know Nora is safe." He glanced at Nora and she felt herself go red. "As for you, my girl, you'd be wise to stay indoors for the rest of the day. There's that butter to churn, for a start."

"Yes, Pa," said Nora. The door scraped shut behind the men, and she went over to retrieve the pail of half-churned cream. Whatever her father said, she knew she would have to go down to the beach again, if only to see whether the sailor had left the cave; he might even be on his way to Aughnanure right now, to a trading ship that would take him back to Spain.

Meg was stirring a basin of broth over the fire. She glanced sideways at Nora as she knelt down and picked up the wooden paddle that was used for churning cream into butter. "You've not told me what happened at the feast yet," she prompted.

Nora blinked, struggling to remember back to the visit to Aughnanure, which seemed a lifetime ago. She avoided replying straight away by beating the paddle so hard that she would have to shout to be heard above the noise of the cream slapping against the sides of the pail. But after a few moments her arm ached too much to carry on, so she let go of the paddle and watched it whirl around in the still-spinning cream.

"There's little to tell," she said discouragingly. "There was hardly any dancing before Brenan Odoyne arrived and everyone started talking about the Spanish ships."

Meg frowned. "Did you see any of the gallowglasses?" she persisted.

"A few. One of them got into an argument with a bard and was tipped into the river under the floor. He wore a fox pelt around his shoulders, the same color as his hair."

"Oh yes, I know the one you mean."

Nora looked up and saw that her sister was gazing into the fire with a distant look in her eyes. Clearly she had her own memories of the fox-haired gallowglass. Sighing, Nora started pounding at the butter again. She stopped when she felt someone touch her shoulder. It was her mother.

"Could you go to Nuala Foyle and ask her for more chamomile, please? Walt's arm is too sore for him to sleep."

Nodding, Nora lifted the paddle out of the thick, yellow butter and laid it on the hearth. Her legs had pins and needles from crouching over the pail, and she stamped her feet on the rushes.

Father Francis stood up as well. "I'll walk with you," he offered, clicking his fingers to Alex who flew obediently onto his shoulder.

Nora glanced uncertainly at the priest, wondering if he didn't trust her not to vanish again.

"I promised Nuala I'd pray with her this evening," he went on, as if he could read Nora's thoughts. He picked up his hazel staff which he had left propped behind the door.

She followed him outside and across the grass to Donal Foyle's cottage. The light was fading and, although the wind had dropped, the high tide sent the waves crashing onto the beach like thunder. Donal Foyle was on his way to fetch a load of peat and Father Francis stopped to talk to him, so Nora arrived at the door of the cottage alone. When she knocked, the door was opened by Clara Foyle.

"Oh, it's you," she said. She sounded surprised, as if she thought that Nora would be kept indoors like a prisoner after her grievous sin of disappearing halfway through churning a pail of butter.

"Mother has sent me to fetch more chamomile for Walt," she explained, trying to look over Clara's shoulder to see if Nuala was inside.

Clara opened the door wider. "You'd better come in then," she said grudgingly.

Nuala was sitting at the far end of the room, by the hearth. The cottage was identical in shape and size to Nora's—a large room with a fire at one end and two windows along each long side—but instead of the salty tang of mussels and oysters carried in by Colm and Walt after a long day's fishing, the Foyles' cottage was scented with the rich, sharp fragrance of Nuala's herbs. Thick, leafy bunches of dandelion leaves hung from the roof beams next to brittle cowslip flowers, turning from butter-yellow to palest cream as they dried.

"Good day to you, Nora," said Clara's mother. She had the same round face and dark brown hair as her daughter, but her eyes shone warmly and her hair glowed like beech leaves next to the flames. "Have you come for something for your brother?"

Nora nodded and went over to the hearth, craning her neck to look up at the herbs above her. Tansy, knapweed, comfrey, milk thistle—leaves that would cure everything from a fever to melancholy. Nuala was mixing a thick, green paste in a birch-bark bowl, adding pinches of crumbled leaves before pounding them in with a stout wooden pestle.

"What's that for?" Nora asked curiously.

"'Tis a compound for cuts and grazes," Nuala explained, pausing to tuck a loose strand of hair behind her ear. She glanced at Nora's hands, red and scraped from where she had tripped on the cliff path. "Would you like some yourself? It will keep away infection and help the skin heal over."

Nora didn't think her hands needed the precious paste, but it was exactly right for the shallow wound on Lir's shoulder—if she ever saw the stallion again, of course. She thought of the way she had pushed the fir tree away from the entrance to the cave, and bit her lip.

"Nora?" prompted Nuala, holding out the bowl.

"Could I take some away with me?" Nora asked, thinking fast. "I . . . I could put it on my hands before I go to sleep, then it won't get wiped off so quickly."

"Of course." Nuala picked up a dock leaf and tipped some of the paste onto it, then folded the broad green leaf around it. "There you go. And what was it you wanted for Walt?"

"Chamomile, please, and maybe some comfrey, if you can spare any?" Nora knew there were few herbs better at knitting bones.

The medicine woman nodded and got up to unhook two bunches of leaves from the roof beams. Nora saw Clara glaring at her from the other end of the room where she was sitting on the rushes, halfheartedly combing out some strands of flax. The door opened and Donal Foyle came in with the priest. The squall-crow fluttered in after them and flew straight up to a roof beam where he started pecking at the string holding a bunch of milk thistle.

"Alex, come back here!" ordered Father Francis, tapping his staff on the floor. The bird swooped once around the room, brushing against Clara's hair so that she shrieked and ducked, before landing on the priest's shoulder with a soft *chack*.

"Father Francis has come to pray with us," Donal Foyle explained.

Nuala smiled at the visitor. "Thank you, Father. Nora, you'll join us, won't you?"

Nora wrapped her fingers more tightly around the folded dock leaf. She wanted to go back to the cave and see if the stallion was still there, and tell the Spanish sailor that Murray ne Doe might be able to help him. But Father Francis was watching her, one eyebrow raised questioningly as if he knew what she was thinking.

Nora forced herself to smile. "Yes, I'll stay," she said.

During the prayers, Nora kept one eye on the sky outside the window. Soon it would be too dark to go down to the beach, not without making her parents send out another search party for her. As soon as the last amen had been said, she picked up the herbs for Walt and went over to the door. But Father Francis joined her, fastening his brat around his shoulders and retrieving his staff from the corner.

"Are you leaving already, Father?" asked Nuala, echoing Nora's own silent, dismayed question. There was no way she could slip down to the beach if the priest was watching her.

"Yes, I'm expected at Ardagh tonight," said Father Francis, referring to a village at the most inland part of the bay. He opened the door, and Nora had no choice but to thank Nuala and say good-bye, then follow the priest outside.

"Will you walk with an old man as far as the ridge?" said Father Francis as they skirted Donal Foyle's cabbage patch.

Nora laughed in spite of her frustration at not being able to go down to the beach. "You're not old!" she said.

He stopped walking and looked at her, his sky-colored eyes unusually grave. "Too old for some things, Nora," he said quietly. "'Twas bad enough when we had just the English. I fear these unlucky Spanish sailors will bring even more bloodshed to innocent folk."

Nora felt her skin prickle. She knew she would be putting herself in great danger by helping the boy in the cave, but now that Father Francis had told her there was a chance Murray ne Doe might be able to help, she couldn't turn her back on him. She couldn't think of anything to say so they walked on in silence, up through the hazel copse and onto the stony track that ran the length of the peninsula.

Father Francis stopped when they reached the track and peered into the dusk, toward the point where Sean, Rua, and Mor lived. "It looks like I won't be traveling alone," he remarked.

Nora followed his gaze and saw two horses coming toward them out of the thickening shadows. One was a sturdy work-pony, with a broad, square nose and a thick, furry coat like Ballach, and it was being ridden by a slim, cloaked figure holding a rope attached to the other horse's halter. Nora frowned, trying to work out why the second horse looked familiar. It was dark bay, taller than its companion by at least two hands and with a long forelock reaching almost to its muzzle. It lifted its hooves high over the stones, but it seemed tired because every so often it stumbled and the lead rope jerked taut against its halter.

"Hallo there!" called the rider, and Nora recognized the voice of Dan Devlin, the horse trader.

Suddenly Nora realized why the horse Dan was leading looked so familiar: Even though its coat was dark brown rather than cloud-gray, it was the image of the horse in the cave. They had the same wide-set, oval eyes and small ears that arched inward at the tip. And no Irish pony had a mane that hung below its neck, or a tail that brushed the ground, as thick at the bottom as at the top.

Dan Devlin reined the horses to a halt and nodded to them. "Good evening, Father, Nora. I wasn't expecting to have company on the road this night."

"I'll walk with you as far as Ardagh," said Father Francis. "But Nora is just on her way home."

Nora nodded, feeling shy under the horse-trader's holly-colored gaze. She was burning to ask him where the bay horse came from, but before she could say anything Alex flew out of the shadows and swooped onto the priest's shoulder. The gelding snorted and leaped backward in alarm, its eyes rolling and its hooves clattering on the stones.

"Whoa there!" shouted Dan Devlin, clutching the lead rope close to his waist.

Without thinking, Nora ran forward and placed one hand on the horse's neck. His skin was hot and slippery and there was a graze on his flank similar to the wound on Lir's shoulder. "It's all right," she murmured. "It's only a bird."

"Careful, Nora," warned Dan.

"That's a fine-looking animal," remarked Father Francis. "Where did he come from?"

Dan Devlin grinned, his teeth flashing wolfishly. "Those sailors weren't the only flotsam washed up by the storm. Would you believe I found him on the beach just beyond the point?"

"Then he's come a long way," remarked Father Francis, raising his eyebrows.

Nora said nothing, but carried on smoothing the horse's silky, brown coat. Had he come from the same ship as Lir? What was Dan going to do with him now?

To her alarm, the horse trader said, "Well, Nora? Would Meg like him as a wedding present, do you think?"

Nora looked up at him. "I . . . I'm not sure," she stammered.

Dan winked. "Worth a try, wouldn't you say? She'd have the finest riding horse this side of Galway."

As if he could sense Nora's confusion, Father Francis put in, "There'll be plenty of people who'd like to own this creature, for sure."

"Oh yes," said Dan, sounding almost hungry. "Murray ne

Doe would pay handsomely for a war horse better than any other chieftain's. And that English captain has an eye for a good horse, too. You'll let me know if you find any other flotsam like this, won't you, Nora?"

She stared at him, appalled at the thought of Lir being sold to a quarrelsome chieftain or an English soldier. Even Murray ne Doe's war horses lasted only a few seasons before being crippled by galloping over rough ground, or even injured in battle. Nora felt a stab of dismay when she realized that Lir might have left the cave already and could stray across Dan Devlin's path at any time. She was saved from answering the horse trader when the Spanish horse sidestepped impatiently, banging his hindquarters into Dan's pony.

Dan cursed under his breath and clapped his heels against his pony's sides to keep him from stepping off the track. "I must be off, if we're going to make Sraith Salach tonight," he said. "You're more than welcome to walk with me, Father Francis, but forgive me if I don't offer you a ride on this fellow."

"Oh, I can see he's more than a match for me," the priest agreed. He turned to Nora and rested his hand on her shoulder. "You'll go straight home now, won't you? Your parents will be expecting you, and 'tis not fair to worry them twice in one day." He smiled. "Those wild ponies will still be there tomorrow, I'm sure."

Nora forced herself to nod and smile back. It was much easier to let Father Francis think that she wanted to slip away to be with the mountain ponies. She said good-bye to the priest and watched him walk away behind the horses, his staff tapping on the stones and the squall-crow sitting on his shoulder, looking around with short, quick movements of his head. Nora knew she'd missed her chance to go down to the shore tonight—even if she risked the tide, it would be too dark inside the cave to tell if boy or horse were still there—but she would try again tomorrow at first light. There were two souls needing her help now, hunted by English soldiers and horse-traders with equal hunger.

⬭⬭⬭

NORA SLEPT FITFULLY, OPENING her eyes every few moments to see if the sky was growing light around the edges of the window. At last the hides were outlined with gray and she could just make out Ballach's ghostly shape against the wall. Pushing aside the blanket, she eased herself away from Meg and crawled to the edge of the room. She would make less noise if she walked on bare earth rather than over the treacherous crackling rushes. She picked up a hunk of oatbread left over from dinner the night before and tiptoed past the sleeping forms of her brothers and father. Tom Donovan was snoring so loudly that Nora felt quite safe pulling open the door even though it scraped on the uneven earthen floor.

Outside, there was a ribbon of palest yellow above the mountains where the sun was waiting to rise, and the air was so still and cold that Nora could see her breath billowing in smoky clouds. Clutching her brat around her to keep warm and pausing only to snatch up a few handfuls of grass, she ran past Donal Foyle's cottage and down the cliff path. The edges of the waves were white against the dark gray water, and the boulders looked like hunchbacked wolves, crouched on the sand with mussels for teeth and pelts of trailing seaweed.

As she splashed her way around the headland, flinching as her soaked skirt plastered itself against her legs, Nora saw the fir tree rolling against the foot of the cliff. It reminded her that Lir and the boy might be long gone, and she ran faster, as if by getting there more quickly, she would be more likely to find them. She was breathless by the time she reached the mouth of the cave and stood panting for a few moments, her mind filled with dreadful images of a dappled-gray horse being spurred over stony ground by an English soldier, or a dark-haired boy shuffling along in chains.

Then a pale shape detached itself from the shadows at the back of the cave and Lir stepped forward with his neck arched and his nostrils flaring.

"You're still here!" Nora exclaimed in delight. She dropped the grass onto the sand and reached out with both hands as the stallion drew near.

He stopped and blinked warily, then stretched his head forward to let Nora run her hands again and again down his smooth, muscular neck. He blew into her hair and she felt her heart leap. The wound on his shoulder was cooler but there was still some swelling under the skin so she took out the folded dock leaf, her fingers trembling in her hurry to unwrap the scented green paste. Lir stood still as she smeared the ointment onto the wound, watching her curiously with his dark, liquid eyes. Nora fed him the dock leaf as well, guessing that he was hungry enough to ignore the bitter taste.

She wiped her fingers on her skirt and stood back to watch him eat the grass she had brought, admiring the slope of his shoulder and his broad hindquarters. Dan Devlin was right, she thought. This was a horse fit for a chieftain. She wanted to fetch more grass and water for him, but she knew she should look for the Spanish boy first. Patting Lir on his neck, she walked past him toward the back of the cave.

The sun had risen high enough to turn the waves green-gray rather than nearly black, and pale fingers of light stretched across the sand, chasing away the shadows where the rock sloped down to meet the floor of the cave. Nora didn't know whether to feel relieved or anxious when she saw the sailor curled up asleep on the nets; he hadn't been caught by the English soldiers yet, but would she be able to explain that he had to go to Aughnanure if he wanted to find a ship to take him home?

Lir wandered up behind her, his hooves crunching on the wet sand, and the boy's eyes shot open in alarm. Nora saw his fingers close on a thick piece of driftwood and she cried out, "No! Stop!"

She spoke in Irish but the boy seemed to understand because he left the stick lying on the sand and turned his head to stare at her, his eyes dark-circled with pain. Nora rested her hand against Lir's neck, letting the warmth of his skin give her courage. She told herself that the sailor was weak and injured, and she would be able to outrun him easily if he tried to attack her. However certain she was that the Spaniards had no quarrel with her countrymen, the boy reminded her of a cornered animal, ready to let fly with teeth and claws.

"You came back," he whispered. He spoke in his own language, but Nora understood in spite of the way the words rasped against his dry throat.

"Wh-who are you?" she asked in Spanish.

The boy struggled up until he was half-sitting, half-lying against the heap of nets. In spite of his torn shirt and blood-soaked trews, there was a strange sort of dignity in the way he held his head. "I am José Sebastian Medovar," he replied. "Son of Don Pedro Sebastian Medovar of Cádiz, one of the most powerful lords of Andalusia."

Suddenly his eyes closed and he swayed. Without thinking, Nora rushed forward and knelt down beside him. She put her hands on his shoulders and laid him gently back down on the nets. His skin was cold and clammy under the ripped cloth and there was a sheen of sweat on his forehead, from pain or fever. "Keep still," she urged him, forgetting to translate what she was saying into Spanish. She had reached the limit of the vocabulary she had learned from the herring fishermen anyway.

"You're too weak to sit up."

"My leg," the boy muttered as he let his head roll back. "It is hurt."

Nora stared at him in astonishment. He had spoken to her in Irish, with a thick, almost musical accent. Something echoed in her head, a memory of him calling to her when he was struggling in the waves.

"You can speak Irish!" she burst out.

José made a tiny movement with his head. "Yes." He looked up at her with a gleam of amusement in his bloodshot eyes. "And you speak Spanish."

Nora shook her head. "Only a little, from the herring fishermen."

"My aunt comes from Galway," José explained. He tried to unfold his injured leg from underneath him but the movement made him curse in his own language and he stopped. "My uncle is a wine merchant. Many times he came here in his ship. He brought my aunt back to Cádiz before I was born and she looked after me when my mother died. That song you were singing when you came before, she sings it too."

A warm muzzle pushed against Nora's shoulder and she turned to shoo Lir away. "I'll fetch you some water in a moment," she promised.

José stirred and lifted one hand. "The horse," he croaked. "He is still here?"

"Yes." Nora bent closer. "Did he come from your ship?"

"Maybe, I don't know. There were many horses, but I did not look after them." He shifted on his bed of nets and winced. "Can you help me? Please."

"I . . . I'm not sure," said Nora. "I've brought you some bread, look." She took the hunk of loaf out of her cloak and stopped, suddenly aware that the boy was lying very still with his eyes closed. She knelt down beside him, bunching her skirt under her knees against the wet sand. Gingerly, she reached out and touched his forehead. It was burning hot. She wished she had brought tansy and loosestrife for him, like she had given one of the wild mares when she lost her foal. Nora shook José's shoulder, trying to rouse him, remembering that Nuala Foyle had told her it was important to keep people awake if they had a fever.

"José," she said urgently. "Don't go to sleep."

The boy stirred and muttered something in Spanish. She tore off a piece of bread and held it against his lips. Lir stretched his head over her shoulder, his nostrils quivering. Nora laughed, in spite of her concern for José, and pushed his nose away.

"Leave my food alone," José mumbled, and Nora turned to see that his eyes were open, although his lips were pinched and white with pain.

"Try to eat," she said, and he obediently opened his mouth

so that she could give him the morsel of bread like a mother bird feeding a chick. He chewed slowly and swallowed, and Nora fed him piece by piece until there was no bread left.

"Water?" said José, looking hopefully at Nora.

She shook her head. "I'll fetch some in a moment, for Lir as well."

"Lir?" José frowned.

"The horse," Nora explained, blushing. "I . . . I gave him a name when I found him."

The boy stretched his dry, cracked lips into a smile. "The name of a sea god? You think highly of that horse."

"Of course!" Nora said in surprise.

José twitched his shoulders in a shrug. "He's just a horse."

"How can you say such a thing?" Nora exclaimed hotly. "He's magnificent."

"There are many, many horses like him in my country. If he is one of the horses from my ship, then he was bred in Andalusia, where I come from. There are no better war horses in the world, but still, they are just horses. . . ." He trailed off, as if talking had exhausted him. He took a long, shuddering breath and looked straight at Nora, his eyes as dark as peat. "I need to find a ship to take me home. Can you help me?"

Nora twisted the hem of her brat in her hands. "Maybe. There is a man called Murray ne Doe O'Flaherty who lives two days' ride from here, at Aughnanure. He trades with Spanish merchants. I . . . I have heard that other men from the ship-wreck are making their way to his castle."

José struggled to sit up. "There are more people from my ship? Where? Can you take me to them?" His torn breeches stretched against the wound on his leg and Nora saw fresh blood stain the cloth like rose petals.

She pressed gently on his shoulder to make him lie down again. "Keep still, or you'll make your leg worse. I have not seen the men myself, and they will be halfway to Aughnanure by now." As long as the English soldiers have not caught up with them, she added grimly to herself.

"I must go after them," muttered José, his teeth clenched with pain. "Tell me, which way is this castle?"

Nora opened her mouth to explain, then changed her mind. "I'll not tell you yet," she said. "You must rest first. I'll bring you more food and water, and herbs to ease the pain in your leg." She felt oddly calm, and almost smiled when she thought how surprised her brothers and sisters would be to see timid little Nora being so resourceful and determined.

José closed his eyes, his breathing quick and shallow, and lay back down as if he was too weak to argue. Nora stood up, shaking the sand from her skirt, and picked up the empty bucket that she had left there two days before.

"Wait. I don't know your name."

Nora looked down at him. "Honora," she said. "But usually

I'm just called Nora."

"Nora," the boy echoed, turning the word over as if he was tasting something unfamiliar. "Don't be long, please," he added, suddenly looking very young and scared.

"I won't," Nora promised. She went over to Lir, who snorted and shifted sideways when she reached out to stroke his neck. He seemed restless, and Nora guessed that he was feeling stronger as well as hungry and thirsty. She didn't try to touch him again, but went to retrieve the fir tree to block the entrance of the cave again. The tide was still going out, and she didn't want Lir to be tempted to wander off, not when Dan Devlin was looking for more washed-up Spanish horses.

"I'll come back soon," she told the stallion, who was watching over the fir tree with his ears pricked forward. His willingness to be barricaded in the cave told Nora that wherever he came from, he had been kept in a stable—she couldn't imagine any of the mountain ponies waiting patiently behind a fallen tree. But he might not stay there much longer, especially when Nuala's herb paste healed the pain in his shoulder. Soon hunger and boredom would make him dangerously restless, and then Nora would have to decide where else she could hide the precious horse.

13

To Nora's relief, the rest of her family were only just waking up when she returned to the cottage. She muttered something about going out to the midden in answer to her mother's questioning look, and busied herself with shooing Ballach and the cow outside while Anne and Meg put away the blankets and hung a pan of buttermilk to heat over the fire. Walt had slept well thanks to Nuala's herbs, and when Nora took him a bowl of buttermilk he told her that his arm was aching less than the night before.

"I think I'll get up today," he said. "If I lie on these rushes much longer, the mice will start eating my trews!" He winked and Nora forced herself to laugh at the old family joke.

She glanced at the half-used bundle of chamomile and comfrey that had been left on the windowsill and asked, "Will you be wanting more of the herbs now, Walt?"

Her brother shook his head. "No, not yet. Could you fetch Colm to give me a hand up? I need to visit the midden."

Nora called her eldest brother and stood by the windowsill while the two men shuffled slowly outside, going at the pace that caused Walt the least pain. She checked that no one was watching and stuffed the herbs into her shirt. She could fetch more for Walt later on.

"Nora?" said her mother.

Startled, Nora turned around. Maria Donovan was holding out a bowl of warm buttermilk. "Thank you," Nora said, taking the bowl. "I . . . I thought I'd go down to the beach this morning and collect some more mussels."

To her relief, her mother nodded. "You can bring back some seaweed too, even if it'll make your father complain that we're turning into merfolk. It's that or go hungry, though. There are hardly any cabbages left, with all the slugs eating them."

Nora took the pail she had used for mussels the day before and went outside, still carrying her bowl of buttermilk. She would take it to José, along with two pails of water and as much grass for Lir as she could wrap in her cloak. There would be no more oatbread until the afternoon, but the seaweed that she had used to tempt Lir into the cave was sweet enough to eat raw, and she could collect some on her way.

With both hands laden, it was a much more difficult journey down to the beach and Nora held her breath the whole way, expecting someone from her family—or worse still, Clara Foyle—to spot her from the cliff and shout down to ask her what she was doing. But she quickly forgot her chafed hands and aching shoulders when she saw the beautiful, gray stallion watching her over the spindly branches of the fir tree. As soon as Nora put the pails of water in front of him, he put his head down to drink, draining one bucket straight off and nearly finishing the other.

Nora grabbed a handful of mane and pulled his head away. "Leave some for José," she told him.

Tipping most of the seaweed onto the sand for Lir, Nora carried the pail and the bowl of buttermilk to the back of the cave. José was awake, propped up on one elbow, and Nora was relieved to see that his forehead seemed drier than before. She handed him the buttermilk and he took a thirsty gulp before thrusting the bowl away with a look of disgust, spilling the pale liquid onto the sand.

"*Madre de Díos*, why are you giving me sour milk?" he exclaimed.

"It's not sour," Nora told him. "It's buttermilk."

José frowned. "In my country, we would throw this away."

"Well, you're not in your country, are you?" Nora said impatiently. She pushed the pail of water toward him and fished in her cloak for the bundle of chamomile and comfrey. "I've brought you some herbs that will help your leg, or will you complain about those as well?"

José looked chastened. "Forgive me. I do not mean to be ungrateful. Without you, I would have died. I am sorry."

Feeling awkward, Nora untied the bundle of leaves and crushed them in her hand to draw out the juice. The cave filled with their sharp fragrant scent and Lir's ears flicked back and forth, though he didn't stop eating. José swallowed the leaves with a mouthful of water from the pail. He raised his eyebrows when Nora offered him a handful of seaweed but started chewing obediently.

She looked at José's injured leg. The stains on his breeches had faded to brown which meant the wound had stopped bleeding, but it would need to be bandaged before he tried to move. She would have to bring some scraps of linen next time, and some of Nuala's herb paste.

José finished the seaweed and lay back on the nets. "Now will you tell me how to get to this castle?" he said.

Nora looked at his pale, strained face and then at the wound on his thigh. "It's a long way," she warned. "You're not well enough yet to go that far."

"But I have to! If I don't go soon, the others will leave without me." He reached out and gripped Nora's wrist, his thin brown fingers surprisingly strong.

Nora pulled her arm away and scrambled to her feet. "You can't even stand!" she exclaimed, hearing her voice echo around the cave. "You wouldn't be able to walk to the end of the beach." She felt her heart beat faster; the boy was desperate, reminding her again of a frightened, wounded animal. Her eyes fell on the thick piece of driftwood lying close to José's hand and she took a step backward.

He followed her gaze and shook his head. "Do you think I will force you to tell me, Nora? How could I, when you could crawl away faster than I could walk? You judge me unfairly if you think that is how I would repay your kindness."

Nora blushed. "I . . . I'm sorry," she began, but José silenced her with an impatient flick of his hand.

"No matter. I know I cannot walk to this castle, wherever it is. But I could ride, couldn't I?"

"What, on Lir?" Nora asked, feeling an unexpected rush of jealousy.

José shook his head. "I do not think I am a strong enough match for the stallion," he said. "I ride at home, but I will not say that I am skilled. This journey is going to be hard enough, I think. Does your family not have other horses, some mare perhaps you could let me have?"

Nora stared at him in disbelief. How wealthy did he think her family was? There was no chance of him taking Ballach. Even if Nora had been willing to let him ride the elderly mare all the way to Aughnanure so soon after her last journey to the castle, there was not an excuse on earth she could give her parents if their pony suddenly disappeared. But a small voice inside her pointed out that there was another mare who could be ridden, who would easily carry him that far.

"Well?" José prompted.

Nora shook her head. Dunlin was not used to being told where to go, even if she could explain to José how to reach Aughnanure. It would have been easier if she could have told him to follow the road through Sraith Salach, but he would need to take the smaller, hidden paths through the mountains to avoid the English soldiers.

"'Tis a foolish idea," she said out loud. "There is a pony, but she lives in the mountains and I don't know if she'd let you ride her. And the way to Aughnanure is very complicated if you can't use the main road, you will get lost in the mountains—"

"Wait, slow down," said José, holding up one hand. "I do not understand when you speak so fast. What pony is this?"

Nora folded her skirt under her and sat down on the nets beside him. She could see Lir watching them but the stallion stayed near the entrance to the cave, letting the pale sun warm his coat. "It's one of the mountain ponies, Dunlin. She doesn't belong to anyone, though she lets me ride her sometimes. But even if she could take you to Aughnanure, I don't think I can tell you the safest way to go. . . . " She trailed off and stared dismally at her shoes, which were stained black from seawater and crusted with a rime of salt like frost.

José leaned toward her, his eyes very wide. "Nora, if there is any chance I can get back to Spain, I have to go to this castle. If I stay here too long, the English soldiers will find me. And maybe they will find you, as well." His eyes darkened, and Nora felt a chill run through her. "If this journey is as difficult as you say, there is only one thing you can do. You will have to come with me."

───⊶⊷───

"COME WITH YOU? T-to Aughnanure?" Nora stammered.

José nodded. "You can show me which way to go." He sounded confident, as if he was used to giving orders. Nora realized his family must be very wealthy indeed if they had servants, and more than one horse. "I cannot give you anything in return," he went on, "but my father will send you money from Spain, I promise."

Nora shook her head. "I've no need for your father's money. But Dunlin is not strong enough to carry us both such a long way."

"Then you must ride the stallion," said José. He sounded surprised, as if it was the obvious answer. "I can see already that you are more used to horses than I am. If you have tamed a wild pony, you could ride him, no?"

Nora opened her mouth to argue, then stopped. She stared at the horse, his dappled coat the color of clouds, and felt excitement leap inside her. Could she really ride Lir herself? She already knew he couldn't stay in the cave for much longer; if she took him to Aughnanure with José, she could find somewhere better to hide him on the way back, in the mountains where there was plenty of grass and water.

But even while her mind raced ahead, Nora knew it would be impossible. How could she be away from home for four days and nights without telling her parents where she was going? She forced herself to meet the Spanish boy's piercing brown gaze. "I'm sorry, I can't come with you."

José clenched his fists so tightly that his knuckles turned white. Nora shrank away from him, the nets crackling beneath her.

"I have to try to get home," said José, his voice low and urgent. "I know you have risked much for me already, but please, you must help me."

"You don't understand." Nora stood up and nervously pleated the fabric of her skirt between her fingers. "I can't leave Errislannan for so many days, with nobody knowing where I have gone."

José narrowed his eyes. "Are you afraid of the English soldiers?"

"No . . . I . . ." Nora trailed off. "Look, I have to go." She pointed to the pale yellow sunbeams that stretched into the cave, nearly all the way to the heap of nets. "I've been here too long. My mother and father don't know where I am."

"It sounds as if you are more scared of them than the English," José remarked. "Do you always do what you are told, Nora?"

"No, I do not!" Nora hissed furiously. "I rescued you, didn't

I? There's no one else in Iar-Connacht who'd have risked their life against Manannan mac Lir. And now I'm here with stolen bread and a cup of buttermilk you wouldn't drink, and herbs that were meant for my brother."

She broke off breathlessly when José held up his hands in confusion. "Stop, stop, I cannot understand. How old are you, Nora?" he asked unexpectedly.

"Fourteen," Nora replied warily. There were two spots of bright red on his cheeks and his eyes were unnaturally bright. She hoped the fever was not returning.

"I am sixteen," said José. "Just two years older. I am not a soldier, nor a sailor, but my father sent me on the Armada because he believed I was old enough to make my own fortune in the world. We were promised wealth and land in return for restoring the people of England to the Catholic faith. I was scared to be sailing to a country I had never seen, where the people would greet us with cannons and musket fire. And now I am lost in your country, further away from my home than I could ever imagine. But I must do whatever I can to return home because that is what my father expects from me. Would your father not expect you to have the same courage?" His face was white and his breathing came in labored gasps after such a long speech, but he didn't take his eyes from Nora's.

She stared back at him in distress. "My father would never send me away from my home!" was all she could think to say.

"Think of me what you will, but I cannot take you to Aughnanure."

She snatched up the empty bowl and the water pail and ran to the mouth of the cave. Lir shifted sideways to let her past, his eyes curious, but she did not slow down to pat him. Instead she dragged the fir tree across the entrance behind her, then clutched her skirt to her knees and ran back across the stretch of wet sand to the beach. She could not stay and listen to José's arguments anymore.

WHEN SHE ARRIVED AT HER cottage she was surprised to find Donal Foyle sharing a cup of whiskey and milk with Tom Donovan, and Nora wondered why her father hadn't gone out in the fishing boat with Colm.

Mr. Donovan looked up as Nora came in and smiled. "Donal and I have decided that you and Clara shall go to Sraith Salach for a while. You can stay with Fionn and Mainie, and Clara will stay with her cousin Ronan mac Nichol."

"Go to Sraith Salach? Why?" Nora exclaimed, thinking at once of Lir and José who were relying on her to bring them food and water.

Nora's mother walked toward her across the rushes. Her fingers were dusty with flour, and there was a brownish-gray lump of dough on the hearth. "There are stories of Spanish sailors coming ashore all along the coast," Maria Donovan explained gently. "There's been a score or more spotted across the bay, and at least a dozen at Curhownagh," she added, naming a village on the other side of Errislannan. "'Tis not them we're afraid of, but they'll bring English soldiers after them, and 'tis safer for you and Clara to go inland." She gave a strained, unconvincing smile. "And think how much you'll enjoy being around the babes. You'll be a great help to Mainie."

Nora forced herself to smile back, but inside she was seething. She'd rather face a galleon of Spanish sailors pursued by the entire English army than be cooped up in her sister's tiny cottage with three squalling tots.

Tom Donovan went on, oblivious to his daughter's silent protest. "You'll be leaving tomorrow at first light. Ronan mac Nichol is coming to Errislannan with a new plowshare and will take you and Clara back with him."

Nora nodded, not trusting herself to speak. Clara Foyle's cousin was a blacksmith, a lumpen, slow-witted man in spite of his important skills. Blacksmiths were supposed to be protected from fairy magic because they worked with iron, which fairies couldn't abide, but Nora secretly thought that any fairy would keel over on Ronan mac Nichol's threshold from scornful laughter rather than fear of his metalwork. She comforted herself with the thought that Clara would be well-suited to his household in Sraith Salach, Ronan's wife being no more lively than her husband.

"Is there anything you'll be wanting me to take to Mainie?" she sighed, knowing it was no use trying to argue.

"Anne and Meg have taken Ballach to fetch a barrel of oysters from Sean," said Nora's mother, bustling back to the fire, "and I thought you could collect some more seaweed. 'Tis good for the children's bones, and it will save Mainie from having to use Brenan Odoyne's spices in her broth." She held out a small oilcloth sack to Nora. "Here, this will be lighter for Ronan's cart than a pail."

As Nora reached out to take the sack, she froze with her fingers brushing the cold, stiff material. Maybe it wasn't so bad that she was being sent away after all. It could be a chance to take José to Aughnanure and find another hiding place for Lir! She could easily make some excuse to Ronan mac Nichol about traveling on her own—for once, it would serve her well that everyone was used to her running wild with the mountain ponies—and with luck, her sister Mainie would not know exactly when to expect her. Aughnanure was only a day's ride from Sraith Salach, so she could be there and back before Ronan mac Nichol remembered to check that Nora had safely reached her sister's house. *You'll not accuse me of lacking courage, José Medovar*, she thought fiercely, taking the sack from her mother at last and rolling it into a tight bundle.

"I'll fetch the seaweed now, shall I?" she said out loud, and Maria Donovan nodded.

"Thank you, my love," she started to say, but Nora was

already hauling open the door, her long, black hair flying.

She headed first to the hazel copse, where the sweetest grass grew. Holding open the sack with one hand, she snatched at the grass with the other, stuffing each handful into the sack until it bulged like a pillow fit for the head of a chieftain. There was good reason for her urgency: Even though she would not be setting out until tomorrow morning, so that her parents at least saw her leaving in the company of Ronan mac Nichol, she could not risk taking Lir unless she had ridden him first.

Nora's heart pounded as she followed the familiar path down the cliff to the beach, though whether it was from the speed of her running or the thought of riding the stallion she wasn't sure. Lir gave her a whicker of welcome and José stared in surprise when he saw her dragging the fir tree aside.

"I was not expecting you back so soon," he said cautiously, pushing himself up until he was sitting on the nets with his injured leg straight out in front of him.

He seemed much more subdued than earlier that morning, and Nora wondered if she should apologize for the outburst which had sent her running from the cave. But there was no time for explanations.

"We're going to Aughnanure," she announced, and felt a gleam of satisfaction when José looked stunned.

"What? When?" he exclaimed.

Nora held the oilcloth sack upside down and shook it so that bright green blades of grass rained down on the sand. Lir put his head down at once and began to eat, his ears twitching as he kept one eye on her. She reached out and touched his neck, and he stamped a foreleg in acknowledgement.

"Tomorrow. My parents are sending me to stay with my sister and her husband in a village that lies halfway to Aughnanure. I am supposed to be traveling with my neighbor and her cousin, but I shall come back with Dunlin to fetch you. You'll find her easy enough to ride, as long as I'm with you."

José closed his eyes and murmured a quiet prayer, suddenly looking very young. Nora felt the first qualm of doubt as she realized how completely he trusted her to deliver him safely to Murray ne Doe's castle. There was still a long way to go before they reached Aughnanure, and it all depended on her being able to handle the Spanish horse. She trailed her fingers through Lir's mane and said quietly, "I need to see if I can ride Lir first, José. I don't know for sure that I can, and without him I cannot come with you."

"But of course you will be able to ride him!" said José, opening his eyes and spreading his hands wide. "Do you think that we do not train our horses well in Andalusia?"

Nora kept running her hands through the stallion's long, long mane. "But this isn't Andalusia," she pointed out, "and I am not the person who is most used to riding Lir. I have no saddle, not even a bridle. Maybe he won't understand what I want him to do."

José frowned. "You are looking for reasons to fail, Nora," he said sternly, and she almost laughed. "Where is your courage? You have made friends with the horse already." His lips twisted into a smile. "You may find that it is I who struggles without a saddle, not Lir."

Nora swept up her hair and twisted it expertly back into a plait. "All right," she said. "I'll try riding him now." She carried on, speaking as much to Lir and herself as to José, who watched her with narrowed eyes as if he was having trouble understanding her rapid words. "I'll take him the other way out of the cave, to Carraig Sands. There are no houses there, so we won't be seen."

She knotted her fingers in Lir's mane and clicked her tongue. "Come on, boy," she said. "Time for you to stretch your legs." She walked toward the entrance of the cave and he followed her quite willingly, pricking his ears forward with interest when she used her free hand to shove the fir tree out of the way.

"Good luck!" José called from the back of the cave, and Nora glanced over her shoulder to smile uncertainly at him.

When she led Lir out into the pale sunshine, he tossed his head and snorted, sending up spurts of sand from his hooves. Nora clung grimly to his mane, hoping that the stallion would not be so delighted to be out of the cave that he took flight altogether.

"Steady, Lir," she murmured, and for a moment she wished she knew his Spanish name.

The horse stood still and looked at her, his nostrils flaring with each rapid breath.

"This way," said Nora, leading him away from the beach below her cottage toward the long stretch of white sand that ran almost all the way to the point. The tide had only just started to come in, so the waves barely reached Lir's fetlocks as they made their way around the headland. Nora halted Lir beside a rock, suddenly aware of just how much taller he was than Dunlin. There was no way she was going to be able to swing herself straight up onto his back like she did with the bracken-colored mare.

Keeping hold of his mane, Nora climbed onto the top of the rock and looked down at the stallion's broad gray back for the first time. He snorted and scraped one hoof on the sand, and for a heartbeat Nora's courage failed her completely. This was a stupid idea, put into her head by some mean-spirited fairy who wanted to show how foolish she was ever to have thought she might ride a horse as fine as this. But then Lir stopped and looked around at her with his huge peat-dark eyes, and Nora knew that she had to trust him—for José's sake, if nothing else. She bunched up her dress and jumped off the rock, landing on Lir's back in a flurry of skirt and long, tangled mane.

At once Lir let out a startled whinny and reared straight up into the air.

15

NORA BURIED HER HANDS in sharp strands of flaxen mane and crouched forward over the stallion's withers, her sense of balance telling her that this would force Lir to drop back onto all four legs. His front hooves crashed down with a thump that knocked the breath out of her, before he wheeled around and set off down the beach at a breakneck gallop.

Nora gripped with her knees as hard as she could to stop herself from sliding off Lir's back, which was as smooth and slippery as a seal. She told herself that she had startled him by jumping on so suddenly; with Dunlin, she had spent several days just walking beside her, leaning more and more of her weight across the mare's back the way she had seen her brother Sean prepare an unbroken pony for being ridden.

"Steady, Lir, steady," she gasped, but her words were snatched away by the wind. Too late, she thought she should have asked José to tell her the Spanish words that meant walk and slow down—the herring fishermen had never talked about horse training, and the Spanish songs that Nora had learned from them were no help now.

Halfway along the beach, the rhythm of Lir's hooves changed and slowed down. He seemed to realize that Nora was sitting still and quiet, and his panic eased. He dropped his nose so that his neck was no longer stretched out flat, and Nora felt his quarters bunch underneath her until his weight was carried on his hindlegs. The muscles along the top of his neck and on either side of his spine relaxed, and Nora began to hope that the stallion was not about to throw her off like a troublesome fly. Still keeping a tight hold on his mane, she tried to sit up straighter and let her legs stretch down behind his powerful shoulders.

It felt so different from riding Dunlin! Nora had never known the wild mare to get tired, but she didn't have the same smooth round muscles on her shoulders and hindquarters that bulged and flexed in time with the drumming hooves. Lir's stride was so long and powerful that Nora found herself thrown toward his withers, her legs slipping against his flanks. They were cantering now rather than galloping—Nora could tell because the hoofbeats came in a pattern of three, not four—but it was only the fact that her fingers were knotted painfully in Lir's mane that stopped her from slithering off.

The end of the beach loomed toward them, a sharply angled headland with the harbor on the other side. Nora didn't have enough breath left to tell Lir to slow down, but to her relief his stride faltered as they neared the rocks and he dropped into a trot, lifting his knees high and flicking his hooves in front of him.

He stopped abruptly a few yards from the rocks and stood stiff-legged in the sand, staring at the cliff with his ears pricked forward. Nora risked letting go of the mane with one hand to pat his damp, solid neck. "G-good boy," she whispered.

The stallion threw up his head and snorted, scattering sticky yellow foam back over his neck. His sides were heaving and Nora realized uneasily that he had probably run faster and for longer than he should have after the shipwreck and two days pent up in the cave. She glanced down at the scrape on his shoulder and was relieved to see that the newly healed skin, still tinged green from Nuala's paste, had not broken open again.

Her legs were trembling and the pale sand seemed a long way below her feet, so she decided to stay on the horse and hope that he took her back to the cave of his own accord. Unsure how to make him turn, she sat still and waited until he seemed to realize that he couldn't go any further and wheeled around to follow his hoofprints back along the beach.

Lir walked at the edge of the waves with his head stretched low and his tail brushing the faintest trail in the sand. Nora tried to relax into his stride but she was still being jolted helplessly with every step. Doubts crowded like gulls in her mind. Could she really ride the Spanish horse all the way to Aughnanure? It didn't matter if he was the most highly trained horse in the world if she hadn't the faintest idea how to command him. Perhaps she should try riding one of the other mountain ponies; the dappled-gray mare who had lost her foal was well used to Nora and might not object to carrying her weight.

Suddenly she realized that they were nearly at the little cave. For a brief moment, she wondered if Lir would refuse to stop and she would have to fling herself off to save being carried along the beach below her cottage and onto the moor. But Lir seemed to recognize his temporary home and halted beside the entrance. Nora quickly swung her right leg over his withers and slipped thankfully to the ground.

Her legs were trembling so she stood still for a moment, leaning her forehead against his neck and letting the shallow waves wash over her shoes. Lir jumped and pricked up his ears when a voice sounded behind them.

"I said you would be able to ride him, no?"

Nora turned, keeping one hand on Lir's shoulder. José was standing just inside the cave, clinging to the wall for support with his injured leg held off the ground. "I'm not sure—" she began, but José cut her off with an impatient wave.

"You did not fall, and he has brought you back. That is enough. We go tomorrow."

Nora bristled. Who did this Spanish boy think he was, ordering her about like a slave? Then she saw that his eyes looked hollow with pain, and his torn shirt hung off his scrawny body like linen drying on a thorn bush. Lir nudged her in the middle of her back, his breath warm through her dress and undershirt, and Nora began to feel more determined. José was right: She had ridden the stallion without falling off, and pulling the Spanish boy out of the sea was only the beginning of saving his life. He would not be truly safe until he was far from here, and away from the English soldiers.

"Yes, we leave tomorrow," she said simply, and she was rewarded by José breaking into a smile, his peat-dark eyes warm in spite of the shadows that circled them.

IN THE END, IT TURNED OUT to be easier to get away from Ronan mac Nichol and Clara Foyle than Nora had feared. They set out just before dawn, the distant mountains dark gray shapes against a paler gray sky. Maria Donovan hugged Nora fiercely as if she was suddenly afraid that sending her youngest daughter away was a mistake. Nora crossed her fingers under her brat that her mother wasn't about to change her mind and make her stay. But Tom Donovan hefted the barrel of oysters onto Ronan's cart and came to peel his wife away, saying, "Come on, Maria. Nora will be safe enough with Mainie. And it won't be long before all this is over."

So Nora walked behind Ronan's cart, up through the copse of hazel trees and onto the ridge to join the road that led to Sraith Salach. There was no room for her on the cart thanks to the gifts of food and cloth that Maria Donovan and Nuala

Foyle were sending to their families, so she walked behind, keeping to the grass at the edge of the track to avoid the deepest mud and the ankle-turning stones. Clara had insisted on traveling in the cart in spite of her cousin's feeble protests that it was laden enough, and she was sitting on an upturned pail with her skirt spread around her. Nora thought uncharitably that she looked like a jellyfish washed up on a rock.

They traveled in silence, apart from the creaking of the wooden cartwheels and the suck and clop of the pony's hooves. Clara yawned until her head tipped forward on her chest with her eyes closed, and Ronan mac Nichol seemed content to trudge alongside the black-and-white pony with his cloak pulled over his head against the chill morning air.

As they neared the forest, Nora looked around her for the wild ponies. She had seen them grazing on the open ground late last night, and she hoped they had not gone all the way back to the mountains. She saw a soft-edged shape moving in a hollow and, putting her fingers to her mouth, she let out a piercing whistle.

Clara's head shot up and she nearly fell off the upturned pail. "Jesus, Mary, and Joseph, what are you doing?" she spluttered.

But she was too concerned with settling herself back on the bucket to notice the herd of ponies that emerged from the shadows, like fairy creatures taking shape from the tussocks of grass. Nora swung herself up onto Dunlin's back and called to

Ronan, "I'll make my own way to Sraith Salach, thank you."
Her heart was thudding as she realized that her perilous journey was about to begin.

Ronan mac Nichol raised one hand in acknowledgement,
then clicked his tongue at the black-and-white pony, who had
stopped dead when Fiach's herd cantered up. The blacksmith
didn't seem remotely surprised that Nora might choose to
travel with wild horses, and she told herself that it was as well
her reputation had spread as far as Ronan's village. Checking
that the oilcloth sack she had brought with her was fastened
securely about her waist, she kicked her heels against Dunlin's
sides, silently warning the mountain pony that, today, Nora
was going to be deciding where they went, and how fast.

Startled, the bracken-colored mare flattened her ears and
hunched her back, but Nora kept her legs closed tight against
Dunlin's flanks until the pony set off at a canter along the edge
of the trees. The herd ran with them, and Fiach pulled alongside Dunlin and regarded Nora curiously with one dark eye.
When a silvery stretch of water opened out on their left, Nora
leaned her weight that way and Dunlin swung around, so that
she was heading straight for the beach that led along Ardbear
Bay to the headland.

The ponies knew this route well and picked up speed, leaping and scrambling over the uneven, marshy ground so close to
each other that their shoulders brushed together. Dunlin's

stride felt short and choppy compared with Lir's, and the ground seemed so near that Nora instinctively lifted up her feet when they came to a patch of heather. The mare's shoulders had never seemed this narrow before, and her ears were barely an arm's length away.

Fiach slowed down when they came to the beach and, still at a trot, dropped his head to sniff at the seaweed. Nora kicked Dunlin on, away from the herd, until they reached the cave. The tide was halfway in but there was barely any wind so the waves rolled lazily with skirts of white froth. Dunlin walked into the sea with her neck arched and her nostrils flared, and even though Nora drew up her knees, the hem of her skirt was soon drenched.

José was waiting for them at the mouth of the cave. Nora slid off Dunlin's back as they splashed onto the narrow strip of sand and led the mare over to the fir tree, which she had dragged across the entrance again to keep Lir there for one more night.

"You came," said the Spanish sailor, his voice rough with thirst.

Nora nodded. "We don't have much time," she said, untying the sack from around her waist. "People will be about on the cliffs soon and we can't let them see us." She pushed the fir tree out of the way with her free hand and clicked her tongue to encourage Dunlin into the cave. The mare threw up her head and snorted when she saw Lir's pale shape in the shadows, but let Nora calm her with a reassuring pat.

From the bag, Nora took several handfuls of grass, which she threw onto the sand for Lir, half a loaf of oatbread, and a long strip of linen. She gave the bread to José who bit into it hungrily. "We'll have plenty of water in the mountains," she told him. "Here, I've brought this to bandage your leg."

She held up the linen when José raised his eyebrows over the hunk of bread. He stood still while she knelt down and wound the cloth firmly around his thigh. The edges of the wound felt hot and swollen, and Nora wished she could have brought some of Nuala's herb paste. She would have to look out for knapweed and chamomile as they rode. Then she went over to Lir and ran her hand down his injured shoulder. To her relief, the skin was cool and flat, with no sign of flaring up again after their gallop the day before. There was no reason to delay their journey. Nora swallowed, the blood roaring in her ears so that it felt as if she were standing inside a giant seashell, the walls and roof of the cave pressing down on her.

She turned to see that José had limped over to Dunlin, who was nuzzling the scraps of seaweed left over from Lir's meal the day before. Nora watched as he reached out and hesitantly patted her shoulder. "She'll not hurt you," she told him.

José looked over his shoulder. "At home, we do not ride wild horses."

"Then don't think of her as wild," said Nora. She tied the

oilcloth sack around her waist again, lighter now but still with the comforting bulge of another loaf of bread, a clean strip of linen, and a coil of hempen rope that she would use to tether Lir when they stopped at night. "You've got to ride one of them, and if it's not Dunlin, then you'll have to ride Lir."

"You spoil me for choice," José joked feebly, white-faced, and Nora realized that he was more scared than he would admit. He had been safe in the cave, and now he was about to ride a wild pony across open countryside, where there would be English soldiers and curious eyes on all sides. She decided not to mention the wolves in the forest or the thick fog that might make them lose their way in the mountains.

"You are right," he went on. "You have already proved you can ride Lir. I will ride the mare."

"Here, lean on me," Nora said, going over and standing on the same side as his wounded leg. He was only a couple of handspans taller than her, and a good deal thinner judging by his bony ribs, so she was sure Dunlin would be able to carry his weight. José hissed sharply between clenched teeth as Nora helped him to hop around until he was standing next to Dunlin's shoulder.

"Are you sure you are well enough for this?" she asked, suddenly afraid that his injury was worse than it first seemed.

José nodded. "I have to be," he muttered. He grabbed a handful of Dunlin's mane. "You will have to help me," he said.

He swayed as he tried to lift his injured leg over Dunlin's rump, and Nora had to heave him up. He landed crookedly on the mare's back and she sidestepped under his weight with her ears flat back. Nora quickly reached out and laid her hand against Dunlin's neck. "It's all right, little one," she murmured.

José cursed under his breath, his eyes shut tight, until Dunlin was standing still again. Then he opened them and smiled wanly down at Nora. "I am ready," he said.

She went back into the cave and took hold of Lir's mane. "Come on, boy," she said. Her voice sounded squeaky and high-pitched, and Nora told herself not to be nervous because it would upset the stallion. But he followed her calmly enough down the sand, past Dunlin and José, and out of the cave. José kicked his left leg against the mare's flank so that she walked after them, her ears swiveling back toward the unfamiliar rider but apparently willing to carry his weight.

Above the mountains, the sky was the color of unbleached linen hemmed with gold where the sun was starting to rise. Any moment now, Nora's father and her brother Colm would be leaving the cottage and heading along the cliff to the harbor. She led Lir over to a rock, curling and uncurling her fingers in his mane to stop them from trembling. This time she pulled herself onto the broad gray back more carefully, and although Lir's head lifted in surprise, he didn't rear up.

Nora looked over her shoulder at José. "Ready?" she asked,

keeping her voice low even though she knew they were too far from the cottages to be heard.

The boy nodded, his mouth set in a determined line. He sat lopsidedly on the mare's narrow back, but Nora guessed that was because of his injured leg—at least his back was straight, with his shoulders square and his hands wrapped firmly in Dunlin's short, coarse mane.

She closed her heels against the stallion's sides and he walked through the waves toward the beach. Grazing on the seaweed near the bottom of the cliffs, Fiach's herd raised their heads and stared curiously at the two horses. Nora's gaze instinctively followed the cliff path up toward the cottages, and felt her heart nearly stop.

There was someone at the top of the path, looking straight at her.

⤜⫸⤛

"COME ON, JOSÉ!" SHE CRIED. Their only hope was to gallop along the shore and trust the half-light to keep them hidden in the shadows at the bottom of the cliffs. She saw him frown, puzzled, but there was no time to explain. Hoping desperately that Dunlin would follow, she wound her fingers deeper into Lir's mane and clapped her heels against his flanks.

"Run, Lir, run!" Nora begged, and the stallion leaped forward with his neck arched and his forelegs thrusting through the waves as if he really were the horse of Manannan mac Lir. Suddenly they were out of the water and his hooves were drumming on hard sand. Nora clung to Lir's mane as he stretched out his neck and flattened his body, swerving between the boulders without breaking his stride. She glanced over her shoulder and saw Dunlin galloping behind them, her nostrils flared and her ears flat back against her neck. José was crouched over her mane with his feet dangling below the mare's belly, almost as low as her knees. Nora winced as she thought how painful this must be for his wounded leg, but they couldn't risk being caught, not now, before they had even started their journey.

She turned back and leaned her whole body toward the cliffs to urge Lir further up the beach. To her relief he shifted direction and headed away from the edge of the waves. A rapid beat of hooves behind told her that Dunlin was still following doggedly.

Nearer and nearer the cliff path they galloped. Nora risked glancing up, and she saw at once that it was Donal Foyle looking down at them, his long hair streaming out like a banshee and his hand reaching instinctively for the broad-bladed knife he carried at his waist. He wouldn't be able to recognize Nora from up there, thanks to the shadows under the cliff, but he would have heard enough about Spanish sailors and shipwrecked horses to guess that these fugitives would fetch a good price with the English army captain or Dan Devlin.

Nora gritted her teeth and kicked Lir on, ignoring his ragged gasps for breath. Straight through Fiach's herd they galloped, scattering the mountain ponies across the sand. Fiach let out a furious whinny and Nora felt Lir tense as he recognized the challenge from another stallion, but she dug her heels into his flanks and did not give him a chance to slow down. She sent up a silent prayer that Dunlin would keep following and not break off to rejoin her herd. As Lir shot clear of the wild ponies, Nora listened carefully and relaxed a tiny bit when she heard the bracken-colored mare's hooves still drumming after them. She looked back quickly and saw that José was swinging his legs against Dunlin's flanks, kicking her on past the other horses. He looked uncomfortable and his face was stretched taut with pain, but Nora was reassured that he could at least ride well enough to stay on at a breakneck pace, in spite of his injured leg.

They reached the end of the beach, where the stretch of open moorland lay between the bay and the forest. Nora let Lir slow down as the sand gave way to treacherous scoops of boggy peat dotted with hard, knobbly tussocks. Dunlin could probably keep galloping all the way to the trees, but there was no point letting José get too far ahead. Lir dropped into a trot, arching his head and snorting crossly at the uneven ground. He stumbled when his hooves clipped the grassy tussocks, and Nora had to grab hold of his mane and heave herself back into the middle of his slippery back.

Dunlin drew alongside them, her eyes so wide that the whites showed. She was half-trotting, half-cantering over the lumpy bogland, and Nora could see that José was struggling to stay on. She held her heels away from Lir's sides and forced herself to relax her grip on his mane, and the stallion slowed to a walk. Dunlin walked too, keeping close to the gray horse's shoulder.

"Is it safe now?" José asked, his eyes almost as huge as Dunlin's.

"I think so," said Nora. "We'll be hidden in the trees soon." She didn't add that the people of Errislannan rarely went into the forest because of the wolves. There was a single road that led straight through to the mountains and Sraith Salach, but Nora and José would have to stay away from that, moving as quickly as they could along the paths used by deer and the wild ponies.

Becoming more used to the stallion's long, swinging stride, Nora risked reaching down with one hand to stroke Dunlin's mane. The mare, who looked no bigger than a wolfhound next to Lir, tossed her head and flicked her ears forward as if Nora's touch had reassured her.

The edge of the forest loomed ahead of them, black and forbidding where the dawn light had not yet pierced the canopy of leaves. The trees were mainly oak, their leaves a thousand shades of orange and saffron, occasionally divided by a glossy dark holly tree like a rogue thread in a rich man's tapestry. In the east, a long way beyond Connemara and the Maam Tuirc mountains, Queen Elizabeth's father Henry had harvested the mighty forests of Irish oak to build a fleet of warships, and Nora wondered how long it would be before his ambitious daughter sent men to chop down these trees as well.

Lir hesitated when they reached the edge of the forest, blowing warily down his nostrils. Nora let him stand for a moment and patted him. "It's all right," she murmured. "We'll be straight through quite safely, you'll see."

Beside her, José raised his eyebrows disbelievingly, and Nora guessed that they had wolves in Spanish forests as well. She found herself smiling, and said, "'Tis better that some of us aren't scared, at least."

José smiled back and shrugged. "We are hunted on all sides, no? But this little mare will look after me, I think." He leaned forward and slapped his hand resoundingly against Dunlin's neck. At once the mare flattened her ears and her head shot around with her teeth bared, snapping shut barely a handspan from José's leg. The Spanish boy looked up at Nora with an alarmed expression in his eyes.

"Take no notice," she said quickly. "Dunlin's not used to anyone except me, and you should be glad she's agreed to let you ride her at all." A wisp of smoke drifting behind him caught her eye, and she realized that someone had stoked the fire in one of the cottages. "Come on," she said, straightening her brat and checking that the oilcloth sack was still safely tied around her waist. "We must keep going." She did not think Donal Foyle would set out after them, but it was bad enough he had seen them and might describe the rider with long black hair to her father.

She clicked her tongue and closed her heels against Lir's sides, and the stallion stepped forward into the shelter of the trees. Sweat was running down his neck, making the hem of

Nora's skirt cling to her legs, and she decided to let him walk for a while to let him cool down. They would have to stop to let the horses eat before too long, but she wanted to wait until they were clear of the forest. José kicked Dunlin more gently than he had on the beach, wincing as the bandage pulled against his injured leg. Nora reminded herself to look out for knapweed and chamomile, which sometimes grew in the shelter of bramble thickets.

The trees closed up behind them and soon they were walking through eerie orange-tinted shadows, the sky lightening above the whispering canopy of branches. They rode in silence aside from the horses' hooves padding on fallen leaves, and Nora tried not to think about the creatures that might be watching them with hard yellow eyes. This forest wasn't as daunting as the yew trees that surrounded Aughnanure Castle, but Nora wasn't traveling with her brothers now, armed with stout cudgels and making her feel safe with their careless chatter and shouts of laughter. She pulled her cloak more tightly around her and told herself that she had to be brave, for José's sake and for Lir's.

Suddenly José held up his hand and sat taller, bringing Dunlin to a halt. The mare lifted her head with her ears pricked up and stared straight ahead. Nora followed her gaze, straining her ears until she heard a faint snuffling coming from some bramble bushes. It could be a badger or a red squirrel—

or a wolf. She glanced at José and he shook his head, warning her to keep quiet.

Lir stood too, his nostrils quivering and every muscle tense. Nora slowly slid one hand under his mane and let it rest against his damp neck, hoping that she was giving him courage rather than scaring him even more with her trembling fingers.

Ahead of them, one of the bramble bushes started to shake violently, then the leaves parted and a slender red shape emerged. A thin nose sniffed the air before the animal turned and trotted away, its long bushy tail scoring a faint trail in the leaves.

Nora breathed out in relief. "Only a fox," she whispered. José frowned, and she guessed that it wasn't a word he knew in Irish. But she didn't want to waste time explaining—the sooner they were out of the forest, the better because the next creature to cross their path might not be so timid. She kicked Lir into a trot and dug in her knees to stop herself from being bounced off, suddenly realizing why the English soldiers rode with saddles and stirrups on the high-stepping Munster war horses. José looked equally uncomfortable beside her, his face white with pain as he tried to wrap his legs around Dunlin's sides. Nora knew it would be easier if they cantered, but the trees grew too close together to go any faster, and they needed to take care that the horses didn't trip over any sticking-up roots.

"You're doing well," she said encouragingly.

José took his eyes off Dunlin's ears to glance doubtfully at her. "In Spain, we ride with—" he broke off and patted Dunlin's withers in the shape of a saddle. "Even then, I am not a good rider like my father. Not long ago, we had a big quarrel because he found me sword fighting with my cousins instead of riding the horse he had bought for me."

"Do you have any brothers and sisters?" Nora asked curiously.

José shook his head. "My mother died when I was very young. That is when my uncle and my aunt Cristina came to live with my father. They have two sons, Ernesto and Jaime." His eyes clouded and he looked down at his hands, clutching Dunlin's mane. "They will think I am dead. It will break my father's heart."

Nora didn't know what to say. She watched José jolting along with his head bowed and prayed that Murray ne Doe would soon find a ship to take him home.

Dunlin drew ahead, following a path invisible to Nora's eyes but she knew they were heading straight through the forest because the moss on the tree trunks was all growing on the same side. Heavy drops of rain pattered on the leaves above them, and she didn't relish the thought of swapping the shelter for the open mountains. But they were drawing near the edge of the trees now because she could see watery, gray light between the trunks ahead. She tried to slow Lir down before they burst out into the open by sitting taller and tensing her stomach muscles so that she was offering a tiny resistance to his movement. To her delight, the stallion's neat, gray ears twitched and he dropped to a walk.

Nora leaned forward and patted him close to the top of his neck, where his coat wasn't slick with sweat like his shoulder. "Good boy," she whispered.

Dunlin slowed down as well and José twisted around to look at Nora. Behind him, the trees ended abruptly, giving way to open bogland that stretched across a narrow valley and reached halfway up the flanks of the round, gray-topped mountains. Binn Ghleann Uisce was nearest to them, with Binn Gabhar and Binn Doire Chlair behind.

"Which way now?" he asked.

Nora saw that his breath was coming in shallow, ragged gasps and there was a sheen of sweat on his forehead. "Would you like to rest for a while?" she said, knowing it would be safer to make straight for the mountains but worried that the boy was close to a fever. She reached down and ran her hand over the scrape on Lir's shoulder, but to her relief it felt no warmer than the rest of his skin.

José shook his head, his eyes fixed on the mountains. "No, we keep going."

Nora fished in the sack at her waist and broke off a chunk of oatbread. "At least eat this," she said, holding it out to him.

He took it and chewed unenthusiastically at the crust, then met Nora's gaze and gave a twisted smile. "I will feast for a month when I get home," he vowed.

"What do you eat there?" Nora asked, nudging Lir forward, out of the trees. She hoped that she might distract José from the pain in his leg if she kept him talking.

The boy's eyes shone and his smile grew broader. "Fish from the sea, longer than my arm, and bread as soft as—" he broke off and pointed up at the sky, and Nora guessed, "Clouds?"

He nodded. "And . . . and—" again he fumbled for the Irish word, then gave up and said in Spanish, "*Naranjas.*"

"*¿Naranjas?*" Nora echoed, the word sounding sharp and strange on her tongue.

"*Sí.*" José's face grew animated and he let go of Dunlin's mane with both hands to make a round shape in the air. "Gold like the sun, on trees with dark green leaves. They are the best to eat of anything."

He looked so excited that Nora laughed. She wondered what sort of fruit these *naranjas* were—they didn't sound anything like the dusty red apples or sour little damsons that she was used to.

It was much colder on the open bogland, and a strong wind blew the rain into their faces and down their necks. José started shivering almost at once, with nothing but a torn undershirt flapping against his ribs, and Nora scolded herself for not bringing a blanket.

"Is there no sun in this country?" José complained, turning

to look at Nora with his eyes half-shut against the cold, stinging raindrops.

"In the summer, yes," she said. "But it's autumn now."

"In Spain, there is sun all the time. The houses have white
walls, and often it is so bright that you cannot look at them. And
the ground is brown and dry, not green everywhere like this."

"What do the horses eat, if there is no grass?" said Nora.

José shrugged. "I don't know. The servants feed the animals,
not me."

"Does your father have many servants?"

"Of course. We live in a big house beside the sea, which is
always blue, not cold and gray like your sea. There are many, many
rooms in the house, and outside we have fields where my cousins
and I play at sword fighting. . . ." His voice trailed away, and Nora
began to wish she hadn't encouraged him to think about his home.
He went on, quietly, "The window of my father's room looks over
the sea. He will be sitting there every day, waiting for me to come
back. Even if people tell him that I am dead, I do not think he will
believe them for a long, long time."

Nora felt her heart twist as she thought of José's father, grief-
stricken once already by the death of his wife. *I will send your son
home to you,* she promised silently. *Keep watching—he will come back.*

The horses trudged toward the mountains with their heads
down and their tails clamped against their hindquarters.
Dunlin plodded quite willingly beside the big gray stallion, and

· *163* ·

Nora felt a glow of gratitude that the mare had not tried to go back to her herd. There was another group of ponies grazing halfway up the mountain ahead of them, but the mare had done nothing more than lift her head and prick her ears to watch them for a few moments before walking on again.

When they reached the foot of Binn Ghleann Uisce, Dunlin took the lead, following a narrow trail that climbed steadily across the flank of the mountain, away from the grazing ponies. Nora looked back over her shoulder to see the valley of Imleach Dha Ru spread out below, scored from end to end by the road that ran from Errislannan to Sraith Salach. There was no one in sight from horizon to horizon, but she knew she would feel safer once they couldn't see the track at all. She tucked her chin into her brat and let Lir's steady stride lull her as he picked his way steadily up the mountain.

She gave a start when she heard José exclaim in alarm, and realized that she must have nearly dozed off.

"Nora!" he called again, his voice tight with urgency. "Where are we?"

Nora opened her eyes and looked around. The horses had come to a stop, still on a stony mountain path but how far up they were, it was impossible to tell. The clouds had come down, and they were marooned in a thick, white wilderness of fog.

17

NORA FOUGHT DOWN THE PANIC that fluttered inside her on dark, anxious wings and remembered what Father Francis had told her about getting lost in the fog. He had told her always to head down into a valley, below the clouds or at least out of the thickest part, where there was less chance of missing your step and plunging straight down the side of a mountain. But she didn't want to go back the way they had come—if they could even be sure of finding the same path—because that would take them back to the road. They had to keep going and hope that the clouds lifted before they went too far the wrong way.

Lir shifted uneasily, sending a shower of pebbles rattling off the side of the path. Nora listened to them fall for a long time and felt her stomach turn to ice.

"Nora?" José said again, and she saw him peer through the fog toward her. Dunlin was little more than a blurred brown shape, beads of mist clinging to her coat.

"It's the fog," Nora said. When José looked puzzled, she added, "Clouds, yes?"

"Clouds," José echoed. "But which way?"

Nora urged Lir a few steps forward. Ahead of them, the path sloped steeply up into the mist. "I . . . I think we should keep going. Once we reach the other side of this mountain, we might be able to see where we are."

José frowned. "But how, if we can't see the path?"

Nora bit her lip in despair. She had been stupid to think she could take José to Aughnanure through the mountains. There was a reason the road had been built through the valley; too many lives had been lost up here, where weather and rock conspired against travelers and cowherds. She tried not to see shapes reaching toward her with sharp, clawing fingers as the air swirled and thickened. Everyone knew that bog-wraiths could make their bodies thin enough to hide in fog, waiting to snatch unwary travelers off the path.

Dunlin interrupted her thoughts by giving a soft snort and edging forward, placing her hooves confidently on the loose stones that covered the path. Nora stared at the mare and felt hope grow inside her like an uncurling fern. Of course! Dunlin knew every mountain path in rain, fog, or blackest midnight.

"We must let the mare show us the way," she told José. "We may be lost, but I don't think she is."

The Spanish boy looked doubtful.

"No, really," Nora urged. "Just sit still and let her keep going. Lir will follow, I'm sure."

She watched as José took hold of Dunlin's mane and closed

his legs against her sides. He was sitting more confidently on her narrow back now, although he still kicked more strongly with his uninjured leg. Dunlin tossed her head and set off, her hooves tapping rhythmically on the pebbles.

Nora bent down and stroked Lir high on his neck, under his long mane. "Come on, boy," she whispered. "Dunlin will keep us safe, I promise."

ON AND ON THEY CLIMBED, until Nora expected them to pop up through the top of the cloud into a strange sort of sunshine. But the fog just grew thicker until their clothes were as wet as if they had swum the length of Lough Corrib and drops of water hung along Lir's mane like fragile, trembling pearls. When Nora found herself slipping toward the stallion's withers, she realized that the path was heading down again, although it was impossible to see what lay below them.

Then there was boggy, tussocky grass under the horses' hooves instead of stones, and the cloud started to drift and thin in the breeze until Nora saw a long, empty valley spread out in front of them. A lake the color of unpolished metal carved a narrow slice out of the bogland, and Nora knew at last where she was. This was the Inagh valley and the water was Lough Inagh, which stretched nearly all the way from Sraith Salach to Killary Harbor in the north. The little mare had brought them safely through the mountains, and they were almost halfway to Aughnanure.

Nora slid off Lir's back and rushed over to Dunlin, wrapping her arms around the mare's sticky neck and burying her face in the coarse, tufty mane. "Thank you, little one, thank you," she murmured.

Above her, José coughed awkwardly. "We are safe, then?" he asked. "This is Aughnanure already?"

Nora pushed her hair back over her shoulders and looked up at him. "No, not yet," she admitted. "But I know exactly where we are, and if we rest here for the night, then we will reach Aughnanure tomorrow."

The Spanish sailor looked around with his eyebrows raised so far, they almost vanished into his thick dark fringe. "Rest here?" he echoed. "But there is no shelter."

Nora pointed to a small copse on the far side of the valley. "There's a booly in those trees," she began, then noticed that José looked baffled and quickly explained. "In the summer, the chieftains send their cattle to be grazed up here. The kerns who come with the herds live in huts that stay empty for the rest of the year. That's what a booly is."

"Boo-ley," José repeated, rolling the word on his tongue in the same way that Nora had with *naranjas*. Then he straightened up, and Nora felt a pang of concern at the shadows that bloomed under his eyes from the long day's ride. "Come on, Señora Dunlin," he said, running his hand along the mare's neck. "We go to the booly."

Nora balanced on the tallest tussock she could find to heave herself onto Lir's back again. She managed it with an ungainly scramble, and was glad that the stallion was too tired to object to her lack of dignity. The two horses crossed the valley at a trot as if they knew that the copse of pine trees offered shelter and a chance to rest. Dunlin led the way once again, lifting her small hooves easily over the tussocks and breaking into a canter whenever the ground smoothed out.

As soon as they reached the trees, Nora slithered off Lir's back and led him by his mane to the small stone hut. There was no door and it looked dark and uninviting inside, but the thatch had been newly repaired with fresh reeds and Nora guessed it was only a month since it had been used by one of Murray ne Doe's kerns, perhaps even her friend Con Foyle. She untied the sack from her waist and took out the rope, looping one end into a rough halter that she slipped over the stallion's ears.

"What are you doing?" said José, watching her from Dunlin's back.

"I need to tether Lir for the night," Nora explained as she tied the other end of the rope to a tree branch. The stallion put his head down at once and began to crop the sweet grass, more palatable than the tussocks out on the bogland thanks to the shelter offered by the trees. There was a small spring at the side of the cottage, trickling over the rocks into a muddy pool that would serve both horses and people well for drinking water.

"Will you tie up Dunlin as well?" José asked, swinging his right leg carefully over the mare's neck and lowering himself to the ground. His breath hissed between his teeth as he put his weight onto his injured leg, and Nora reached into the sack again for the herbs that would help him sleep.

"The mare doesn't need tethering," she told him. "These mountains are her home. I can't tell her to stay in one place."

José looked worried. "But what if she goes away and does not come back?"

"Oh, she'll come when I whistle," Nora promised, hoping that she sounded more confident than she felt. She had been counting on Dunlin staying close to the booly, but there was always a chance she would go back into the mountains to find her herd. The mare wandered over and pressed her forehead against Nora's chest, and Nora rubbed her small, furry ears absentmindedly.

"You'll stay with us, won't you, girl?" she murmured, and Dunlin blew warmly against her skirt in reply.

Nora left the mare grazing close to Lir and followed José into the hut. He had hopped unsteadily through the doorway, clinging to the wall for support, and almost vanished in the shadows. Nora waited for a few moments until her eyes got used to the dim light, then saw him half sitting, half lying on a heap of dirty straw in the corner furthest from the door. There was no hearth, but Nora had no means of lighting a fire anyway. She did notice something that made her heart leap, though—a torn and filthy blanket half hidden under the straw.

José screwed up his nose when Nora dragged it out and gave it a shake, but he lay still while she spread it over him. "I will stink like a cow forever," he murmured, and she smiled.

"Murray ne Doe will let you bathe like a most honored guest at his castle," she promised him. After all, she told herself, the chieftain would doubtless be interested in earning the handsome reward that might be offered by José's wealthy father.

José laid his head against the wall and closed his eyes.

"Do you think you can eat something?" asked Nora, offering him the rest of the oatbread and the watercress.

The boy shook his head, his eyes still shut. "Water," he muttered, and Nora ran outside to scoop some water out of the pool. She should have brought a bowl, she thought angrily, but enough water stayed in her hands for José to swallow a couple of mouthfuls. He drifted off almost at once into a light, feverish sleep, and Nora settled down beside him, trying to keep him warm with the length of her body as well as the stinking blanket. She smiled into the dark at the thought of what her sisters would say if they saw Nora sleeping so close to a young man, then a pang of alarm clutched at her insides; did Mainie know that Ronan mac Nichol had reached Sraith Salach without her? Nora shook her head to drive out the useless worries and made herself finish the dry, unappetizing oatbread.

It seemed strange to be going to sleep with just one other person beside her, and without the flickering orange light from a fire. Nora whispered a hasty prayer to keep away fairies and dark spirits, then shut her eyes and let exhausted sleep rush in like black waves from the edges of her mind.

When she woke, Nora felt chilled to the bone and every muscle protested as she uncurled and sat up. For a moment she couldn't work out why the cottage was so cold and quiet, until she remembered where she was. The room was still dark but through the doorway she could see that the far side of the valley was flooded with light which meant that dawn was long past. They would have to set off as quickly as possible if she wanted to deliver the Spanish sailor to Murray ne Doe and return to Sraith Salach by nightfall. She woke José, who seemed refreshed by his rest and in less pain from his injured leg, and they were on the horses following a narrow path into the Maam Tuirc mountains before the sun clipped the top of the pine trees.

The horses seemed well rested too, and Lir's flanks had filled out after a night of grazing. To Nora's relief, Dunlin had strayed no further than the edge of the trees, as if she had accepted the two humans and the Spanish stallion as her temporary herd. The day was much brighter than the previous one and there was no sign of the fog that had nearly swallowed them whole, so they were able to trot and canter through the hidden valleys and bleak swaths of marshland. Nora knew that these mountains were as unfamiliar to Dunlin as they were to her, but she trusted the wild pony's instincts to keep them out of the most dangerous bogs; several times, the bracken-colored mare stopped dead and swerved around a patch of ground that looked no more sinister than any other part of the flat, scrubby grass.

They headed steadily east, stopping briefly beside a stream to let the horses drink, where Nora found a clump of watercress which she pulled up and offered to José. He chewed the sharp-tasting leaves willingly enough, although Nora heard him mutter "*naranjas*" under his breath as if he were imagining a different flavor altogether. Finally they stood with the Maam Tuircs behind them and looked across an empty stretch of moorland at a hazy, dark strip of green. It was the edge of the yew forest around Aughnanure Castle.

Nora glanced at José and knew that triumph was making her eyes shine. "We're nearly there!" she promised. She wondered what her brothers and sisters would say if they knew that mousy little Nora, their timid blackbird, had ridden all the way to Murray ne Doe's castle with only a shipwrecked sailor for company.

José grinned. "I hear the sound of Spanish sails already," he replied, and he leaned forward and kicked Dunlin's flanks to send her cantering forward.

Lir threw up his head and bunched his quarters beneath him as if he wanted to follow. Nora was so used to his powerful strides now that she sat easily on his back, keeping herself still with her knees and wrapping her hands more firmly around a hank of mane. She was about to let him gallop after the mare when something caught her eye. There was a dark, ragged-edge shape on the road that led across the moor from Aughnanure to Sraith Salach; the stony track was a good half-league from the path José and Dunlin were taking, but it ran parallel with a clear, treeless view from one to the other. Once Nora and José left the slopes of the mountains, there would be nowhere to hide until they reached the yew forest.

The shadow grew nearer and the wind carried a distinctive jangle of metal against leather and the crack of iron-shod hooves to Nora's ears. She had heard that sound before, on the same road after her last visit to Aughnanure.

English soldiers!

CHAPTER
18

〰️

"JOSÉ!" SCREAMED NORA. "COME BACK!"

But the boy didn't hear her, didn't even look back, as he crouched over Dunlin's withers and urged her faster and faster toward the line of trees. Nora was sure he hadn't spotted the people on the road—he would be wary enough of meeting Galway folk, let alone his most feared enemies. She clapped her heels against Lir's sides and the stallion half reared, his forelegs plunging through the air, before leaping forward like a breaking wave.

Nora nearly slid straight off his back. She managed to cling on with strands of mane biting into her fingers and lashing against her face like sharp, tiny brambles. They were galloping faster than she had ever gone before, even faster than her first ride along the beach when Lir had been weak from hunger and lack of exercise. Nora's legs slipped helplessly against his smooth flanks and every time she opened her mouth to call out to José, the wind snatched her words away and made her gasp.

Dunlin was racing along flat out, but Lir's strides were longer and he was carrying less weight so Nora caught up with the mare before she was two thirds of the way to the trees. She kicked Lir on until he was galloping alongside the mountain pony; her neck was stretched out and she seemed low enough to run straight under the stallion's belly. Nora risked a glance sideways at the road. She could see the soldiers clearly now, seven or eight of them cantering on broad-chested war horses led by a tall figure on a bay gelding with a white blaze. Nora recognized the horse rather than the rider and knew this must be Captain Money, who had passed her family on the way back from the feast and who had threatened the fiercest punishments to people found helping the shipwrecked Spanish men. It seemed impossible that the soldiers had not yet seen him, but in a few moments they would be level, barely a quarter of a league apart, and Nora and José would be discovered for sure.

Nora hoped that the soldiers would have more sense than to turn their horses off the road and try to cross the moor in pursuit; there were patches of bog between the tracks that would sink a hare, let alone a heavily saddled war horse. With luck they would realize that they would have to turn around and follow the road back to the forest before hunting down their Spanish prey. José and Nora's only hope lay in reaching the trees well before they did and hiding in the thick, green sea of trunk and branch where only the wolves and wood-spirits dared to go.

More afraid of being captured by English soldiers than anything an Irish forest might hold, Nora turned to José. He looked up at her questioningly, and Nora realized that he hadn't noticed the soldiers, who were now hidden behind her and Lir.

"We have to get to the forest!" she gasped, and José frowned, unable to hear her above the drumming hoofbeats and the noise of the wind.

There was no time to explain. Nora's sharp ears had picked up a shout from the road and the clatter of hooves on stone as the war horses were jerked roughly to a halt. Flattening her body against Lir's neck, she pushed him on even faster and prayed that Dunlin would follow. A hoarse cry beside her told her that José had seen the soldiers at last and she caught a glimpse of his face, seafoam-white under his dark fringe, as the horses galloped flank against flank across the moor.

Nora didn't dare turn around to see if the soldiers were pursuing them. The trees raced toward them, the dark green line dividing into huge black trunks and branches sweeping low to the ground before vanishing into shadow beyond. She swallowed and gritted her teeth, reminding herself of what would happen if she and José were caught by the English captain. The Spanish boy clearly thought wolves and wood-spirits were a much better prospect because he kept drumming his feet against the mare's sides, which were black with sweat and peat, as they hurtled into the trees.

The open moorland was still visible through the trees behind them when the horses were forced to drop into a trot and then walk to pick their way through the brambles that covered the forest floor. Dunlin's breath was coming in hoarse, ragged gasps and her eyes were wide with alarm. Nora reached down from Lir's back to touch the mare's ears, hoping she could keep going until they reached Murray ne Doe's castle. Lir was breathing heavily, too, but his ears were pricked forward as he looked warily about him, walking with short, quick strides that suggested he could still take flight at any moment.

"Will they follow us?" said José, his voice barely more than a whisper.

Nora looked over her shoulder at the rapidly fading light at the edge of the forest, tinged yellow from the prickly bogland grass. There was no sign of movement out there, no shadowy figures galloping toward them with swords drawn. The soldiers must have gone back along the road to pursue them through the forest, where the ground was less treacherous even though the brambles under the trees would slow their horses down.

"I can't see them," Nora said, then forced herself to add, "but that doesn't mean they're not after us." A silent scream rose inside her. They were being hunted like one of the stags that the English insisted belonged to their queen, far away on the other side of the sea. She took a deep, trembling breath and pressed her knuckles into Lir's neck for comfort. "We must get to the castle as quickly as we can. Murray ne Doe will protect us once we're there."

At least, she hoped he would, and it all depended on her being able to work out which way to go through this pathless, midnight-dark part of the forest.

"Do you know the way?" José asked as if he could read her thoughts.

Nora blinked and looked hard at the tree trunks. Just like in the forest near Errislannan, the moss would grow on the side of the trees away from the cold north wind. The castle lay not far from the shore of Lough Corrib, which still must be to the east since they had not already come across the long stretch of water. So as long as they kept the bare sides of the trunks on their right, they should end up at the lake if not the castle itself. "That way," she said, pointing ahead.

She closed her legs against Lir's sides and the stallion walked on, lifting his hooves high over the brambles and occasionally stumbling when a barbed strand caught around one of his fet-locks. Nora sat as still and as lightly as she could, concentrating on keeping her balance and steering him back onto a straight line whenever they had to veer around a particularly thick clump of brambles or a glossy holly tree. Dunlin plodded behind them, her head low with exhaustion and her hooves thudding dully against the dry, leafy floor. José rode in silence, turning his head from side to side as he kept watch for any sign of their pursuers. Nora thought he looked like a frightened deer, his brown eyes huge and the skin stretched taut over his cheekbones, and she felt a new wave of rage and indignation against the English soldiers. How could it be right that a boy barely more than her own age was hunted like prey, when all he wanted to do was return home?

The light at the edge of the forest soon vanished among the thickening tree trunks, and shadows reached down from the dark-needled branches until Lir glowed ghostly gray in the half-light. Nora tried not to shriek out loud when thorny fingers clutched at her skirt, but it was only a bramble, not a wood-spirit dragging her into its hollow tree home. She wrenched the cloth free with shaking hands and rode on, instinctively drawing her knees higher to keep them away from the bushes.

Suddenly Lir stopped dead and his head shot up. The tips of his ears were almost touching as he listened to something Nora couldn't hear.

Dunlin stopped, too, and out of the corner of her eye Nora saw her lift her head and tense every muscle along her damp, furry neck.

"What is it?" José started to whisper, but before he had finished speaking they both heard the sounds of something crashing through the forest—not just one pursuer but several, giant horses breaking through low-hanging branches and stamping over brambles, ridden by men who shouted in low voices and drew swords with the whisper of steel against leather.

For a heartbeat, Nora froze, imagining blades slicing through skin and the agony of knowing that she had failed, that she had brought José into far greater danger by taking him away from the cave. But then her mind cleared as if washed by a cool wave, and she found herself scooping up great handfuls of Lir's mane and kicking him forward into the darkening forest.

"Come on, José, quick!" she cried over her shoulder. They were not caught yet—this prey still had fleet-footed horses and the thickening shadows on their side. And most important of all, the English soldiers did not have dogs. They could try to follow the direction of the sound Lir and Dunlin made as they galloped, but they could not hunt them down by their scent like Murray ne Doe's wolfhounds tracked deer and hares with their long, keen noses.

Through the trees they fled, and Nora was grateful that at least the noise they were making would scare off any wolves awake in the daytime. Lir jumped and scrambled through the brambles, not slowing even when they tore at his skin and left a necklace of red beads welling against his pale gray hair. Nora started to brush the blood away with her hands, but stopped when it made the mane scarlet and slippery to hold. She guessed that Dunlin would fare even worse, with her soft nose and belly so much closer to the snagging thorns, and she sent a silent apology to the loyal mare.

All at once the shouts of the soldiers echoed terrifyingly loud and close, and Nora clapped her right heel against Lir to send him swerving away around a huge holly tree. She took no notice of the moss on the tree trunks now. There would be time enough to find their way to the castle as soon as they were sure they were no longer being hunted.

Suddenly the trees came to an abrupt halt for the space of a cart-width, perhaps more, and Lir's hoofbeats rang on stone, not leaves. Nora realized they had come to the road that led to the castle. She glanced left and right, but there was no one around. This was the quickest route by far to the safety of Murray ne Doe's walls, but they would be much more easily spotted by the English soldiers. Nora halted Lir by sitting up tall and letting her legs hang straight without touching his flanks. Dunlin skittered to a stop beside them, and Nora thought longingly and fleetingly of Nuala's healing paste when she saw the angry red scratches across the mare's nose and shoulders.

José opened his mouth to speak but Nora held up her hand to stop him. The sound of the English soldiers was fainter now, and seemed to be growing quieter as if they were heading in a different direction. "Come on," she called to José as she kicked

Lir into a canter along the road. His hoofbeats rang on the hard-packed stones so Nora steered him into the muddy ruts carved out by passing wheels. Before long, the castle wall appeared in the narrow gap between the trees, tall and gray and the most welcoming sight that Nora had ever seen.

Even better, the wooden gate was open to let in a group of men, six or seven on foot and a few on horseback. As they drew nearer, Nora saw that it was a hunting party: The men on foot were leading wolfhounds the size of foals or carried leather-hooded hawks on their gloved hands, held aloft like precious trophies. Two of the men were bent double under the weight of deer carcasses draped over their shoulders; it was clear that Murray ne Doe still considered the forest to be his own hunting ground, not the English queen's.

Of the men on horseback, two rode sturdy, shaggy-coated ponies with simple bridles but no saddles, and had bows and quivers of arrows slung on their backs. One of them was the fox-haired gallowglass who had fallen through the trapdoor at the feast. The third man was on a tall brown horse with a broad chest and sturdy quarters like the Munster-bred war horses. He wore a cloak lined with russet fur and his head was bare, with gray-black hair flowing down over his shoulders. It was Murray ne Doe O'Flaherty himself, and Nora sagged with relief as she realized that she would be able to take the Spanish boy straight to the chieftain.

She followed the deer-bearers through the gate, nodding to José over her shoulder to tell him that he should keep close beside her. The courtyard was heaving with noise and bustle after the dark forest; servants carried pails of water and hay into the byres where cows lowed impatiently for their feed, mothers ran after their grubby-faced children who were in turn chasing squawking chickens across the muddy ground, and everywhere voices added to the din so that it was impossible to make out any single conversation.

At first Nora and José sat on their horses unnoticed, and Nora was conscious only of the feeling of safety that washed over her as the gates were shut firmly behind them. Then one of the men carrying the dead deer nudged his companion, who called to a gallowglass on a horse, and suddenly the men in the hunting party fell silent and turned to stare at the visitors.

"Who are you?" said the man who had been helping to bar the gates. He walked up to Lir and frowned at Nora. "What do you want?"

The fox-haired gallowglass—was his name Campbell? Nora tried to remember—narrowed his eyes above his bushy red beard and said, "You were at the feast, weren't you?" He turned to call to Murray ne Doe, "My lord, this girl belongs to your clan."

Nora nodded, not daring to speak because her heart was thudding so hard she feared it would spring right out of her throat if she opened her mouth.

Murray ne Doe O'Flaherty kicked his horse forward and reined it to a halt next to Lir. The bay gelding was almost the same height as the gray stallion, but its chest was narrower and its quarters less muscular, and Nora felt an unexpected and somewhat ill-timed jolt of pride that she was riding a horse even finer than a chieftain's favorite war horse.

"Your father is Tom Donovan, is he not?" said Murray ne Doe, leaning forward to peer at her with his hard, black eyes.

Nora swallowed. "Yes, he is." She reminded herself that Murray ne Doe had won this castle by good fortune and clever dealing with the English, and before that he had lived on a croft not much bigger than her father's. There was no need for her to feel afraid of speaking to him or asking for his help.

"Have you come alone, all the way from Errislannan?" the chieftain went on, raising his eyebrows. "Who is this young man?" He gestured toward José, who seemed to have shrunk under the weight of so many curious eyes.

Nora took a deep breath and squared her shoulders. "I . . . he . . . I found him on the beach. He was shipwrecked—from a Spanish ship," she added, in case Murray ne Doe thought she was trying to foist a random washed-up Irishman onto him. She glanced around as she spoke, looking for a sign that there were other Spanish sailors at the castle waiting for a ship to take them home. She couldn't see anyone who didn't look as though they belonged to Murray ne Doe's household. The door to the banqueting hall was firmly shut and a kern stood outside, his fighting stick clasped across his chest and a dagger stuck in his belt.

"A shipwrecked sailor, you say?" the chieftain echoed, and Nora was suddenly afraid that he was about to refuse to help. The blood roared in her ears and she barely heard his next words.

"And if I help him, what can you give me in return?"

Nora started to tremble so hard that she almost slithered off the stallion's back to land at the feet of the fox-haired gallowglass, who had dismounted and come over to stand at Lir's head. But she hung onto his mane, her relief quickly replaced with a cold feeling of dread. She had nothing to offer as payment—as Murray ne Doe well knew.

There was the sound of hooves behind her and José nudged Dunlin forward until she was standing in front of the chieftain's bay gelding. The boy looked exhausted and barely old enough to be a kern, his undershirt clinging to his ribs like a torn sail and the bandage on his thigh grubby with peat and an ominous bright red stain. But he held himself with the same dignity Nora had seen before in the cave, and his voice was clear as he introduced himself to the people in the courtyard.

"My name is José Sebastian Medovar. My father is Don Pedro Sebastian Medovar of Andalusia. Whatever price you wish for me to return home, he will pay it."

A murmur spread through the watching people like wind through leaves. "God's bones, he speaks Irish!" Nora heard one of the deer-carriers exclaim under his breath.

Their chieftain didn't show a flicker of surprise that a Spanish sailor should be able to speak his language. He held up one hand for silence and leaned forward to peer down at José. "Brave words, my friend, but why should I believe your empty promises? We have only just met, after all." His voice wasn't scornful, but as calm and emotionless as though they were discussing nothing more important than the price of a barrel of wine. He gestured toward the banqueting hall on the other side of the courtyard. "The others came ashore with jewels and gold coins, which have helped pay for their journey home."

Nora's heart leaped. So Murray ne Doe was indeed helping Spanish sailors—many of them, by the sounds of it. They were probably under guard in the banqueting hall for their own safety, in case any English soldiers chanced to visit the castle. The thought reminded her of their pursuers in the forest, but Nora guessed they would have reached the gate already if they had had any suspicions that this was where the fugitives had been heading. Perhaps they assumed that Murray ne Doe was enough of a friend to the English to turn away any Spanish sailors that sought help from him.

José was shaking his head. "I have no gold," he told the

chieftain. "What I had, I lost in the sea."

The old man frowned. "If I find a ship to take you back to Spain, I will be putting myself and my family in great danger, and for that I need payment now, not the promise of payment later."

"But we have nothing, can't you see?" The words burst out of Nora before she could stop herself, and she felt her cheeks go bright red with embarrassment. She looked down at Lir's mane and waited for a gallowglass to berate her for being discourteous to the chieftain. But to her surprise there was silence, and when she looked up, Murray ne Doe was smiling at her, his broad face creased like the bark of an ancient yew tree.

"I wouldn't say that you have nothing, young lady," he said, and Nora let herself be warmed by the honey-smooth tone of his voice. His gaze swept over Lir from his head to his long, ground-sweeping tail.

"That's a finer stallion than any mountain pony I've ever seen," he remarked. "In fact, I'd guess he came from a long way farther than Connemara, did he not?" Without waiting for a reply, he went on, "I'll take the stallion in exchange for the boy's voyage home. That's the price of my help."

CHAPTER

19

⠶⠶⠶

YOU CAN'T! HE'S MINE! Nora wanted to shout, instinctively gripping her knees tighter against Lir's smooth, warm sides. The
stallion turned his head and rubbed his muzzle against her leg.
She thought back to the first time she had seen him, when she
had mistaken him for a fairy horse belonging to Manannan
mac Lir, and then her first ride, when she had nearly fallen off
because his stride was so powerful and unfamiliar. But they had
grown to know each other well on the long journey from
Errislannan, so that now Nora felt as if his four legs were
extensions of her own body, and she could steer him along the
narrowest of paths with just a touch of her heel and pressure
from her knees.

Then she looked at José, hunched and white-faced on
Dunlin, his eyes huge with fear, and she knew that she had no
choice but to give the stallion up so that he could go home. She
had risked her life to rescue him from the sea; she could not fail
him now. And if she refused Murray ne Doe's request, he
would send them back into the forest, where the English soldiers would be waiting. Lir and Dunlin had outrun them once

already today—Nora didn't think they had enough strength to be hunted all the way back to Errislannan.

José reached up and touched Nora's hand. "You don't have to do this, Nonita," he whispered, and she jumped to hear him say the affectionate Spanish form of her name that the herring fishermen had used.

She drew her hand away and swung her right leg over Lir's withers so that she could drop to the ground. "I do," she whispered back.

Murray ne Doe flicked his hand and a slave ran forward with a halter which he slipped over Lir's head. The stallion let himself be led away to a byre and Nora felt tears of humiliation brim behind her eyes. Lir stumbled when his toe clipped a stray piece of wood, his legs iron-heavy from tiredness. His cloud-colored coat was stained with mud and sweat, but he was still the most beautiful horse Nora had ever seen. She just hoped that Murray ne Doe would know how fortunate he was to have the finest horse in Iar-Connacht, maybe even the whole of Ireland, and treat him more carefully than his other horses. But deep down, she doubted the chieftain would be able to resist showing him off if he rode against a neighboring clan, and she felt her insides weigh heavy with grief at the thought of the gray stallion being galloped into battle.

José slipped off Dunlin and came to stand beside her. "I'm so sorry, Nora," he murmured. "I did not wish for this, I promise you."

Nora didn't trust herself to speak so she said nothing, just shook her head.

From astride his horse, Murray ne Doe ordered, "Take him to the banqueting hall with the others."

José stretched one hand toward Nora and was about to say something else when two kerns stepped forward and took hold of his arms. With a look of surprise, José tried to break free but they gripped him more tightly until he winced in pain.

"Wait!" cried Nora, startled out of her sorrow. Why was José being treated like a prisoner? "What are you doing?" She moved toward one of the kerns, but a hand on her shoulder stopped her.

It was the red-haired gallowglass. He was wearing the fox pelt around his shoulders, and the creature's beady, black eyes seemed to stare accusingly at Nora as the man said, in his gruff, accented Irish, "They'll not hurt him. He'll stay with the others until a ship comes, that's all."

Nora stood and watched the kerns take the boy across the courtyard to the banqueting hall. Her fingers plucked nervously at the sack tied around her waist, and she wished she had had time to give José the rest of the herbs she had brought for him. Murray ne Doe clapped his heels against his war horse and sent the gelding cantering toward the far end of the courtyard, where a gate led through the second wall to the tower house. Just below the gate was the narrow harbor where the river washed right into the grounds of the castle. There were no Spanish ships there now, just a short-masted fishing boat like the one Nora's brothers used to gather oysters.

"Are you coming, Alaric?" asked the fair-haired gatekeeper as he followed the chieftain toward the inner courtyard.

The fox-haired gallowglass nodded and let go of Nora's shoulder. "God be with you on your journey," he said. He glanced at Dunlin and smiled. "That mare looks clever enough to look after you."

"Yes, she is," Nora agreed, but her mind was filled with thoughts of a gray Spanish stallion and a scared boy being led away and shut up in Murray ne Doe's strong-walled buildings. Alaric Campbell strode away, the fox pelt's tiny paws swinging in time with his steps, and Nora rested her hand on Dunlin's neck. Exhaustion dragged at every bone in her body, and she was not looking forward to the long journey back to Sraith Salach. But if she left now, she could reach Mainie and Fionn's house by nightfall, hopefully before they noticed that Ronan mac Nichol and Clara Foyle had reached the village without her.

Nobody seemed to be paying Nora any attention now that the boy and the horse had been taken away, so she swung herself onto Dunlin's back and tucked her brat around her. The mare seemed tiny after two days of riding Lir, and Nora felt as though she would be able to touch her toes under Dunlin's belly if she turned her feet inward. She patted the familiar, bracken-colored neck and Dunlin's ears flicked once in recognition.

"Come on, precious girl, we'll be fine now," Nora murmured. But the words sounded dull and unconvincing because, much as she loved the loyal mountain pony, her heart was breaking at the thought of leaving Lir behind.

A kern opened the gate for them and Nora rode through into the forest. Dunlin's hooves tapped lightly over the stones, the echoes quickly swallowed up by the yew trees on either side of the road. Suddenly there was a shout from behind them.

"Nora Donovan? What are you doing here?"

She twisted around to see Con Foyle standing on top of the tower beside the gate. She was too worn out to explain about the Spanish sailor and the horse; if he had missed the exchange in the courtyard, he would find out about Murray ne Doe's bargain soon enough from one of the other kerns. She pretended that she hadn't heard his question, but instead called out, "Good day to you, Con! I'm away back to Sraith Salach now. God be with you."

"Nora, wait!" came the faint reply, but Nora pressed her heels against Dunlin's sides and sent the little mare trotting further into the forest until the gate, the wall and Con Foyle were far out of sight and earshot.

As THE ROAD EMERGED from the trees, Nora passed the troop of English soldiers again. They had dismounted to let their horses drink from a narrow stream. The men looked hot and red-faced, their clothes torn and untidy from plowing through branches and thorn bushes. Some of them had taken off their helmets so that their hair stood up in sticky tufts. Nora was too tired and dejected to feel frightened. She doubted they had got a clear enough look at the fugitives to recognize her now that she was riding the pale dun pony. She tucked her chin deeper into her cloak and resisted the temptation to push Dunlin into a canter.

But the captain—Nora recognized him from his dark blue eyes and narrow shoulders—watched her closely as she passed, and her heart began to writhe like a trapped eel when he stepped into the road and held up one hand.

"Stop!" he said in slow, heavily accented Irish. "Have you seen a white horse?"

Nora stared at him, feeling her eyes grow huge with fear. She was sure that the soldier would be able to guess what she had done from her face as clearly as if she had told him everything in his own language. Then one of the other soldiers wandered over with the reins of his horse looped over his arm.

"It's no use asking her, Peter," he said in English. "Look at her, she's as dumb as a turnip. You'll get no sense out of her."

Nora stayed absolutely still and gave no sign that she had understood his words. She fiddled with a piece of Dunlin's mane and held the captain's gaze until he looked down and kicked at a clump of grass. The sharp metal spur on his boot jangled and Dunlin pricked her ears, but Nora didn't move.

"If that was really a Spaniard we saw, he'll be lost in the forest by now," the second soldier went on. "Do you think we should see if he's gone to ask O'Flaherty for help?"

The captain shook his head. "No, I told you, O'Flaherty knows how much he owes us. He'd not be foolish enough to help those Spanish dogs, not if it would mean losing his precious castle."

Nora had understood pretty much everything that had been said, and in spite of her fear she smiled to herself. These English hogs were arrogant and stupid to think an Irish chieftain like Murray ne Doe O'Flaherty could be bought for the price of a tower house.

Captain Money suddenly seemed to notice that Nora was still there, and he dismissed her with an impatient wave. She nodded as humbly as she could manage, the narrowness of her escape making her want to scream out loud, then sent Dunlin trotting along the road, further and further away from Aughnanure, José, and Lir.

NIGHT WAS FALLING AND NORA was nearly slipping off Dunlin's back with exhaustion by the time they reached Sraith Salach. The mare plodded along with her head down and the tips of her hooves dragging against the stones every few steps, but Nora didn't trust her legs to carry her if she tried to walk on her own. When Fionn mac Gowan's cottage loomed out of the dusk at the foot of the mountain, Nora waited until they were nearly at the front door before she slid to the ground and wrapped her arms around Dunlin's neck.

"Thank you, thank you," she whispered, her heart aching with love for the brave little mare—along with a dull, hollow feeling where she felt the pain of having to leave both José and Lir behind. Dunlin blew gently into Nora's hair, then wheeled away and vanished into the shadows. Nora listened as her hoof-beats quickened to a canter, much lighter without the weight of a rider, until they, too, faded and she was left alone to push open the door of the cottage and step into the noise and warmth generated by three tiny children and a mildly curious cow.

Mainie greeted her youngest sister with the same distracted air of tiredness that Nora remembered from her last visit, and Una and Alis swarmed over their aunt with fingers that didn't seem to have been washed since then, either. To her relief, the blacksmith had not yet delivered the barrel of oysters sent by her parents so Fionn and Mainie had no idea that Nora should have arrived a whole day earlier. She sang lullabies to Una and Alis until she was fighting to keep her own eyes open, and cradled the baby Fergal while his mother ate a bowl of broth as if she hadn't seen food for a week.

Judging by Mainie's bony wrists and gaunt cheekbones, Nora thought this might well be likely. She wondered if Fionn had noticed how tired and ill his wife was looking, but the barrel maker seemed as cheerful and untroubled as ever. Nora resolved to help Mainie as much as she could until it was safe to go home to Errislannan, and give her sister a chance to recover at least some of her strength before the cold winter weather set in.

And at the back of Nora's mind, a tiny voice pointed out that the more she kept herself busy, the less time she would have to imagine what was happening to José and Lir—whether Murray ne Doe had kept his promise of finding a Spanish ship to take the boy home, or whether she had given up the beautiful stallion for nothing.

TWO DAYS LATER, NORA WAS BRINGING in the pail and stool after milking the cow when she noticed a small crowd further along the road, clustered around Ronan mac Nichol's open-fronted forge. It was raining, not heavily but with stubborn relentlessness so that Nora's brat hung limply from her shoulders and her hair felt damp and uncomfortable against her neck. She felt a flicker of curiosity about what could have brought so many people outside in the rain, so she set down the stool and the pail of milk in the doorway to Mainie's cottage and stood on tiptoe to see what was going on.

The door to the cottage was open, and when Una saw her aunt standing there she walked unsteadily up to the pail and dipped her plump hand into the milk. "This for Una?" she asked, looking up at Nora with enormous blue eyes.

Nora picked up the pail to keep it out of the little girl's reach. "Not yet," she said. She carried it into the cottage and put it on a ledge beside the hearth. Mainie was feeding Fergal, propped on a pillow of folded blankets, while Alis played a complicated private game that involved weaving rushes together and pulling them apart with a satisfying sound of ripping stalks. Nora's sister was looking less tired already, but Nora suspected that she was the one now going around with black-circled eyes and pale cheeks; the children were exhausting enough to look after, and at night she couldn't sleep for thinking about José and Lir.

"Did you hear who's come to the village?" Mainie asked excitedly.

Nora shook her head as she scooped up a bowl of milk for Una. The little girl held out her hands to take it, before sitting down heavily on the rushes to drink her breakfast.

"Brenan Odoyne!" announced Mainie.

Nora was surprised. It was less than two weeks since the feast at Aughnanure, and the peddler usually took longer than that to restock his bundle in the markets in Galway town.

"Clara Foyle came to tell me he was here," Mainie went on. "That was kind of her, don't you think?"

Privately, Nora didn't think so at all—she thought that her

neighbor from Errislannan more likely wanted to show how important her cousin was, that the peddler called at his house before everyone else's. Then Nora chided herself for being so mean-spirited and said, "Will you be wanting me to go along and see what he has?"

"Yes, please," said Mainie. She shifted Fergal onto her other arm. "I'll go along myself when this young man has finished, but I don't want to miss out if he has any of that pepper Anne bought from him last time."

Nora twisted her hair into a plait and laid it on top of her brat to keep the cold, wet tendrils away from her neck. "I'll tell Brenan not to pack up before he's seen you," she promised, and slipped back outside into the rain.

When she reached the forge, it seemed as if the whole village was there, not just the wives but men as well, running their hands over the pieces of iron that Brenan sold to make spades and plowshares. As usual, the gray merchant brought more than spices and metal with him. Everyone wanted news about the Spanish sailors, and whether the English soldiers had rounded up any more of the wild-eyed, ragged men that had been seen wandering on beaches all along the coast.

"It looks as if a certain chieftain is going to make hunting Spaniards much easier for those English hogs," Brenan Odoyne was saying when Nora squeezed through the crowd to stand at the front, close to his unrolled oilcloth pack.

"What do you mean?" asked a red-haired man, whose face was almost as ruddy as his hair from the heat that was coming from Ronan mac Nichol's fire.

Brenan Odoyne's eyes lit up with an unpleasant gleam, and Nora felt her palms tingle ominously. "'Tis no secret that Murray ne Doe O'Flaherty has been storing up Spaniards, ready to send home on one of the wine merchants' ships that come to his precious harbor. Even the English soldiers have come to hear of it, and Sir Richard Bingham has sent word to Murray ne Doe that he must hand over every one of the ship-wrecked men or risk losing his castle to an English attack. Those Spaniards at Aughnanure will be going nowhere except the gallows in Galway town."

Nora turned and pushed her way blindly out of the forge. As usual, she had shown no more sense than a clod of peat. No one else in her family would have been stupid enough to trust Murray ne Doe O'Flaherty. What on earth had made her think she could save José, when the whole of the English army was set on capturing him? José was going to be hanged, and Manannan mac Lir would have his soul after all.

CHAPTER

20

⎯⎯⟨∞∞⟩⎯⎯

WITH HER HEAD DOWN AND HER eyes blurred by tears and rain, Nora ran straight past Mainie's front door toward the mountain that rose steeply above the village. She wanted to find Dunlin and be comforted by her warm, unquestioning company. When she reached the narrow path that led up and across the flank of the mountain, she heard a high-pitched squawk. She looked up and saw a black dot circling nearer and nearer. With a soft rush of wings, a squall-crow landed on a large rock not far from the path and studied Nora with its head tipped to one side.

"Hello, Alex," she murmured, holding out her hand. With a gentle *chack*, the bird unfolded its wings and flew away. Nora followed the small black shape around the side of the mountain and saw it land neatly on the shoulder of the man walking toward her.

"Good day to you, Nora," called the priest, raising his staff in greeting. "I heard you'd gone to stay with your sister Mainie. How is she, and the babe?"

Nora looked down at her hands, hoping Father Francis

wouldn't notice her reddened eyes and flushed face. "They're fine, thank you, Father," she said.

On the priest's shoulder, Alex rustled his wings with a sound like dry leaves rubbing together and chattered gently in the man's ear. Father Francis reached out and laid one thin, brown hand on Nora's arm. She jumped and tried not to pull away. Had the bird just told him that she'd been crying? She warned herself not to be so fanciful, and made herself lift her head and meet the priest's gaze when he said, "Is there something wrong, Nora?"

"No, Father, of course not. I'm just tired from looking after the children, that's all."

Father Francis nodded understandingly. "Three of them so small must be quite a handful." He took his hand away and pulled his brat more tightly around his bony shoulders. "Has Brenan Odoyne come to the village this morning?" he asked, peering down the side of the mountain to the gray stone cottages half-hidden by the rain.

"Yes, he was at Ronan mac Nichol's forge when I left," said Nora. A lump rose in her throat as the gray merchant's words echoed in her head, and she was blinded by a picture of English soldiers wrenching open the door to the banqueting hall and dragging out the shipwrecked men, their faces twisted with terror. Nora dug her nails into her palms. *I'm so sorry, José!* she thought desperately.

"No doubt you'll have heard about Murray ne Doe, then," said the priest, his calm voice bringing Nora back to the rainy mountainside.

"What, that he's declared his loyalty to the English queen yet again?" she spat, surprising herself with the bitterness of her tone.

Father Francis raised his eyebrows. "Well, 'tis the Spaniards that he's brought trouble to this time," he pointed out.

Nora felt herself grow hot with anger. "But the English are our enemies too!"

"The world of chieftains is more complex than you or I could know," the priest said gently. "Let us thank God that we do not have the responsibilities carried by Murray ne Doe. You might say that he wasn't betraying the Spanish sailors, but protecting his family and household. Why should he risk the lives of those he loves for the sake of some shipwrecked strangers?"

Because I did! Nora wanted to scream. *I challenged Manannan mac Lir, I was hunted by English soldiers, and I gave up Lir, all to save José's life.*

Father Francis looked grave as he read the defiance in her face. "I am not completely without pity, Nora. I shall say a Mass for the souls of those poor men tomorrow."

"Tomorrow?"

The priest nodded. "I've heard that soldiers will come to Aughnanure at first light, when more troops have arrived from Dublin. Clearly that English captain thinks he'll need more than half a dozen armed men to manage a handful of half-drowned Spaniards."

Nora barely heard the scorn in the priest's voice. Her mind was racing ahead, fleet-footed with hope. If José was still at Aughnanure, she could rescue him before the English soldiers came! A silent voice demanded to know how a mere girl was going to break into Murray ne Doe's well-guarded tower house and escape with a wounded sailor who already had a price on his head.

Because I won't use the gate or the walls, Nora found herself answering. An image sprang into her head of a hole opening up in the banqueting hall, and a fox-haired man plummeting into the river below. That's how she'd get in—through the trapdoor that led straight into the hall where the sailors were being kept. With luck, the rope that had been lowered to rescue the gallowglass would still be there, and José would be able to follow her out the same way.

"Go well, Nora," said Father Francis as he started to walk down the path toward Sraith Salach. "Take care in the mountains today. It looks like this rain is going to set in for a while yet."

"Oh, yes, Father," Nora said. "I'll be careful, I promise."

She waited until he had disappeared around the flank of the hill, the squall-crow hunched on his shoulder like a second, thinner head, then put her fingers to her mouth and whistled as loudly as she could. She was a long way from Fiach's usual territory, but she had glimpsed the herd on the other side of Lough Inagh the day before, and there was a chance that Dunlin would hear her from there. But there was no answering whinny or drum of hoofbeats over the scrubby mountain grass.

Nora picked up her skirt with both hands and scrambled further up the mountain. *Please, Dunlin,* she begged silently. She stood still, gasping for breath for a couple of moments until she could whistle again. She was nearly at the top of the mountain now, and the thin, reedy sound spilled into the valleys on every side, echoing over and over again until it was swallowed by the peat and the grass and the endless shimmering water of the lake.

Nora's shoulders slumped with frustration. Had she really imagined that she could break into Murray ne Doe's tower house and rescue a Spanish prisoner? Why couldn't she just accept that Manannan mac Lir had won, that she couldn't save José no matter what she did? She pictured the boy's thin face, his wide-set brown eyes and his brilliant smile when he had seen the forest of Aughnanure after their long journey across the mountains. And as for Lir, well, wasn't Murray ne Doe fortunate to have a war horse that would be envied by every chieftain in Iar-Connacht, and every English soldier?

Blinded by tears of bitter anger and sorrow, she started to

trudge back down the mountain to Mainie's cottage. In the distance, a small group of ponies standing with their quarters hunched against the rain lifted their heads to watch her. The rain drummed harder, beating against the peaty ground like a bodhran, louder and louder until it sounded like hoofbeats galloping. . . .

Hoofbeats! Nora spun around and shouted for joy as a pale, brown shape emerged from the rain and skittered to a halt next to her. "Dunlin, you came!" she cried, wrapping her arms around the mare's slippery neck and pressing her face against the hot, damp fur. The mare tossed her head and snorted as if she couldn't understand why Nora was making such a fuss.

She stepped back, feeling her heart pound as she realized that here was her chance to rescue José after all. She started to think of everything that might go wrong—she might even end up captured by the English herself—but then she remembered José's face when he spoke about his home, and she knew that she would do anything to help him feel the warm Spanish sun and taste *naranjas* again. Manannan mac Lir had not won yet!

Bunching up her skirt, she leaped onto Dunlin's back and sent the mare down the path at a brisk canter. She wanted to reach the castle by dusk—there would be less chance of being seen if she waited until nightfall, but she would need a little light to find her way through the underground river. Mainie and Fionn would worry when Nora didn't return before dark, but Father Francis might tell them he'd seen her heading into the mountains; she hoped they would assume that she had been caught unaware by sunset and was spending the night with the wild ponies.

Nora followed the same route out of the mountains that she and José had taken three days before. Dunlin cantered quite willingly away from her herd and across the open moorland toward the yew forest. Today the road was empty aside from an ox cart rolling slowly in the direction of Murray ne Doe's castle. Nora passed it on her narrow bogland path and slipped into the thick, green shadows under the trees.

The fading afternoon light scarcely pierced the canopy of branches at all, and she was tempted to use the road that led through the forest to the castle because it would be easier than battling through the brambles and safer from the threat of wolves. But too many people from the castle would remember her from when she had brought José to Murray ne Doe, and she couldn't risk meeting someone who would be curious about why she had returned so soon. Reaching down to pat Dunlin's neck, she let the mare slow to a walk and pick her own way through the undergrowth, deeper and deeper into the forest.

Every rustle in the bushes, every bark from an unseen deer or fox made Nora stiffen and look around in alarm. The forest seemed to stretch forever on all sides, and she realized that fleeing from the English soldiers had carried her and José much more swiftly through the trees. Now she was beginning to feel as if she would be struggling through these trunks and brambles for the rest of her life, until wolves or wood-spirits came out to hunt her like helpless prey. Hot tears of fear and self-pity welled in Nora's eyes and she wiped them away angrily. What had happened to the courage that José had promised she had? She squared her shoulders and sat taller, and Dunlin started to walk more quickly in response, lifting her hooves carefully over the tree roots and pricking her ears forward. Comforted by the mare's loyalty, Nora nudged the mare into a trot and let the drum of hoofbeats drown out the quieter, scarier forest noises.

Suddenly Dunlin halted and Nora was thrown forward onto her neck. She pushed herself upright and looked around. They had come to the edge of the trees, but it had been so dark in the forest that she hadn't noticed night falling outside, and now she was surrounded by thick, empty shadows. Just in front of them, somewhere below Dunlin's front hooves, was the sound of water lapping against stone. Slowly Nora's eyes got used to the darkness, washed with silver from a moon no wider than the tip of a fingernail.

The mare had stopped on the bank of a wide river, the water a soft black shadow against gray stone. On the other side of the river loomed the high walls of Aughnanure Castle. Torchlight

flickered from the windows on each floor of the tower house—
Nora counted five rows of arrow slits, stretching all the way up
to the steeply pointed roof—and from the other side of the
wall came the sounds of the household settling for the night,
occasional shouts of laughter, and a cow lowing for its calf in
one of the byres.

To Nora's left was a gatehouse with a wooden bridge which
led straight into the inner courtyard. She would need to follow
the river the other way, where it flowed under a low stone arch
and disappeared under the outer courtyard wall. But it was too
dark now to swim into the water-filled cave. She would have to
wait until dawn, and hope that she could get into the hall
before the English soldiers arrived. Nora slipped off Dunlin's
back and stood by the mare's head to rub her ears. A bat
swooped low overhead, and behind them in the forest an owl
hooted sadly. Dunlin rested her muzzle against Nora's chest
and stamped a foreleg.

"Come on, girl," Nora whispered. "Let's find somewhere to
sleep."

She led Dunlin by her mane a little way back into the trees
and flattened a clump of ferns into a bed. Trying to ignore the
hunger that gnawed her stomach, Nora settled down on the
crackling fronds and tucked her brat around her. She would
have to rely on the mare's wariness of the forest to keep her
from wandering off in the night, and she reached out to touch

Dunlin's nose as the pony dropped her head to sniff Nora's hair. As fear clouded her thoughts, she reminded herself that on the other side of that wall, José was waiting through another long night for a boat to take him home, unaware that fate was rushing toward him on the hooves of galloping English war horses, not the full-bellied sails of a Spanish ship.

⎯⎯⎯⎯⎯⎯⎯

THE NIGHT DRAGGED PAST AND NORA found herself jumping awake every time she dozed off, startled by the tiniest rustle or squeak. Dunlin didn't stray more than a few paces from Nora's clump of ferns, nosing through the dried bracken in search of the soft forest grass. At last Nora gave up trying to sleep and stood up, stamping her numb feet and wrapping her arms around herself to bring some warmth back to her fingers. She walked to the edge of the trees and looked down at the river. She could see the water quite clearly now, flowing swiftly from the gatehouse bridge to the stone arch. Above, the sky was the dark gray of a pigeon's wing, fading to seashell-cream beyond the roof of the tower house. Murray ne Doe's household was cloaked in the brief hour of silence between the gallowglasses finishing their games of dice and the slaves and women getting up to bake bread and see to the animals.

Nora unfastened her brat and rolled it into a bundle to leave under a tree. She glanced down at her dress, briefly wondering if she should swim in nothing more than her undershirt, then decided that she would rather be modestly clad than half-naked when she found José. She looked over her shoulder at Dunlin, who was watching her curiously with a blade of grass sticking out of the side of her mouth. Nora knew there was nothing she could do to make the wild pony wait for her—even if she had had time to bring a coil of rope, she would not have tried to tether her.

A cockerel crowed on the other side of the wall, making Nora jump and reminding her that there was not much time before the castle woke up. With a last whispered good-bye to Dunlin, she hung onto a trailing yew branch and lowered herself down the sheer, slippery rock and into the river.

The water was colder than anything Nora had felt before— colder than the sea, colder even than the icicles that hung from the cottage roof in the dead of winter, which she and Meg snapped off to suck before they melted against their hands and tongues. Her skirt billowed on the surface like a dark gray sail, and Nora had to push the cloth under the water with both hands until it clung to her legs like trews, sodden and heavy. Her shoes sunk into the peaty mud, churning it up until the water turned cloudy and stained her undershirt dark copper-brown.

Nora let go of the branch and waded further into the river, forcing herself to bend her knees so that the water rushed up and over her shoulders. It was so cold that she wanted to turn around and scramble out again. Her limbs ached and her skin stung as if it had been flailed with brambles. But then she thought of José, and the sandy-haired English captain who was galloping toward the castle in search of some easy Spanish prey. She kicked off from the bottom and pushed the water away with her arms until she was swimming past tree roots that hung like garlands along the stony bank, into the yawning black mouth where the river vanished under the ground.

At once it was so dark that Nora had to blink to make sure that her eyes were still open. She was too cold to be scared, and breathing seemed like an indulgence she would have to save for dry land. Numbly, she scooped and kicked into the invisible black water until her fingers scraped against slimy rock. She fought back the panic that told her she had been buried alive and would never see daylight again. This must be where the river bends to flow under the banqueting hall, she told herself. She pushed against the rock with both hands and followed the pull of the current, letting her fingers trail against the side of the cave because there was a small comfort in knowing that she hadn't swum off the edge of the world into black nothingness.

Suddenly, something heavy and wet slapped against Nora's face. She screamed and instantly choked on a mouthful of river water. Spluttering and coughing, she grabbed whatever had struck her to stop herself from being dragged under the surface. It was coarse and scratchy, no thicker than her wrist, and Nora knew at once what it was. Just as she had hoped, the rope that had been lowered to rescue the fox-haired gallowglass was still hanging down from the tilting flagstone.

Kicking hard with her legs, Nora reached up with both hands and grasped the rope. She was near enough to the wall of the cave that she would be able to push against the rock with her feet to help her climb. The rope tore at her hands as she hauled herself out of the water but she hardly noticed, she was so numb from the cold. Her skirt dragged at her legs and dripped so loudly back into the river that she was convinced someone would hear and open the trapdoor. But the roof above her stayed black and featureless. At first, her shoes slipped on the rock, and she quickly learned to wrap the rope around her wrists and press her weight against the soles of her feet so that she could rest for a moment between each upward heave.

It seemed as if she had been climbing toward empty shadows for ages before Nora felt something brush against her hair. She ducked and reached up carefully with one hand. There was a narrow piece of wood beside her, sloping from the roof to the wall of the cave. She guessed it was the mechanism that released the trapdoor: The flagstone had dropped away, hinged at one edge, when Rhidian the bard had pulled an unseen lever. She shuddered as she thought of the men that Murray ne Doe had sent to a startling, watery death with his clever device.

Wrapping both legs around the rope so that she didn't slide down again, she ran her hand up the timber until her fingertips touched cold, hard stone. The faintest of drafts was coming through a narrow gap around the edge, except where a wooden slat was fitted under the flagstone to hold it in place. Nora tried to move the slat but it wouldn't budge. Gripping the rope more tightly between her knees, she reached up with both hands to grab the piece of wood. At once the rope bucked and twisted away from her. Terrified of plunging into the black water below, Nora kicked out and her feet struck against the trapdoor mechanism. There was a gritty, scraping noise, the slat was wrenched out of her hands, and the flagstone tipped down toward her, spilling gray light into the cave.

In the same instant, the rope slipped away and hurtled toward the river. Nora made a desperate grab for the edge of the floor, kicking frantically with her legs as her fingertips scraped against the cold, hard stone. There was a splash as the rope hit the water, then silence broken only by Nora's labored breathing and the steady rush of the water. She hung there for a moment, waiting for surprised shouts from above and startled faces to appear in the hole. But none came, so she braced her feet against the wall and started to heave herself up into the hall. Without the rope, there was only one way out of the cave—through Murray ne Doe's castle. There was no way she could expect José to jump all the way down into the water with his injured leg, even if she thought she could manage the drop herself.

As soon as she was high enough, Nora propped her arms on the edge of the hole and cautiously raised her head. There was just enough light to make out the shapes of more than a score of men lying on the rushes at the other end of the hall. Several of them were stirring, muttering, and looking around, and Nora ducked her head down, her heart pounding like a bolting horse and feeling her cheeks burn with fear and humiliation. She hadn't given any thought to how she would attract José's attention without being seen by all the other shipwrecked men.

Outside, a dog started to bark and one of Murray ne Doe's kerns shouted crossly for it to be quiet. Nora heard some of the men stand up and walk over to the door, calling in Spanish to whoever was on the other side of the door. Their accents were thicker than those of the herring fishermen and Nora couldn't understand every word, but they didn't seem angry or alarmed; she heard the words for food and ship, and she guessed that the sailors had not been told there was no ship coming for them, that today they would go no further than Galway, and meet their death at the hands of the English soldiers.

The knowledge that Murray ne Doe had deceived them filled Nora with furious strength, and she heaved herself up to land in an undignified heap on the floor with her cheek pressed against a heap of dirty rushes and one foot dangling over the edge of the hole. Nora saw all the men by the door turn toward her and stare in disbelief. For a moment, she had no idea what to do next.

Then one of the men pushed his way to the front and exclaimed, "Nora! What are you doing here?"

Like a many-headed monster, his companions swiveled

their heads to look at him. José ignored them and ran over to the trapdoor. He knelt down and put his hand under Nora's elbow to help her up. "Where . . . how . . . what . . . ?" he stammered in Spanish, and she looked up at him as she scrambled to her feet. She noticed that at least Murray ne Doe hadn't been starving his guests, because José looked less pale and better fed than when she had pulled him out of the sea.

"I've come to rescue you," she blurted out, her throat sore and croaky from swallowing the river water.

José's eyebrows drew together in a frown. "What do you mean?" he asked in Irish. "We are staying here until a ship comes from Spain."

"You don't understand! There's no ship coming. Murray ne Doe has lied to you!" Nora exclaimed wildly, and the men by the door started murmuring, aware of the panic in her voice even if they couldn't understand the words. "You have to leave now," she told him. "There's no time to explain."

But even as she spoke, the dog in the courtyard started barking again, rapidly joined by its companions, and above the chorus of barks came the sound of hammering at the gate and a man shouting in English.

Nora stared at José in dismay. She was too late. The soldiers had already arrived.

22

"THE ENGLISH ARE HERE?" José whispered, his eyes stretching wide with horror.

Nora nodded. "Murray ne Doe is going to let them take you in return for not attacking the castle."

"But the ship . . . he took gold from the other men, and he promised . . ." His voice trailed away, and he looked very young and confused.

"I'm so sorry," Nora murmured. Angry tears sprung to her eyes. Everything had gone wrong, and now she was about to be captured by English soldiers. "I didn't know this would happen."

José's eyes hardened and he grabbed Nora's hand. "They have not caught us yet, Nonita," he declared. "We can still escape."

"But how?" said Nora. "The rope has fallen into the river, so we can't go through the trapdoor." She looked around help-lessly. Through a gap at the edge of the hide across the window, she could see slaves and kerns running across the courtyard to open the gate.

"You know people here, don't you?" said José, and Nora nodded. "Then if we can get out of here, they will help us to leave the castle," he went on. Nora felt a flash of uncertainty—the only friend she could count on was Con Foyle, and if he was ordered away by a gallowglass, or by Murray ne Doe himself, they would be left at the mercy of the soldiers.

But José was already dragging her across the floor to the windows on the other side of the hall. They were as tall as a man at the highest point of the arch and finely carved with grapes and leaves on slender curling stalks. José pulled the hide away and Nora shivered as a cold wind rushed through the gap.

"Look!" he ordered, pushing her closer to the window.

Outside, there was a small open space between the banqueting hall and the outer wall. A narrow thatched roof jutted out from the wall and beneath this Murray ne Doe's horses were tethered in a long row, from small thick-coated ponies to the broad-chested bay war horse that the chieftain had been riding when Nora brought José to Aughnanure.

Nora's heart leaped as she recognized a round, gray rump with a long, thick tail the color of seafoam. "Lir!" she cried, and to her delight the stallion turned his beautiful head toward her with his ears pricked.

"Lir," José echoed, nodding. "I have been watching him, for your sake. He has been well fed." A brief smile flashed across his face. "But he is not liked by the servants. He kicked one of them over yesterday." He made a tipping motion with his hand like a tree falling.

"I want to take him with us," Nora said suddenly.

José looked startled. "How? It will be hard enough for us to get out alone."

"I don't know —" she began, but she was interrupted by the sound of the door crashing open and the Spanish men scrambling out of the way over the rushes.

José shoved Nora behind him and stood with his back to the wall. "Don't move," he hissed out of the corner of his mouth.

Shaking with fear, she listened to the shipwrecked men raising their voices in confusion and then anger as the English soldiers ordered them outside. The air was thick with shouts in Spanish, Irish, and English, against a deafening chorus of dogs barking, chickens clucking in alarm, and children wailing. It was obvious that the sailors had realized what was happening because Nora heard a furious cry of "Get him!" in English as one of them tried to run across the courtyard.

The air was split with a crack of musket fire that echoed around the walls like thunder, and in the ringing silence that followed Nora heard José muttering, "*Madre de Dios, Madre de Dios, Madre de Dios,*" under his breath.

A woman screamed and the Spanish sailors started shouting again, not in anger now but pleading for their lives as they were herded out of the banqueting hall. Heavy footsteps crunched over the rushes and Nora froze. She had heard that jangle of spurs before, and she pictured the English captain walking toward her with his thin lips twisted in a smile and one hand resting lightly on the hilt of his sword.

José reached behind him and pushed Nora along the wall. "Keep moving," he murmured, and Nora obeyed, stumbling in his shadow along the side of the hall until they were nearly at the door. She kept her head down, hoping that her wet hair would make her look like a boy and that it was too dark for the soldiers to see her long skirt. They joined the crowd of men waiting to go through the door, and Nora waited breathlessly for one of them to point her out, to trade their unexpected prisoner for freedom. But if the Spanish sailors knew she was there, they said nothing, and Nora shuffled forward with them, stumbling on the rushes and breathing the stench of sweat and fear and bodies that had seen neither daylight nor water for several days.

They reached the doorway and Nora stepped hesitantly through. At once José shoved her roughly to the left, around the corner toward the yard where the horses were kept. They were shielded from the main courtyard by the other sailors, and Nora dared to lift her head to look at José. But before she could say anything, her eyes met the startled gaze of Con Foyle, standing just behind José's shoulder. His eyes were filled with a thousand questions, and he looked so terrified that Nora was certain he had not expected the English soldiers to start shooting the Spanish prisoners before they had even left the castle.

José stopped and stood very still, knowing that Nora had been spotted.

Very slowly, she slid her gaze sideways toward the horses. Con's eyes narrowed, then his head twitched in the tiniest nod. Nora took José's hand and pulled him away from the other men, dragging him at a run until they were out of sight behind the wall of the banqueting hall. The horses under the thatched roof bunched together in alarm, and Nora hoped that there was enough noise in the main courtyard to hide the sound of their hooves slipping on the muddy ground. She ran over to Lir and reached up to lay her hand on his nose. The horse snorted and backed away as far as the rope tied to his halter would allow, his nostrils flared and a white rim showed around his eyes.

"It's all right, Lir, it's only me," Nora whispered, fighting down the panic that rose inside her with every heartbeat. The stallion tossed his head and his ears twitched in recognition.

"We don't have time for this," José muttered, coming up behind Nora, his face white and desperate. "They will come after us soon."

Nora looked around the yard. It was empty except for the horses and a few small piles of hay. "But we can't hide here. They'd find us at once!"

José's mouth was set in a hard, determined line. "We are not going to hide. We are going to ride out of here on the stallion."

Nora stared at him in disbelief as he went on, "The gate is open, and the soldiers have enough to do with keeping the other men together. Once we are in the forest, Lir can run faster than any of the English horses."

Nora knew he was right, but the distance to the gate of the castle suddenly seemed further than she had ever ridden before. The courtyard was full of soldiers and Murray ne Doe's gallowglasses—and the soldiers had muskets. She shook her head. "No, it's too dangerous," she began.

José seized her by the shoulders and put his face very near to hers. From this close, his face looked long and pointed like a fox's, and his eyes burned. "It is our only chance," he hissed through clenched teeth.

Nora pulled herself away and turned around to untie the rope that tethered Lir to a rail next to the wall. "You'll have to help me up," she said. She was filled with a bleak sense of despair that left her hollow and unable to argue any more. Whatever they did, they would be caught. At least this way Lir might have a chance of escaping on his own. She felt José's hands around her waist, and he lifted her high enough to scramble onto Lir's back. He pulled himself up behind her, wincing as he took all his weight on his injured leg, and Nora found herself glancing down to check that there was no fresh bleeding. The strip of linen she had used for a bandage had long since fallen off but the stains on his breeches were dull brown rather than fresh scarlet.

José wrapped one arm around her waist and grasped hold of Lir's mane with his other hand. Nora felt his breath warm and quick against his cheek. "You are very brave, Nonita, to have come here for my sake," he whispered. "I will never forget what you have done. Never."

She swallowed, not trusting herself to speak, and twisted around to meet his solemn, dark-eyed gaze. She felt as if every thudding heartbeat was counting out the last moments of her life, and she prayed that her death, when it came, would be swift.

José nodded once and Nora closed her legs against Lir's sides, using the halter rope to steer him out of the line of horses and across the yard to the narrow gap between the banqueting hall and the wall of the inner courtyard. They paused at the corner of the hall and listened to the sounds of heavy-saddled war horses stamping and men shouting in three different languages. The English soldiers were clearly having more difficulty rounding up the prisoners than they had expected. Nora felt her heart miss a beat as she realized they had no idea how many soldiers were waiting in the courtyard.

But it was too late to change her mind. The shadowy figure at the far end of the gap turned toward her, and Nora saw with dismay that it wasn't Con Foyle, but an English soldier who raised his sword and gave a shout as soon as he saw them.

"*¡Vaya!*" shouted José, tightening his hold on Nora's waist and kicking Lir so hard that the stallion leaped straight into a flat out gallop.

Nora leaned forward and buried her hands in Lir's mane, letting sharp tendrils of hair flail against her face so that she wouldn't see the flash of the sword blade as it sliced toward her. The hollow echo of hoofbeats as they raced through the gap suddenly vanished amid a clamor of shouts and barking and the whinny of horses, and she lifted her head enough to see that they had shot straight past the soldier into the middle of the courtyard, scattering sailors and kerns around them like autumn leaves.

The gate lay straight ahead of them, half open, with the English captain sitting on his bay war horse in the middle of the gap. Nora was too far away to tell if he was smiling, but he was already drawing his sword and digging his heels into his horse's flanks to turn it around to face them. There was nothing she could do to stop Lir or slow him down; startled by the noise and the people running in all directions, the stallion was bolting with his head stretched out and his hooves hardly seeming to touch the ground.

He tore through the Spanish sailors, their faces a pale blur at the level of Nora's feet, and galloped toward the gate. Nora felt José tense behind her, and out of the corner of her eye she saw an English soldier kneeling beside the wall with a long-barreled musket raised to his shoulder. *Oh Lord, no*, she begged, and she didn't know if she had prayed silently or screamed the words out loud.

Suddenly a tall, brown-cloaked figure swooped down from the top of the wall, his arms stretched out to slow his fall and a mane of red hair streamed behind him. He landed on his feet, right on top of the kneeling soldier so that the man tumbled over and the musket slipped from his hands into the mud. A pair of tiny unseeing eyes gleamed at Nora as the red-haired man straightened the fox pelt around his neck and stepped away from the soldier with his hands raised as if his landing had been nothing but an unfortunate mistake. The gallowglass turned and met Nora's gaze, his expression giving nothing away except for what might have been the faintest glimmer of amusement in his fox-colored gaze. Then, without any warning, he bent down to pick up the English soldier's sword and threw it to José.

The boy snatched it out of the air so quickly that Nora was conscious of little more than a flash of silver beside her. There were just a few strides now between them and the captain. Lir had seen the half-open gate behind the war horse and was heading for the gap with no sign of slowing. The captain slowly raised his sword, and now Nora could see that he was indeed smiling under his domed helmet, as though he relished the prospect of striking down two prisoners with a single blow.

Her mind went numb with terror, and she barely had time to wonder if the soldier knew she was a girl, not a Spanish sailor, before Lir's pounding hooves carried them level with the war horse's head, then his shoulder, and the blade came closer and closer, slicing through the air like a heron's wing—and suddenly José's arm shot up and there was a mighty clang as the two blades crashed together. Lir stumbled and Nora nearly went shooting over his shoulder but José hung on to her with his other arm and thrust away the captain's sword with a deafening screech of iron against iron. The war horse shied away and Lir galloped on, through the gate and out into the forest.

23

THE SHOUTS BEHIND THEM quickly faded as they were swallowed by a green sea of branch and shadow. Lir's stride faltered, brambles clutching at his legs, but José kicked him on, his knuckles white where he clutched the English soldier's sword. "They will be following us," he said tensely, and Nora was too scared and exhausted to argue.

They crashed through the trees, away from the road, and Nora realized they were coming close to the place where the river disappeared underground. She straightened up and stared around wildly. "Dunlin might be waiting for me," she cried.

"We don't have time to stop and look," José warned, and Nora knew he was right. The mare would have been scared by the sound of musket fire and shouting, and had probably fled deeper into the forest. She dug her nails into her palms as she pictured the mountain pony galloping blindly through the trees, watched by the yellow eyes of a hundred hungry wolves. Nora reminded herself that it was still daylight, and any wakeful wolves would likely have been just startled into flight by the sounds of fighting, but she couldn't help staring into the shadows, desperate for a glimpse of a bracken-colored coat, as Lir half-trotted, half-cantered through the undergrowth.

After a while, the trees thinned and the bleak moorland spread out before them, with the rounded gray peaks of the Maam Tuircs beyond. Lir slowed to a walk, his sides heaving with tiredness and his head held low. Nora's anxious fingers sought out the old wound on his shoulder but the skin felt cold and firm; his exhaustion was due to being pent up in the little courtyard for two days.

She let the stallion halt at the edge of the trees, his nostrils flaring rapidly in and out as he sniffed the air. José stirred behind her, and she wondered if he had dozed off, slumped against her back. But when she twisted around, his eyes were as huge and wakeful as ever, and his skin stretched so taut over his cheekbones that it looked like a pale dried leaf. His right hand was still wrapped around the hilt of the sword, the unsheathed blade resting carefully across his thigh.

"Where now?" he asked, and his voice was flat with despair.

Nora gazed at him with a heavy lump of sorrow in her chest. They had risked everything to escape the soldiers, but Murray ne Doe had been José's only hope of returning to Spain. Now she did not know what to do to help him. However, she was certain of one thing, which was that they had to get as far as possible from Aughnanure before someone found them.

"I'll take you back to the booly by Lough Inagh," she said. "I can bring you food from my sister's house, and then—" José's eyes lit up for a moment as if he thought she might already know another way for him to get home, and Nora felt her heart sink as she went on—"I'll try and think of someone else who might help you."

The boy nodded without saying anything and Nora turned around again to urge Lir into a trot across the bogland. She felt José drop his head onto her shoulder, his body rocking gently in time with the stallion's strides, and she stretched out one hand to smooth the warm, damp skin under Lir's mane. The horse snorted and tossed his head, and Nora loved him fiercely for being so trusting and tireless.

You shall not have them yet, Manannan mac Lír, she vowed silently. *You have enough Spanish souls now—the horse and the boy are mine.*

"BY OUR LADY, NORA, WHERE have you been?" Mainie snatched hold of Nora's shoulders and almost wrenched her off her feet as she dragged her into the cottage.

"I . . . I'm sorry," Nora stammered, fumbling her words through exhaustion rather than shame. "I was with the mountain ponies," she added, sensing that her sister was waiting for an explanation.

Mainie clicked her tongue crossly. "You're just so thoughtless, Nora. I've been worried sick about you all last night, and when you didn't turn up this morning I was all set to send out a search party in case you'd been fool enough to fall over and break your leg."

Mainie turned away and angrily clattered some pots on the hearth. Nora realized that her sister had been genuinely worried and she reached out to touch Mainie's arm. "I'm sorry," she said again. "Is there anything you'd like me to do?"

She was so tired that all she wanted to do was sink onto the rushes and sleep for a day and a night, but she knew that she had to go back to the booly before nightfall to take food to José, and a rope to tether Lir. She hoped that after the long journey from Aughnanure with a double burden, weariness alone would keep the stallion from straying too far from the hut. She had left him hungrily cropping the grass under the fir trees, José leaning against the open doorway to watch. He had acquired an oversized jacket from one of his fellow prisoners so at least he wouldn't be as cold as his last night in the booly, but Nora wanted to take him a clean blanket as well. After all, she didn't know how many nights he would have to spend on the mountainside before she found another way of sending him home.

A small, plump hand tugged at Nora's skirt and a high-pitched voice said, "Nora home?"

She looked down and saw Una gazing up at her. "Yes, Nora home," she agreed.

She bent down to wipe a smudge of cinders off the little girl's cheek but Mainie stopped her, saying, "Here, you'd best eat this. I doubt the wild ponies gave you supper last night." She held out a piece of warm oatbread spread thickly with butter, and Nora took it gratefully.

"And when you've finished that," Mainie went on briskly as Nora bit into the bread, "you can take this to Ronan mac Nichol to be sharpened." She pointed to a short-handled knife lying on the hearth with its blade wrapped in a piece of sacking. Four more loaves of oatbread were cooling on a wooden trencher behind it, as were two pails of creamy yellow butter. Mainie bent down and scooped up two of the loaves and one of the pails of butter. "I'm taking this to Orla mac Nichol, the blacksmith's mother. She sat with the children this morning while I did the baking." Nora was starting to think that she found her sister easier to cope with when she was exhausted from looking after the children on her own.

With her free hand, Mainie unhooked a brat from a nail behind the door. "Leave Una with her father in the back. He's got Alis and Fergal with him already. When you've taken the knife, you could pick some shamrock. There's a good patch under the ash tree on the far side of Ronan's cottage."

She drew a breath as she unlatched the front door, and Nora said quickly, "I lost my brat on the mountain last night—" she thought guiltily of the sodden bundle that would be lying under a tree near Aughnanure— "so would I be able to borrow one of yours?"

Mainie tutted and gestured to a wooden chest under the window. "What will Mother say when she hears how careless you've been? It's not as if you spin enough wool in a twelve-month to make a new one." Still muttering, she opened the door and vanished outside.

Nora waited until her sister's footsteps had faded away toward the cottage where the blacksmith's elderly mother lived, then ran over to the chest, and heaved open the lid. It was well stuffed with blankets, and she hoped that Mainie wouldn't miss one. She took out a brat as well and fastened it around her shoulders. With a quick glance to make sure that Una wasn't watching, she picked up one of the remaining loaves of bread and wrapped it in the blanket. Calling to the little girl, Nora led her niece out of the cottage and around to her father's workshop. Una ran over to join her sister Alis, who was drawing shapes in a heap of ash.

Fionn looked up briefly from the strip of wood he was hammering into place on the frame of a barrel. "Back then, Nora?" he said mildly.

"Oh, yes," she said. She held up the cloth-wrapped knife. "I'm just taking this to Ronan mac Nichol."

Fionn nodded, his attention already returned to the half-made barrel. Nora paused to retrieve the coil of rope that she had left under a tree behind the midden and ran down the road to the blacksmith's cottage. The meal of oatbread had revived her and she felt almost cheerful as she handed the knife to Clara Foyle—who seemed less than pleased at being asked to pass on the request for sharpening—before heading out of the village along the narrow path that led to Lough Inagh.

A hooded figure was sitting on a boulder beside the path, his hands folded over the top of a hazel staff. A small, black bird pecked at the ground by his feet. Nora tucked the blanket more securely under her arm and called out, "Good day to you, Father Francis."

The priest turned, his face creasing into a smile. "And good day to you, Nora Donovan." If he wondered why she was carrying a coil of rope on her shoulder, he gave no sign of it. "I was just praying for the souls of the Spanish men at Aughnanure," he added.

Nora blinked and told herself he couldn't possibly have found out that she had just helped one of those men to escape. But of all the people she knew, Father Francis was the most likely to hear of any plans to help the sailors get back to Spain—even if he had misjudged Murray ne Doe's loyalty. "The English soldiers seem set on capturing all the shipwrecked men," she said carefully. "Do . . . do you think there's any hope for the ones who haven't been caught yet?"

Father Francis narrowed his eyes. At his feet, Alex stretched out his wings and let out a series of rapid *chacks*. Nora forced herself to hold the priest's gaze and refused to believe that the squall-crow was telling Father Francis exactly what she was up to.

"There are still some who would help the Spaniards," he said at last. "Not everyone is watched by the English as closely as Murray ne Doe O'Flaherty." He reached down to smooth Alex's sooty black feathers and Nora waited, hardly daring to breathe, for him to go on. "There is a Spanish merchant called Juan de Luca who has a shop on the quay in Galway. I've heard that he knows of a ship that is coming for the shipwrecked men."

Nora almost cursed out loud with frustration. Father Francis knew as well as she did that she was unable to enter the city since the merchant families had passed the ban against the O'Flahertys.

Father Francis pushed himself to his feet and pulled his brat around him. The squall-crow flew onto his shoulder and turned its head to look down at Nora with one shiny black eye. The priest laid his hand on her arm. "Be careful, Nora," he said quietly. "Even the kindest of hearts has enemies." Then he walked past her and down the path toward the village, his staff tapping lightly on the stones in time with his footsteps.

Nora clutched her cloak around her and ran as fast as she could around the flank of the mountain and along the valley beside Lough Inagh to the booly. A herd of ponies was grazing on the other side of the valley, and Nora paused for a moment to look for the dark gray stallion and a bracken-coated mare that would tell her it was Fiach's herd. Both ponies were there, and Nora felt warmed by the thought of them watching over the booly—and weak with relief that Dunlin had made it safely back through the forest and the Maam Tuircs.

The light was fading quickly, the cloud-veiled sun already well below the peaks of the mountains on the far side of the lake, but Nora saw a pale gray shape moving among the fir trees and knew at once that Lir hadn't wandered off. The stallion lifted his head and whinnied as Nora burst through the line of trees and stopped, panting. She went over and smoothed his nose, whispering to him that he was the most beautiful horse in all of Ireland and that the fairies would be green with envy that they couldn't steal him away to Tír na nÓg.

"Do you think he understands you?" said a bemused voice behind her, and Nora spun around to see José standing in the doorway of the booly.

"What matter if he doesn't?" she said defiantly. "He knows I think the world of him, and that's enough."

José smiled, his eyes warm. "I am sure you are right." His gaze dropped to the bundle under Nora's arm. "Did you bring any food?"

"Of course," said Nora, unwrapping the blanket and holding out the loaf of oatbread. He limped over and bit into it hungrily. "Is your leg troubling you?" she said, concerned.

José looked at her over the hunk of bread. "A little," he admitted.

Nora scolded herself for not thinking to bring some herbs as well as food. She would look for knapweed and chamomile when she went to fetch the shamrock. As she slipped the rope off her shoulder and started to coil one end into a makeshift halter for Lir, José asked, "Any news of Spanish ships?"

He spoke lightly as though he might be joking, but his expression turned to one of pleading hopefulness when Nora turned around and said, "Perhaps. I . . . I'm not sure."

"Not sure? What do you mean?" José frowned and he reached forward to take hold of Nora's sleeve. "Tell me, is there a ship?"

"Yes . . . yes, I think there might be," Nora stammered. "There is a merchant called Juan de Luca who knows when it is coming."

"Where is this man?" José demanded, looking as if he was about to set out there and then in search of him.

Nora looked down at the ground. "In Galway," she answered quietly.

She knew what José would say next, and she lifted her head to see José's eyes burning feverishly into hers as he declared, "Then we must go to Galway and ask him!"

Nora finished tethering Lir to a fir tree and followed José

into the booly where she shook out the blanket and laid it on the heap of straw. The English soldier's sword was propped against the wall, its blade gleaming faintly. "You don't understand," she said. "Galway is a long way away, further even than Aughnanure, and . . . and I am not allowed inside the town walls."

José looked confused. With a sigh, Nora explained how the powerful merchants' council, headed by the wealthy Lynch family, had passed the law in protest against the clan they described as the "ferocious O'Flahertys" because of their reputation for lawlessness and cattle raiding.

When she had finished, the boy was silent for a few moments, twisting a piece of straw over and over in his fingers. Then he said, "These merchants, you know them, yes?"

"Of course not," said Nora, surprised. "I have only been to Galway once, long ago, and they are very important people. Even if I had passed them in the street, they would never have spoken to someone like me or my brothers."

"So they do not know what you look like? There is nothing to say that you belong to Murray ne Doe's clan?"

Nora slowly shook her head, following José's train of thought. "No, they don't know what I look like." She could guess what he was going to say, and she realized that it might just work.

"Then we can go, and they won't know that you are one of

these, what did you say, 'ferocious O'Flahertys.'" José spread his hands wide as if this was an obvious conclusion, and Nora knew as certainly as she had known what he was about to say, that she would agree to go with him.

24

‹‹‹‹‹‹‹‹‹‹‹‹›››

THEY LEFT AT DAWN THE FOLLOWING morning, heading south through the Maam Tuircs again on Lir and Dunlin. Nora had stopped feeling surprised by the mare's willingness to go with them so far from her territory. Her only concern was that Dan Devlin or another horse trader would see her and want to sell her as a riding pony. They didn't usually sell horses straight off the mountain, but to anyone watching, Dunlin looked well-trained enough for a merchant's wife, trotting steadily along with José on her back, his long legs hanging below her belly. He had insisted on riding the mare because he said he was still a little wary of Lir—and it was true that the stallion didn't whinny to him as he did to Nora, or walk over to blow in his hair with an expression of gentle curiosity in his liquid brown eyes.

She had decided they would ride only as far as the tip of Lough Corrib, more than a league north of Aughnanure Castle because the last thing they needed was to be seen by anyone from Murray ne Doe's household. Even if some of the kerns were sympathetic toward the Spanish prisoners, Nora was riding a stolen war horse, and they'd win high praise from their chieftain for taking the stallion back to Aughnanure. When they reached the lake, she explained to José that they would take one of the currachs kept along the shore and row the length of the lough, from north to south. Even though Galway town was as far as Nora had ever been in her life, and she had made the journey just once before, the way was easy enough to remember; from Aughnanure, they had to follow the western shore of Lough Corrib past Murray ne Doe's castle until they reached the Galway River, which led to the town and beyond that, the open sea.

Borrowing a stranger's currach might mean that one of the locals missed a day's salmon fishing, but Nora couldn't think how else to get hold of a boat, and they would return it by nightfall if all went well. They would travel more quickly on the water, and with less risk of meeting English soldiers. She tried not to think what would happen if she or José were caught; luckily it was raining in hard, shimmering rods, which meant people would keep their heads down and hurry through the streets without stopping long enough to notice any strangers.

When they reached the edge of the Maam Tuircs, they headed east along the edge of the yew forest until they came to the shore of the lake. The gleaming channel of water stretched south as far as they could see, dotted with small, brown islands thickly covered with trees. Nora halted Lir in a copse a little way from the shore and slid off his back to tether him to a branch.

José jumped down from the mare and watched her twisting the rope into a halter. "Will Dunlin stay with him, even though she is not tied?" he asked, running one hand down the mare's neck.

"Yes, I think so," said Nora. "She stayed with him before, at the booly. I think the musket fire scared her off in the forest." She came over and placed both hands on Dunlin's muzzle, then lifted the mare's face to blow gently down her nostrils. Dunlin snorted affectionately in reply.

José laughed. "You like horses more than people, don't you?"

Nora looked up at him in surprise. "Well, I suppose so. I've always known that Dunlin was my best friend—and now Lir is, too. It's much easier to trust horses than people."

"You can trust me, Nonita."

José's brown eyes were serious, and Nora felt her cheeks grow warm. She let go of Dunlin's nose and said, "We should find a currach before the fishermen come." She gave Lir one last pat and walked out of the copse toward the edge of the lake. The shining silver water was dotted with raindrops, and a skinny black cormorant skimmed the surface looking for eels. There were half a dozen currachs dragged up on the beach and Nora started to haul the nearest one over the stones toward the water.

José limped forward to help her. "Have you been in one of these before?" he asked, looking doubtfully at the fragile wicker frame wrapped in a thin layer of pitch-covered hide.

"Oh, many times," Nora told him. She reached into the bottom of the currach and held up a short, broad-headed paddle. "Here, this is for you." She saw him raise his eyebrows and added, "Don't worry, there's one for me, too. Did you think I'd make you row all the way on your own?" She grinned at him and realized that in spite of the seriousness of their mission, she was excited at the prospect of going to Galway—maybe all the moreso because she was one of the banned "ferocious O'Flahertys."

They reached the edge of the water and floated the currach on the idly lapping waves. Nora held the little boat steady while José climbed in, cursing in Spanish when it rocked violently and almost spilled him straight out again. "Sit down, quick," she warned him, trying to keep the laughter out of her voice.

He pretended to glare at her, but folded his legs under him and leaned over the side to dig his paddle into the bottom of the lake and hold the currach still for Nora to clamber in. She settled herself with her skirt and brat tucked modestly around her, then dipped her paddle into the water and pushed the boat forward, away from the shore and into the center of the lake.

They rowed through the pigeon-gray dawn without speaking,

the silence broken only by the dip and splash of their paddles and the occasional cry of a water bird. Little scrubby islands loomed toward them and slipped quickly by. No one lived on them, although some had tiny huts where fishermen would stay overnight if the weather was too bad to make it back to the shore, or the salmon were swimming particularly well. When they drew level with Aughnanure Castle, Nora touched José's sleeve and pointed to the tower house roof just visible above the dark green yew trees. He nodded grimly and dug his paddle harder into the water as if he wanted to get past the place where his companions had been betrayed.

By the time they reached the start of the Galway River, Nora's arms burned from her shoulders to her fingertips and her legs were stiff and cramped from sitting cross-legged. Luckily the current flowed more strongly here and they were able to rest their paddles on the edge of the currach and let the water carry them between the low, muddy banks. There were a few people in the fields beside the river, walking behind a herd of plodding cows or carrying eel traps down to set in the water, but none of them paid any attention to the little boat.

When a tall, pointed spire slid past on the north bank, Nora picked up her paddle and steered the currach toward the shore. "We need to get out here, by the abbey," she told José. "We can't row all the way to the quay because there are too many large ships."

He nodded, his face paler now and more serious, and helped Nora to paddle up a narrow sidestream and run the currach into some reeds. The water was only a few handspans deep and they climbed out, leaving the currach well hidden, and splashed through the mud to stand on a patch of grass outside the abbey walls. Nora felt a pang of sadness as she looked at the silent, crumbling stone. The monks had been driven out five years earlier by English soldiers, and now the abbey lay empty, its outbuildings used to store grain rather than shelter black-robed clerics.

She pointed across a wooden bridge to a steep-roofed gate-house, several stories high. "I think that's Little Gate Tower," she said, trying to remember her first and only visit to Galway. Her most vivid memory was of clinging tightly to her brother Colm's hand, terrified of losing him in the deafening, shoving crowd. "The quay is on the other side of the town." She stopped, suddenly afraid that she'd never remember the way and that they'd be discovered at once by the ruling Galway merchants. At least the jacket José was wearing hid his torn undershirt, but the leg of his trews was still stained with blood, and he looked thinner and more haunted than even the hungriest, most desperate crofter.

José saw the fear in her eyes and stepped forward to lay one hand on her arm. "It's all right, Nonita," he said quietly. "Put your cloak closer, like this—" he pulled Nora's brat higher around her face, tucking her plait down her back—"and don't look so scared." He smiled, but his hands were shaking.

She nodded, wanting to reassure him that she would be brave; she would only be ordered out of the town if she were recognized, whereas José was risking his life to find the Spanish merchant. Side by side, they walked across the bridge and into the town, staying unnoticed at the edge of a noisy, chattering family following a laden oxcart. Nora glanced up as the shadow of the city gate passed over them and her step faltered when she saw the raised portcullis gleaming like sharp metal teeth.

Suddenly there was the sound of galloping hooves, and a man shouted in English, "Watch out, there! Stand aside!"

José seized Nora's elbow and shoved her roughly into the wall until her cheek grazed the bricks. "Keep still," he hissed, standing beside her with his head bowed. There was a commotion behind them as the family struggled to heave the oxcart out of the way, and she heard the jangle of a horse's bit terrifyingly close. One of the children trod heavily on her toe as the soldiers kicked their horses nearer, their metal-shod hooves ringing against the cobbles.

Nora held her breath and stared at the rough, gray stone in front of her face, waiting for a leather-gloved hand to grab her shoulder and ask her what she was doing with a Spanish prisoner. Beside her, José curled his fingers into a fist as if he was still holding the English soldier's sword. The noise of hoof-beats grew deafeningly loud, echoing around the gatehouse walls, and there was an indignant bellow from the ox as one of the horses sidestepped into the cart and jolted the shafts against the animal's broad white flanks. Then the soldiers' shouts and the jangle of bridles faded as the last of the war horses passed under the gate and plowed into the people thronging the street.

José took hold of Nora's hand. "Come on," he whispered, and she let him lead her through the gatehouse and into a long, straight street lined with tall houses built of gray stone.

For a moment, she stood stock-still and fought against an urge to turn and run back to the currach, back to the silence and the emptiness of the mountains. There were people *everywhere*, pushing carts, rolling barrels, thronging in and out of shop doorways with cloth-wrapped bundles, and all making such a din that Nora thought her ears would never stop ringing. The rumble of wooden cart wheels sounded like thunder behind a chorus of a thousand voices raised in shouts on every side. She glanced at José, wondering if he found the scene as overwhelming, but he was looking around quite calmly, now that the English soldiers had gone.

He caught her eye and murmured, "It is like Cádiz, where I live. But not like the mountains, no?"

Nora shook her head. The crowd surged around her, and

when it parted briefly she saw a space ahead where another road joined Little Gate Street. There were several rows of stalls piled high with gleaming, silver fish, and a brief memory of her brother Sean rolling a barrel of mussels over cobbles flashed into her mind. "We need to go that way," she told José.

He grasped her hand to prevent her being swept away in an eddy of people, and they battled their way toward the fish stalls like salmon swimming upstream. Just beyond the market, a dark gray tower house loomed higher than all the other buildings and cast a long shadow into the street below. Nora knew this was Lynch's Castle, where the most powerful family in Galway lived. She drew her brat more closely around her face and kept her head down as she walked past; Mayor Lynch's had been one of the loudest voices to call for the O'Flahertys to be banned from Galway. When she came to the corner of another road, she paused and looked around, trying to remember which way she and her brothers had come from the quay.

José pointed to a man pulling a handcart up a road that led away to the right. The cart was laden with glistening, wet barrels, the dark wood crusted with a glaze of salt. "Perhaps he has come from a ship?" he suggested, and Nora nodded. They squeezed past an enormously fat man selling hot pies from a stall—the food smelled delicious and Nora wished she had a coin or something to trade for one—and walked down the road between more lofty, gray houses. When the street divided at a broad space filled with carts of corn and oats, they headed left, following a trail of water spilled on the cobbles and keeping a careful eye out for more English soldiers.

José pulled Nora into the side of the road as a gray pony trotted past; its coat was cloud-colored like Lir's, though it was shorter and sturdier, like the mountain ponies. Nora watched in dismay as the pony's rider, a stout, red-faced woman wearing a fine scarlet cloak, jabbed her spurred boots into its flanks and flapped the reins to make the pony trot faster over the slippery cobbles.

"Wretched animal!" cursed the woman when the pony stumbled over a sticking-up stone. She yanked the reins until the bit clattered against the pony's teeth. Nora winced and was about to cry out in protest when she felt José's fingers press into her arm in warning. She bit her lip and kept silent as the woman bounced away down the street. José stepped away from the wall and led Nora after him, flashing her a sympathetic glance to show that he had been equally dismayed at the rider's treatment of her long-suffering pony.

Suddenly the houses came to an end and they found themselves standing at the edge of a wide, cobbled square enclosed by a high wall. There were two gates in the wall, and through them Nora saw the tall masts and furled sails of many ships. She turned to José. "This is the quay! Now we just have to find Juan de Luca." Her heart sank as she gazed at a long row of shops that lined the square, open-fronted to show the barrels of wine, kegs of salt and spices, and pieces of unworked iron on sale.

"You will have to ask someone where he lives," said José, his mouth set in the tense line that Nora remembered from the castle. He kept his head bowed, so that people didn't see his sun-browned skin and dark eyes.

Feeling hot and clumsy, she stumbled over the cobbles to the nearest shop. An old man with a leathery face and pure white hair was sitting on a barrel just inside the doorway, sharpening a knife against a piece of stone.

"I'm looking for Juan de Luca," Nora blurted out, twisting her hands in the hem of her brat.

The man didn't look up from his knife. "Seems that many people are just now," he remarked.

"Please, it's important," Nora pleaded. She hoped he wasn't going to ask for anything in exchange. She had nothing to give except her cloak, and that was Mainie's.

The merchant sighed and put down his knife, only to pick up another one that lay in a neat row on the floor. "Two shops along," he said gruffly. "Look for the black and yellow sign."

"Thank you, sir," said Nora, letting go of her brat and backing out of the shop. She beckoned to José and they walked along the row of shops until they came to one with a wooden board hanging above the entrance, painted yellow with a black stripe. "This is it," she whispered.

To her surprise, José hung back, biting his lip. "I think you should go in alone. What if it is a trap?"

Nora's heart started to pound as she realized that he was right. She didn't think that Father Francis would deliberately betray them, but the priest had no way of being sure that Juan de Luca was really able to help the shipwrecked men. Even though she was an O'Flaherty, at least she was Irish, and there wasn't the same price on her head as there was on José's. Nora looked at his scared, pale face and before her courage failed her, she turned and walked into the shop.

It was dark inside and at first Nora could see nothing more than the dim shapes of barrels and cloth-wrapped bundles stacked along the walls. There was the sound of footsteps and a tall, dark-robed figure emerged from the shadows at the back of the shop.

"Can I help you?" he asked, in a low-pitched, musical voice that sounded a little like José's.

"I . . . I hope so," Nora stammered. "We . . . I'm looking for Juan de Luca."

The man spread his arms wide but stayed where he was so that his face was cloaked in shadow. "You have found him."

Nora swallowed. "I've heard there is a ship coming for the Spanish sailors who were shipwrecked. Please can you tell me where it will come, and when?"

There was a long pause, broken only by the rumbling purr of a black-and-white cat curled on top of a sack, who watched Nora with unblinking copper eyes.

Then the merchant spoke, and his voice was heavy with suspicion. "But you are not a shipwrecked sailor. Why would you want to know about such a ship, if there was one?"

25

⟨∽∽∽⟩

NORA'S HEART PLUMMETED. It might still be a trap. How could she convince the merchant to tell her about the ship without giving José away?

"Because she has already risked her life trying to help me return home."

José walked up behind Nora, speaking in clear, measured Spanish. She spun around and stared at him in dismay, but the boy held up his hand and continued. "From your accent, I'd guess that you come from Cádiz. That is my home, too. Please, if you know about this ship, you have to tell us." Nora noticed that José didn't tell the merchant his name, or who his father was. She guessed that if the man was going to tell them anything, it would be because he was willing, and brave enough, to help all the shipwrecked sailors rather than because of José's ancestry.

There was a low, rumbling laugh from the shadows and the man at the back of the shop stepped forward into the dim light. Nora gasped when she saw a long, raised scar running from the merchant's ear to the corner of his mouth.

He saw her reaction and smiled, his mouth curving up on the uninjured side of his face. "I have not always been a trader of wine and spices," he said quietly. He looked past her to José, and his brown eyes narrowed. "You are right. I was born in Cádiz, a long time ago." He spoke in Spanish, but Nora understood him quite easily because his accent had been softened by years of speaking her own language—he sounded a little like she did when she spoke to the herring fishermen.

His glance flickered from José to Nora. "You speak Spanish?" She nodded quickly. "If I tell you about the ship," Juan de Luca went on, "you did not hear it from me, and you do not know my name, yes?"

"Of course," José said calmly, and he sounded like the son of a powerful Spanish nobleman rather than a frightened ship-wrecked sailor.

"It will come to Killary Harbor, north of the Connemara mountains, in two days' time. It has been sent by our Catholic friends in Scotland, and will wait for only one night before leaving for Spain." The merchant leaned forward and his scar glowed pink against his tanned skin. "Godspeed, my friend. There are English soldiers everywhere, and I heard they brought another fifty prisoners here yesterday."

Nora glanced at José and knew he was thinking the same thing—that some of those men must have come from Aughnanure, and he could so easily have been among them.

Juan de Luca stepped back as a short, red-haired woman bustled into the shop with a basket over her arm. "Good day to you!" she called cheerfully, squeezing past José and Nora to dip her finger into a bowl of powdered saffron. She raised it to her nose and sniffed appreciatively. "I'll take this, and some cinnamon if you have any."

The merchant nodded and turned to Nora. "I am sorry that I do not have the spice you are looking for," he said in Irish. "But I hope that you have good fortune elsewhere," and Nora knew he was wishing them luck with the Scottish ship.

"Thank you, sir," she said. She heard José move away behind her, and turned to follow him out of the shop.

The noise of the quay burst upon them as they emerged, blinking, in the daylight. There was a commotion in the far corner, and Nora stared curiously as she heard a shrill whinny, quickly answered by another, and the clatter of hooves on the cobbles. A row of shaggy, dun-colored rumps told her that this was the horse market. At the far end of the line of ponies, a broad-shouldered, bearded man was arguing about the price of a beautiful gray horse, darker than Lir, with an arched neck and a long, flowing mane. Nora guessed that this was another Spanish horse that had made it ashore from the shipwrecks.

Then a slight, brown-haired man stepped out from behind the horse's shoulder, and she found herself staring straight into the clear green gaze of Dan Devlin.

Without a word, she grabbed José's hand and dragged him into the crowd. She wasn't willing to stay and find out if Dan had recognized her. The horse trader knew full well that Nora's family wasn't allowed inside the town walls and she was filled with horror that he might ask awkward questions about what she was doing when he next came to Errislannan—and, more worryingly, about her dark-haired companion. There was no way she could ever let her parents know that she had come to Galway, or that she had risked her life to help a Spanish sailor.

"Is something wrong?" José panted as she led him half-walking, half-running through the mass of people, every one of whom seemed to be pushing in the opposite direction.

Nora glanced over her shoulder, afraid that she would see the horse trader weaving his way toward them at any moment. "I saw someone that I know," she admitted. "A horse trader who sometimes comes to Errislannan."

He frowned. "And he saw you, too?"

"I think so." There was nothing they could do except get out of the town as quickly as possible through the throng of people and carts, and gray-brown dogs as thin as hazel stems weaving their way through a forest of legs. They pushed their way back through the corn market to Lynch's Castle, paused for a moment to make sure there were no English soldiers around, then turned left past the fish traders. Most of the day's business had been finished so there were fewer people here now, and half a dozen scrawny cats sniffed hungrily around the stalls, yowling like seagulls.

Under Little Gate Tower they hurried, breaking stride only to jump over a steaming pile of ox dung, then back across the wooden bridge. Nora stopped by the patch of reeds where the currach was hidden and bent double, gasping for breath and clutching her side where it felt as if she'd been run through with a sword. José sank to his knees, his face white with pain, and Nora realized that his injury hardly made him fit to run from one end of Galway to the other. But they couldn't stay here—already people on the bridge were looking toward them and pointing, and it would only take one person with a lively imagination to guess they were fugitives from some crime and call the attention of a town constable or worse, an English soldier.

She tugged at the boy's sleeve. "Come on, get into the currach. I can row us on my own."

At first José sat huddled beside her, his ribs heaving and both hands clasping his injured leg, but after a while he straightened up and picked up his paddle. With a determined look on his face, he dug it strongly into the water and sent the currach back up the river. They took turns to row once they reached the lake, where the current wasn't dragging them so insistently back toward the sea.

José lay back more comfortably in the little boat, trailing one hand in the water so that his fingers flickered below the surface like pale, thin fish. He looked at Nora and smiled. "I think Juan de Luca can be trusted. He is from Cádiz, after all. The ship will come, and I can go home to Spain."

Nora smiled back, hoping more than anything else in the world that he was right. Her heart twisted as she thought of José's father sitting at the window in his white-walled house, waiting for his son to come home across the sparkling blue sea. Two days would be plenty of time for Lir and Dunlin to rest from today's journey, and for José's leg to heal.

The bottom of the currach scraped against pebbles and Nora looked over her shoulder to see that they had reached the northern tip of the lake. José jumped into the shallow water, wincing as he landed on his wounded leg, and held the boat steady while Nora scrambled out. They hauled the currach up the shore, where it sat looking rather lonely, waiting for the other currachs to return from the day's fishing.

Nora was cheered by the thought that they would be back in Sraith Salach before nightfall. She might even have time to help Mainie with some chores, and make sure her sister didn't send her back to Errislannan in a fit of temper before she had a chance to take José to Killary Harbor. They walked up the beach and across the tussocky grass to the copse of trees.

"My father will be very surprised to hear how much riding I have done," José remarked.

Nora didn't reply. She had reached the edge of the trees and

stopped dead, staring around in dismay. The copse was completely deserted apart from a muddy coil of rope lying on the
ground.

Lir and Dunlin had gone.

A TRAIL OF HOOFPRINTS SHOWED that the horses had gal-loped back along the yew forest and into the mountains, the same way they had come. The rope was riddled with teeth marks, which suggested that Lir or Dunlin had chewed at the knot until it came undone—probably by accident more than judgement, but it wasn't hard to imagine them taking advan-tage of the stallion's sudden freedom.

Nora was relieved that at least they hadn't been stolen or strayed into the forest, but it was a long, hard walk back to Connemara, especially for José, whose leg was hurting badly. Before they set out, she whistled as loud as she could, hoping that Dunlin was not too far away, but this time there was no answering drum of hoofbeats. There was no point staying by the lake, which was more than twice as far from Killary than the booly. They trudged through the hammering rain with their heads down and their cloaks pulled up around their ears. Nora listened to the uneven slap of José's footsteps in the mud, plodding on as though he was determined that nothing was going to stop him from reaching Killary Harbor, even if he had to crawl on his hands and knees.

Tears of exhaustion and disappointment ran into the rain-drops on her cheeks, and it was hard to remember their excite-ment at finding out about the Scottish ship. There was a bottomless well of sorrow inside her at the thought of losing Lir—not just because she wanted to ride him to Killary Harbor to see José safely onto the ship, but because she had begun to think of him as different from the mountain ponies. He was better trained, of course, but he had also been dependent on Nora for food and shelter, and that had made the bond between them much stronger. She had risked her life to rescue him from Aughnanure as much as she had for José, and she felt a strange sense of betrayal that he had chosen to go with Dunlin rather than stay with her. She wondered if the mare would take Lir to her herd or leave him to fend for himself in the mountains. Nora couldn't imagine Fiach welcoming the young Spanish horse into his territory, and she winced as she pictured what might happen if the elderly stallion challenged Lir.

It was nearly dark by the time they stumbled down the hill toward the booly, but they were so tired that the hut looked welcoming in spite of the thick, cold shadows inside. José slumped down on the blanket and tucked into the rest of the oatbread that Nora had brought with her that morning.

"I'll come and see you tomorrow," she promised, standing in the doorway. She didn't dare sit down in case her legs gave way completely and she couldn't get up again.

"How will we get to the ship without the horses?" José asked, pausing mid-chew and looking up at her with wide, anxious eyes.

"Oh, we'll have Dunlin, for sure." Nora forced herself to sound confident and avoided mentioning Lir. Now that the Spanish stallion had a taste of freedom, he might not want to be ridden again. And would Dunlin want to leave her new companion for Nora and José? Killary Harbor was more than a day away on foot, so they would have to leave sooner if she couldn't be sure of the mare appearing at the sound of her whistle.

Distracted and very hungry, Nora left José curled under Mainie's blanket, already drifting into sleep, and trudged back around the mountain to the tiny village by the lake. She braced herself for a row as she pushed open the cottage door but Mainie hardly looked up from spooning broth into Alis's mouth. The two youngest children were running a fever, she explained, and she had sent Fionn to Orla mac Nichol for some herbs. She didn't mention the missing loaves of bread or the fact that her wooden chest was short of a blanket as well as the cloak that Nora had borrowed. Feeling guilty that she had been away while the children were sick, Nora quickly took off her brat, then went over to feed Alis so that Mainie could look after Fergal, who was a small, grizzling bundle in the far corner.

It was a long, fretful night in spite of the herbs that Fionn brought from the blacksmith's mother and by morning Nora felt as if she had rubbed handfuls of sand into her eyes. The children fell asleep as dawn began to stretch pale fingers past the window hides; even Una, who had wailed louder than the other two combined when Nora accidentally tripped over her as she went to pick up Fergal in the middle of the night, curled up with her eyes tightly shut.

Even though she knew José would be waiting for her at the booly, hungry and anxious for any more news, Nora could not leave Mainie to make the bread, milk the cow, and do all the other chores on her own. Fionn, who had appeared to shut up his ears like a seal to the children's cries during the night, went off to his workshop as soon as he had finished his bowl of buttermilk, leaving the two tired women to bake, sweep, and air blankets until the watery sun had passed the tops of the mountains. Nora waited until Mainie had settled down with the children playing quietly around her; then, stowing a piece of oatbread and a bowl of warm buttermilk under her brat, she ran past the blacksmith's house and along the path to the booly.

The sky was the color of sea-bleached driftwood, with long fingers of mist trailing across it like newly washed fleece. Nora paused when she reached the copse of fir trees and shaded her eyes to stare across the valley. The wild ponies were grazing on the other side of Lough Inagh, a cluster of soft-edged shadows against the pale green grass. Fiach usually kept a little way apart from the herd, ready to throw up his head and watch for anyone trying to approach, but today Nora couldn't see him. Then a furious whinny echoed along the valley and she followed the sound to a rounded knoll above the lake. The small, gray-black stallion stood there, stiff-legged and with his ears flat back against his neck. In front of him was a pale gray horse the color of clouds, his long seafoam mane lifting in the breeze, and Nora knew in one terrible instant that the stallions were going to fight.

Fiach whinnied again and Lir reared up into the air, striking out with forelegs and answering the challenge with his own deafening neigh. The bowl of buttermilk and the oatbread tumbled onto the grass at Nora's feet and she rushed into the booly, crying, "José! Come quickly!"

In one swift movement, José threw back the blanket and snatched up the sword that was propped against the wall. His eyes were wild as he grabbed Nora and pulled her toward him. "What is it?" he demanded. "Have the soldiers come?"

Nora pulled away and ran back to the door. "No, it's Lir and Fiach. They're fighting, look!" She pointed across the valley, feeling sick with anguish.

"Fiach?" José echoed in confusion, stumbling across the floor to join Nora in the doorway. "Who is Fiach?"

"The stallion in Dunlin's herd," she explained rapidly. "Come on. We have to stop them!" Fiach was older than most of the other mountain stallions, but Lir had no experience battling for a herd of mares, and his injured shoulder would make him dangerously vulnerable to Fiach's sharp teeth and flailing hooves. Nora bundled up her skirt and tore across the grass toward the lake with no clear thought about what she could do to stop two fully grown stallions from attacking each other, but the fear that Lir might be badly hurt in the struggle spurred her on.

José caught up with her and dragged her to a halt on the edge of the lake. Above them, the horses lunged at each other, their front hooves clashing so loudly that a flock of squall-crows were startled out of a nearby tree. Nora watched in horror as Fiach's head stretched forward and he sank his teeth into Lir's neck. "No," she whispered. "Please, stop."

José turned her to face him. "There is nothing we can do," he told her, his brown eyes warm with sympathy. "They will fight, and one of them will win. It is the way of horses, no?"

Nora nodded, knowing he was right but longing with every bone in her body to run up the hillside and somehow force the stallions apart.

"If you try to stop them, you will get hurt," José added.

Further along the lake, the rest of the herd lifted their heads to watch the battling horses. Nora clenched her hands tight as a familiar bracken-colored shape stepped out of the herd and stood with her ears pricked toward the knoll. *This is your fault,*

Dunlin! she wanted to scream. *You shouldn't have taken Lir away. He isn't a mountain horse like you.* But deep down, Nora knew that Lir was only obeying the instincts of any stallion to be the strongest and the bravest. She stood helplessly beside José, whose hand still gripped her arm, and watched the horses fight; one was short-legged and quick, whipping his head around to bite Lir's neck and flank, and the other was several hands taller, reaching out with his long forelegs to carve scars like dark new moons in the older stallion's coat.

Suddenly Fiach spun around and lashed out with both hind legs, striking the Spanish horse squarely on his injured shoulder. Nora gasped as Lir's legs buckled and he crashed to the ground. The wild stallion stood over him, shaking his short, dark gray mane, and Nora wrenched herself out of José's grasp and rushed forward around the edge of the lake, waving her hands above her head.

"Leave him alone!" she screamed. "Go back to your mares!"

Fiach looked at her for a moment, his ears flicking back and forth, before wheeling around and trotting back to the rest of the herd. He broke into a canter as he neared them and let out a loud whinny so that the mares threw up their heads and started running too, away from the knoll and the fallen Spanish horse. Only Dunlin stayed where she was, staring at Lir with her ears pricked. Fiach spun around on his hindlegs and cantered back to nip her crossly on the rump. Dunlin squealed and bucked in protest but galloped out of the valley with the black stallion at her flank, their hooves drumming fainter and fainter over the peat until they were swallowed up by the mist and the valley was quiet again.

Nora broke into a run again, not taking her eyes from the still, gray shape on the knoll. José ran after her, his stride more level than the day before, and quickly caught up with her. They scrambled up the side of the hill and stopped, panting, where the ground flattened out to look at the stallion. Lir was lying with his front legs propped under his chest and his head hanging down. His neck and shoulder were covered with wounds left by Fiach's teeth and hooves, and his coat was stained pink where the blood had mixed with sweat.

Nora lunged forward but José put his hand on her arm. "Be careful," he warned. "He might be angry still."

"I can't just leave him there," Nora argued, but she was interrupted by a snort from Lir, and the sound of his hooves scrabbling in the grass as he heaved himself to his feet. He stood motionless for a moment before shaking himself violently so that his mane and tail whipped the air like storm-tossed branches. He snorted again and nodded his head up and down, then looked straight at Nora through his tangled forelock—and in that moment she knew that he was asking for her help, just as she had helped him after the shipwreck. Wrenching her arm from José's grasp, she ran across the grass and threw her arms around Lir's neck.

"You foolish boy," she murmured, smoothing her hands down his neck over and over again. "What were you thinking of, fighting Fiach like that?" The stallion blew warmly against her neck, and she looked past his broad, scratched nose to José.

"We must take him back to the booly," she said. "I can wash his cuts there, and Fiach won't try to attack him again so close to the hut."

José looked doubtful but he didn't try to stop her as she took hold of Lir's mane and gently encouraged him forward. The horse hesitated, then limped beside her down the knoll and around the shore of the lake. His head nodded painfully with each step, and when Nora put her hand on his shoulder she was alarmed to feel that it was hot and swollen, like it had been after the shipwreck. The names of herbs slid instinctively into her head—Orla mac Nichol would tell her where she could find the rarer plants like chamomile and loosestrife, if she couldn't spare any from her stores.

They came at last to the copse of fir trees and Lir followed Nora quite willingly to the spring beside the booly. She cupped her hands and scooped up handfuls of water to wash the mud and sweat from the stallion's coat, so that it ran in greasy, red rivulets down his legs. José picked some grass and held it under Lir's nose until he halfheartedly started to chew.

"Will he be all right?" he asked, and Nora guessed he was

wondering if Lir would be able to take them to Killary Harbor.

"I think so, after a good night's rest," she said. "His shoulder healed pretty quickly last time, and I should be able to find some herbs in Sraith Salach. I don't think he'll wander far tonight, but I'll bring the rope to tether him tomorrow."

She rested her cheek against the stallion's clean, damp neck and twisted her fingers in the ends of his mane. He was breathing more evenly now, rather than the rapid, shallow breaths when he was winded after the fight. They would be able to leave for Killary Harbor tomorrow night as they had planned, even without Dunlin. There would be just a tiny sliver of moon so it would be a dark night even if there were no clouds, but the route was an easy one, north along Lough Inagh through a wide, treeless valley.

Nora closed her eyes and realized for the first time that part of her didn't want José to go home, because no one in her family understood what the wild ponies meant to her, and no one else had ever told her that she was brave. If she lost Lir as well, she would be left alone with nothing to remind her of the Spanish shipwrecks, and she might forget that her life had changed forever.

She heard José walk back to the booly, pausing at the spring to scoop up some water. Keeping her eyes shut, she pressed her face closer to Lir's neck and let her breathing slow to match his. Suddenly there was a movement among the trees behind her, and Lir stiffened, pricking his ears and turning his head to peer into the shadows.

Very slowly, Nora raised her head and felt her heart sink as a voice said clearly, "That's not a mountain pony, is it, Nora Donovan?"

27

NORA SPUN AROUND AND STARED in dismay at the look of triumph on the girl's pale, plump face. "Clara! What are you doing out here?"

Clara Foyle held up a small leather sack. "Old Mother mac Nichol sent me to collect some watercress." She walked out of the trees and stopped a few paces away from Lir. "Well, this is quite a secret to be keeping. Did you find him washed up on a beach?"

"'Tis none of your business!" Nora spat. She let her fingers rest against Lir's shoulder behind her, drawing comfort from his smooth, warm coat. "And you'll gain nothing by telling anyone about him, so you can go back to the village and forget you ever saw him."

"Oh, I don't think I could do that." Clara stretched her eyes wide with an air of wounded innocence. "There's people looking all over for flotsam from those shipwrecks. Dan Devlin for one would pay a good price for a horse like this. Or perhaps you were thinking of telling him yourself?" She walked up and reached out to touch Lir's mane. The stallion blew down his nostrils and shifted away from her.

Nora clenched her teeth together so hard that pain shot through her temples. "I found him, not Dan Devlin. He'll have nothing to do with this horse."

Clara raised her eyebrows. "Is that so?" She let her gaze drift past the stallion to the booly. Nora felt every muscle in her body strain to turn around and reassure herself that José was out of sight but she made herself stay exactly where she was with her eyes fixed on Clara's face.

Her legs nearly gave way when the girl said, without looking at her, "You seem very nervous, Nora. Are you sure the horse was the only piece of flotsam you found?" Before Nora could say anything, Clara let her hand fall back to her side and started walking across the grass toward the booly.

With a gasp, Nora stumbled after her, peering desperately into the shadows inside the little hut for some sign that José knew what was going on.

Clara stopped at the doorway and looked back at Nora, her teeth gleaming white in the darkness when she spoke. "Now, you wouldn't be keeping any more secrets from me, would you? After all, we're friends as well as neighbors. And we all know the price on the heads of anyone foolish enough to try helping Spanish sailors."

Her voice sounded strained and Nora realized that the girl was scared of what might be hiding inside the booly, though whether her imagination feared fairies or some desperate half-drowned Spanish sailor, it was impossible to tell. There was the faintest movement behind her, more a shifting of shadow than any clear sense of shape or limb. Out of the corner of her eye, Nora saw the unmistakable glint of steel and she knew at once that José was waiting just inside the doorway with the sword. There was no doubt that he would have heard it was only a girl outside, but Nora knew he would do anything to escape being captured again.

"Jesus, Mary, and Joseph, what are you saying?" she exclaimed, forcing her voice to keep steady as she stepped forward and laid one hand on Clara's arm. "Do you think I'd be brave enough to hide a shipwrecked Spaniard as well as a horse?" She felt sick as she waited for Clara to laugh at her and agree that no one would credit Nora Donovan with that amount of wit or courage.

Clara blinked, then a malicious smile spread across her face. "And you've not even managed to hide the horse very well, have you?" She looked at Lir, who was watching them curiously from the other side of the clearing. "Because I know about him now, Nora Donovan. And you can't begin to imagine how much trouble you'll be in when your ma and pa find out what you've been up to." She paused and an unpleasant gleam lit up her eyes. "But maybe I won't tell them first. Dan Devlin might pay me well for letting him know where there's another Spanish stallion to be found. I heard he sold that bay horse to a merchant in Galway for more than he'd get for a dozen work ponies. You might have found this stallion first, Nora, but I know where he is, so he's no more yours than any of those mountain ponies." Without another word, she ran off through the trees, moving more swiftly over the uneven turf than Nora would have expected from the lumpen figure.

"*Madre de Díos*, what will happen now?" José's voice was husky with shock as he emerged from the doorway.

"I don't know," Nora confessed. "But she doesn't know you're here, which is the most important thing. And by tomorrow night, you'll be gone—and Lir, too."

They stood side by side and looked at the cloud-gray stallion, who had lowered his head to crop the grass beneath the fir trees. "Perhaps it's as well if she wants to tell Dan Devlin first," said Nora, trying to sound encouraging for José's sake. "The horses that he's found already will keep him busy in Galway for a while"—she winced at the memory of the horse trader's startled gaze across the crowded marketplace—"so you should be long gone before he comes back here."

And Lir? said a voice inside her. *What will happen to him, now that Clara knows you're hiding a Spanish horse?* Nora felt her heart begin to break as she realized that she could no longer be sure of keeping the stallion safe. As long as she carried on trying to look after Lir, it would be only a matter of time before Clara or

Dan, or whoever else found out about Nora's secret, followed her straight to him.

NORA LEFT JOSÉ WATCHING Lir graze among the fir trees and ran back to Sraith Salach. It was almost too dark to see the road, and the lake below the cottages was a steely black gleam in the starlight. The door to Ronan mac Nichol's forge was open and Nora forced herself to run past without looking in, although her ears strained to hear if Clara was already telling her cousin what she had found in the next valley. There were shouts of laughter from inside the firelit room, but it was impossible to tell what was being said and Nora sent up a silent prayer that Clara would keep to her word and wait until the horse trader came back to Sraith Salach before spilling her secret.

In Fionn's cottage, Una and Alis were playing by the hearth while Mainie nursed the baby on a pile of clean rushes. Rhythmic hammering came from the workshop behind the cottage where Fionn was finishing a set of cart wheels. Nora started to heat some broth for supper and put stones in the embers to warm the girls' buttermilk, hoping that her sister wouldn't notice that her hands were shaking so much she nearly sent the milk spilling into the fire. After supper, she tried to let Una's chatter about fairies and elves distract her, but behind her eyes all she could see was the booly in the shadow-darkened valley, where a cloud-colored horse and a shipwrecked boy waited for her to lead them to one last chance at safety.

THE NEXT MORNING, NORA woke early and went to the booly with a loaf of bread and the coil of rope to tether Lir before Mainie and the children were awake. The stallion whinnied as she came through the trees and stood patiently while she slipped the makeshift halter over his head and tied the other end of the rope to a tree branch, but there was no sign of José until she stood in the doorway and softly called his name.

His eyes were huge and dark-shadowed when he stumbled into the daylight and his hands trembled as he took the bread from her and broke it in half. "I . . . I wasn't sure if it was you," he explained without taking his eyes off the bread.

Nora felt her stomach twist with sympathy for him, together with a longing to slap Clara Foyle's smug pink face. "It's all right, there's only today and then we can leave for Killary Harbor. Lir's wounds seem fine after the fight," she added, nodding at the marks on the stallion's flank left by Fiach's teeth and hooves. She had already run her hands over the injuries and found little heat left in the scars and hardly any swelling under the skin.

José said nothing, just looked at her over the chunk of bread as he started to eat. Nora glanced at the yellow line above the mountains to the east and said, "I'd better go before Mainie wakes. I'll be back tonight, at nightfall. Try and get some rest."

She held José's gaze for a moment, wishing she could promise him that she would keep him safe until the ship came but painfully aware that Clara's discovery meant she was as dangerous to him and the stallion as a whole legion of English soldiers. Then Nora picked up her skirt in one hand and ran out of the clearing, pausing to stroke Lir's neck before slipping through the trees and back around the flank of the mountain to the village.

All day long Nora kept her ears open for the sound of hoof-beats on the road that might announce the arrival of the horse trader. But the only visitor that day was a young man from Curhownagh who brought a barrel of mussels to exchange for the cart wheels Fionn had finished late the night before. Mainie was delighted with the fresh shellfish and set Nora to sorting through the barrel at once, sitting on an upturned pail in a sheltered corner of the yard. While she picked out the smashed shellfish and put the good ones into a bucket of salt-water to boil, Una and Alis played with the empty shells, clacking them together like horses' hooves while they cantered around the yard on unsteady legs. Watching them, Nora would have laughed if she hadn't been so conscious of the sun sinking below the roof of the workshop. There wasn't much time before she would have to set out for the booly, and the barrel of mussels was still half full.

After a while, Mainie called the girls in for their supper and Nora started to sort through the mussels more quickly, scraping her fingers painfully against the sharp open shells. Suddenly a shadow fell across her and she looked up, expecting to see her brother-in-law come to summon her to help with the children.

"Good day to you, Nora Donovan," said Dan Devlin. "I've just had a very interesting conversation with Clara Foyle, wouldn't you know?"

NORA SCRAMBLED TO HER FEET, sending mussel shells scattering across the yard like hard-edged mice. "I . . . I didn't hear you arrive," she stammered.

"Did you not?" The horse trader's tone was as friendly as if he had come to discuss nothing more important than the weather. "Well, 'tis not surprising. Those children of your sister's make enough noise to drown out an army, even without Fionn hammering away at his wheels."

Too late, Nora realized she should have insisted the girls let her sort the mussels in peace so she could listen out for the horse trader. She'd had no reason to think he'd stay longer in Galway, not when there was the chance of finding more ship-wrecked horses along the coast. Just as quickly she told herself there was nothing she could have done to stop Clara from telling him about Lir, even if she had heard him arrive. The only thing she could do now was get to the booly without Dan seeing her, and take José and Lir away. Ignoring the spilled mussels, she picked up an empty pail. "I can't stop now, Dan," she said. "I'm away to milk the cow."

"Is that right?" The horse trader looked sympathetic, as if he thought Mainie was working her too hard. "Then I'll walk with you," he said, and fell into step beside her. He didn't say anything else until they had gone past Fionn's workshop and were crossing the scrubby patch of grass toward the cow, who was standing under some trees.

"I saw you in Galway, did I not?" he began easily, as if he met Nora inside the town walls every day.

She knew there was no point trying to lie. "Yes, you did."

Dan Devlin looked sideways at her. "Would that have anything to do with this Spanish horse Clara tells me you've found?"

Nora stiffened. "Nothing at all, and why would it?" she challenged fiercely.

Dan Devlin waved his hand. "No matter. Whatever the reason, it's of no interest to me." His voice was unthreatening, and for a moment Nora wondered if he was going to agree to keep her visit to the town a secret. But then he said, still in the same mild tone, "It would be of interest to your parents though, would it not?"

Nora stopped dead and faced him with her hands on her hips. "What do you want from me, Dan Devlin?" she demanded, fear and fury making her forget that she would do anything to keep Lir hidden from his greedy eyes.

The horse trader took a step back with his hands in the air

and a look of surprise on his face. "Easy, Nora," he said. "There's no need to get angry. After all, I may yet be part of your family, don't you know?" He winked, and Nora wanted to tell him there and then that her sister Meg had no intention of marrying him. She tightened her grip on the handle of the pail.

Dan Devlin walked on across the field, tucking his hands under his brat, and glanced back over his shoulder with a thoughtful look in his dark green eyes. "You know, I always said to myself that if there was anyone around here who might take it upon themselves to rescue a shipwrecked horse, it was you, Nora Donovan. Take it as a compliment, for sure"—he grinned, and Nora felt the pail twitch in her hand—"but you have to admit that no one else has a way with horses like you do. And by Mary and all the saints, it turns out that I was right all along. Clara says it's a fine animal that you have tucked away in that valley. 'Twould be a shame if I didn't get to see him for myself, don't you think?"

Nora didn't feel obliged to agree, so she kept stony silent.

Dan Devlin went on, "It seems to me that we could come to an arrangement here. You take me to wherever you've hidden this stallion, and I'll not tell your parents you went to Galway."

Nora put the pail down on the grass, fighting an overwhelming urge to clap it against the side of the horse trader's head. She'd never surrender Lir to him, never!

"Why do you need me at all, if Clara's already told you

where he is?" she said.

Dan Devlin spread his hands wide. "Let's just say I like to make life easy for myself wherever I can. These Spanish stallions can be quite a handful, as I'm sure you know. If you've gone to the trouble of taming this one on my behalf, then that could be very useful to me. I'd hate to startle it away into the mountains now, being a stranger and all."

Nora knew she had no choice but to agree, and hope that the horse trader left her alone long enough to get José and Lir far away from the booly by Lough Inagh. She shrugged as if admitting defeat. "Very well. I'll take you to him tomorrow morning."

Dan Devlin smiled, lighting up his bony face. "Excellent. You won't regret helping me, Nora. I can find a better home for that stallion than he'd ever have in the mountains, you must know that."

Nora bit back a furious retort as she pictured Lir as a chieftain's war horse, risking his beautiful legs with every war mongering raid on a rival's cattle herds, or trotting over hard cobbles with a fat merchant's wife jolting on his back. But she nodded and lifted up the pail, saying, "May I milk the cow now?"

"Of course," said the horse trader, raising his eyebrows as if he were surprised that she was asking his permission. He hitched his brat higher on his shoulders and started to walk toward the cottage.

"I'll see you soon, Nora Donovan," he called back to her, and she muttered under her breath, "Not if I see you first."

THE NIGHT WAS BLACK AS A PAIL of pitch, the moon little more than a fingernail scratch in a cloudless sky. Nora ran along the path with her brat billowing behind her; it crossed her mind that anyone who saw her might mistake her for a banshee or a bog-wraith, venturing out on this windy night to make mischief for unwary travelers. The sun seemed to have dived behind the mountains more quickly than usual, and she knew they would have to ride swiftly to reach Killary Harbor by midnight. As soon as she finished milking the cow, she had told Mainie and Fionn that she was going for an evening of music and dancing at the blacksmith's cottage. Nora's sister didn't see anything odd in her sudden wish to spend time with Clara Foyle, and only warned her to be quiet coming back into the cottage so that she didn't disturb the children. Nora had kept well away from the forge as she left the village in case Dan Devlin was watching out for her; at the same time, she was sure he would trust her at least until she failed to keep their arrangement the next morning because he had seemed so confident his threat would work.

Lir snorted and shied in alarm when she reached the fir trees, although the rope kept him from going more than a couple of paces. He looked like a ghost horse, a gray, soft-edged shape breathing steamy clouds into the night air. Nora went over to quiet him and untie the halter, trusting her voice and legs to steer him without the help of the rope.

A voice said from behind her, "I thought you had changed your mind about coming."

She turned and saw José standing in the doorway of the hut. "I am here now," she said. "Are you ready?"

The boy nodded, his face as pale as Lir's coat. He walked toward her across the grass and Nora saw that he was carrying the sword from Aughnanure. Much as she hated the idea of having to use it against another person, even an English soldier, she told herself that it was better to go armed than to rely on Lir's fleet-footedness to carry them out of trouble.

José looked closely at her. "What has happened?" he said. "Something is wrong, I can tell."

Nora watched the end of the rope sliding toward her over the grass as she coiled it up. "I saw Dan Devlin," she said. "He . . . he knows about Lir." She raised her eyes to meet José's startled gaze, and said quickly, "But he doesn't know about you. Clara told him only that I was keeping a Spanish horse here at the booly."

José peered past her, through the trees. "Has he followed you?"

"I don't think so. I told him I'd bring him here tomorrow morning, when it's light."

"We cannot be sure he trusted you enough not to watch for you leaving the village," said José, echoing Nora's earlier fears. "We must go at once." His expression was somber as he put his hands around Nora's waist and lifted her onto the stallion's back. He looked up at her, his fingers brushing her leg, and said quietly, "Have courage, Nonita. It is not your fault that this man found out about the horse. If we leave now, we will be safe."

Nora nodded, trying to let his confidence give her strength. *This is it*, she thought. *If all goes well, this will be the last journey we take together.* And she pushed out of her head the thought that this journey might be the first step toward safety for José, but as far as Lir was concerned, he was in more danger than ever before.

José pulled himself up behind her and they rode out of the fir trees into the valley. Lough Inagh gleamed like the blackest shadow, the water whispering almost inaudibly against the shore. At first Nora's ears were filled with the sound of Lir's hoofbeats, but gradually she became aware of other noises carried by the breeze across the lake—stamping hooves, soft breathing, and the steady champing of grass. Somewhere in the darkness, Fiach had brought his herd to graze.

Nora couldn't resist it. With a quick glance over her shoulder at José, she let go of the stallion's mane and put her fingers in her mouth to give a piercing whistle. The sound echoed down the valley like the shriek of a hundred banshees, and Lir's head shot up in alarm. Nora patted his neck to reassure him and felt José twitch behind her.

"Someone might hear," he began, but Nora put up her hand to silence him.

The steady pad of Lir's hoofbeats hadn't changed, but they had been joined by another set galloping around the side of the lake, closer and closer. Nora peered into the darkness, suddenly afraid that it was Fiach coming to challenge the stallion who had dared to intrude on his territory again. She saw José's grip on the sword tighten as if he was thinking the same thing.

Lir swung around to face the approaching horse, his ears pricked and his nostrils flared rapidly in and out. Then a pale dun shape hurtled out of the shadows and skidded to a halt beside them, her flanks heaving and her legs spattered with wet peat.

"Dunlin!" Nora cried in delight, leaning down to rub the mare's small furry ears. The mountain pony lifted her muzzle and blew on her fingers, and Nora forgave her at once for taking Lir away and putting him in danger from Fiach.

José was already scrambling off Lir's back, holding the sword well clear of the smooth gray flank. He patted Dunlin's neck and jumped onto her back, flashing a grin up at Nora. "Now we can go faster," he said, and clapped his heels against the mare's sides to send her plunging into the shadows.

Nora leaned forward and wrapped her hands in Lir's mane.

"Come on, boy," she whispered, and as if he understood, the stallion bunched his quarters beneath him and leaped into a flat-out gallop, eating up the ground with long, effortless strides. The two horses raced side by side along the valley until they reached the end of the lake; all at once, the grass gave way to knobbly tussocks surrounded by slippery scoops of peat, and the horses slowed down to climb steeper and steeper into the mountains.

Nora let Dunlin take the lead, trusting the mare to follow unseen trails across the scree-covered slopes. At last the wind carried the sound of waves washing against rock, and the riders emerged on a hillside overlooking a broad strip of water that glinted under the sliver of moon like an unpolished sword. The horses halted, and Nora and José looked down at the water in silence. This was Killary Harbor, a long, straight-sided bay that stretched inland for more than two leagues, deep enough for the biggest ships but too steep-sided to be used by traders or fishermen.

"Nora, look!" José's voice was choked with emotion as he lifted his hand to point at the faint outline of a ship riding at anchor in the middle of the bay. While they watched, a shadow detached itself from the ship and started heading toward a narrow stony beach at the bottom of the mountain. Ripples spread out behind the shadow and Nora knew it was a rowing boat coming ashore to collect the shipwrecked sailors. Juan de

Luca had told them the truth, and here at last was José's chance to go home.

Tiny shapes appeared on the beach, first one or two, then more until the pebbles were almost hidden under a throng of men, wading eagerly into the water toward the boat. Nora saw José's face light up. "There are others! Thank God, I am not the only one to survive," he murmured, speaking in Spanish as if he had forgotten Nora was there.

He gathered up a handful of mane, ready to plunge down the side of the mountain and join his countrymen. But Nora had spotted something moving further along the valley and she stretched out a hand to keep him still. She narrowed her eyes and stared into the darkness until the shadows separated into a long line of horses and riders, divided by the faint gleam of starlight on sword and bit.

Oh Lord, no, she thought. *English soldiers!*

The men on the beach hadn't seen the approaching horses; the noise of their feet crunching over the stones and splashing through the shallow water drowned out the drumming hoof-beats and creak of leather that drew steadily nearer. Nora felt the blood in her veins turn to ice. She couldn't stay to watch what happened when the soldiers reached the shipwrecked men. She wheeled Lir around so that he was facing the mountains.

"Come on, José!" she cried. "The soldiers haven't seen us yet. There's still time to hide."

The Spanish boy looked at her over his shoulder, his eyes like black fire. "I ran away once before and let my companions die," he said quietly, shifting his grip on the sword so that the blade gleamed in the shadows. "This time, I will stay and fight." With that, he dug his heels into Dunlin's flanks and sent her leaping straight down the side of the mountain.

Lir threw up his head and snorted as the mare vanished into the darkness. Nora closed her legs around him to keep him still and gazed in horror at the empty space where Dunlin had been. A clatter of stones far below told her that they had nearly reached the bottom of the slope. She shut her eyes for a moment and thought of her father's cottage, safe and quiet on the other side of the mountains. Would she ever see Errislannan again? Memories of her life before the shipwreck seemed fragile as mist, as if they had happened to somebody else. Then Nora opened her eyes, took a deep breath, and kicked Lir after Dunlin.

The ground dropped away in a vertical sheet of scree, and for a moment it felt as if the stallion was falling straight toward the harbor, his hooves barely touching the loose stones. Nora clutched his mane and dug her knees into his withers to keep herself from shooting off his back and reaching the bottom before he did. They seemed to plummet forever and she was aware of nothing but the rattle of stones and the rushing of wind in her ears, but suddenly the ground flattened out and Lir was scrambling to get his haunches under him, his ears pinned back with alarm and his eyes rolling. Nora barely had time to push herself back into the middle of his back before the stallion took off again, galloping over the scrubby grass toward the edge of the harbor.

Ahead of them, Dunlin had nearly reached the shore and José was brandishing the sword above his head, yelling out in desperate, furious Spanish. The sailors on the beach were staring around in confusion and calling anxiously to one another. Out of the corner of her eye, Nora could see the troop of English soldiers thundering along the bottom of the valley, racing in ominous, terrifying silence except for the drumming hooves. In contrast, the Spaniards looked as if they were moving underwater, agonizingly slow and clumsy.

"Look out!" she screamed in Irish. "Run!"

"Who's that?" one of the sailors exclaimed in Spanish, peering into the shadows.

"*Madre de Díos*, I think that's José Medovar!" said another. "But what is that girl doing here?"

Dunlin skidded to a halt on the edge of the stones and José twisted around to look at Nora with fury in his eyes. "Go back!" he shouted. "This is not your fight!"

Lir caught up with the mountain pony in a few strides and stopped so sharply that Nora was thrown forward on his neck. She pushed herself back with an undignified scramble and glared at the Spanish boy. "I'm not leaving you now," she insisted.

And then the English soldiers were upon them and everything vanished in a tempest of shouting and the crunch of hooves on pebbles and the swipe of steel through the air. Some of the men on the beach fled toward the mountain while others snatched up pieces of driftwood and big stones to defend themselves as the soldiers stormed toward them with their swords held up like greedy scythes, their faces invisible behind domed metal helmets.

José charged forward, flying over the stones on the shaggy-coated pony like an ancient Irish warrior. Nora clung on helplessly as Lir hurtled after Dunlin, panicked by the noise and the Spanish sailors scrambling past on every side, their eyes wild with fear. A massive bay war horse, its glossy coat slick with sweat, wheeled away from the other soldiers to face José and Nora, bringing Dunlin and Lir to a sudden, juddering halt. The soldier reined in his horse, his gloved hand yanking the reins so hard that the gelding reared up and Nora glimpsed a flash of steel on its hooves. Her insides twisted with horror when she saw a familiar smile curve beneath the rider's helmet.

"You again," Captain Money said in English. He sounded amused, like a cat playing with a trapped weasel. "You were lucky to get away from me before, but you are a fool if you think you will ever leave this wretched country alive." He turned his heels inward, ready to sink his spurs into the geld-ing's flanks.

"I'll see you dead first!" José promised grimly, and his fingers tightened around the hilt of his sword.

Nora froze. The blood roared in her ears so loudly that the sounds of fighting and fleeing men faded away, and she was aware of nothing but José and the English captain, facing each other with their swords raised. For a moment, she thought her heart had stopped but then she heard it thudding, louder and louder, and she felt faintly puzzled that she could hear it so clearly when everything else seemed to have gone quiet.

It wasn't her heart, but a drum being pounded again and again, echoing through the darkness and making the soldiers lower their swords and look around to see where the noise was coming from. José's eyes stretched wide in disbelief as he stared past Captain Money, and Nora followed his gaze along the valley to a long, treeless ridge that looked down on the harbor, little more than a blacker shadow against the night sky.

Tiny shapes were appearing along the top of the ridge, more and more until it looked like a forest of stocky, leafless trees had sprung up in the space of a dozen heartbeats. One shadow stepped forward, much taller and bulkier than the others until Nora realized that it was a man on horseback, and he raised his arm so that the double-edged blade on his axe glinted in the starlight.

"Attack!" he shouted, and the line of men surged forward with a deafening, wordless roar, straight down the side of the ridge toward the beach. A few rode ponies, short-legged, dun-coated animals like José's mare, but most were on foot, leaping over ditches and tussocks of grass as fast as the ponies could run.

José glanced at Nora and she saw her own horror reflected in his eyes when she whispered, "Murray ne Doe O'Flaherty."

NORA FELT A BOLT OF RAGE toward the faithless chieftain. It wasn't enough for him that he had handed over the prisoners at Aughnanure; now he had brought his kerns and gallow-glasses across the mountains to help the English soldiers slaughter a handful of unarmed men.

Captain Money bared his teeth in triumph and lifted his sword again. Behind him, one of his men called cheerfully to the Irish warriors as they hurtled onto the beach. His cry was cut short and there was the sound of a body falling heavily to the ground. At once the rest of the English soldiers started shouting in fear and their horses crunched frantically over the stones as swords clashed against long-handled axes.

Captain Money's face darkened and he wheeled his gelding around. "What is this?" he roared, slicing the air with his sword as though tiny, winged enemies flocked around him like squall-crows.

A broad-shouldered figure loomed out of the shadows and Murray ne Doe rode up on his dark brown horse. His gaze flickered over José and Nora, his eyes widening very slightly when he saw Lir, and came to rest on the captain. "It seems that your word is worth even less than mine," he growled in English. "You promised my family would be safe if I let you have the Spaniards, but yesterday my nephew's son was struck down by one of your men because he was hunting deer. I have told you more times than I can count that those are *my* deer, in *my* forest. They are nothing to do with your greedy, far-off queen. You are a fool if you think I will not take revenge for his death."

Behind him, the battle cries of his kerns and gallowglasses changed to shouts of victory as one by one the English soldiers spurred their horses into a gallop and fled into the darkness. The Spaniards sensed that the tide had changed and rushed forward, brandishing their pieces of driftwood as if they were the sharpest swords. Nora felt hope soar in her chest like a gull on outstretched wings, but then she saw a soldier rush toward Murray ne Doe with his sword held high and she screamed a warning, knowing it was too late.

Out of nowhere, a pony raced up and its rider brought a battle-axe crashing down on the back of the soldier's head. He folded like a crumpled straw and toppled onto the stones. Murray ne Doe looked around and his eyes met those of the fox-haired gallowglass, who had pulled his pony to a halt behind his chieftain. His eyes were wild and his hair streamed behind him but the fox pelt was still in place around his neck, its fur spattered with scarlet drops of blood.

"You have saved my life again, Alaric," the chieftain said calmly, and Alaric Campbell nodded before turning his pony and galloping back into the thick of the battle.

Murray ne Doe turned back to the English captain. "You would be wise to leave now, before my men have no one left to fight," he advised.

Captain Money stared at him for a long moment, and Nora pictured his cold blue eyes narrowing in the shadow cast by his helmet. "This is not the end," the soldier promised, before clapping his spurs to his horse's flanks and galloping away.

Murray ne Doe watched him disappear into the shadows, then turned back to look at Nora. Their eyes were level because his horse was a hand shorter than Lir. She twisted her fingers in Lir's mane, suddenly afraid of what the chieftain was going to say about finding a girl from his clan in the middle of a battle with English soldiers—and riding a horse that was rightfully his, as well.

"You are a remarkable girl, Honora Donovan," he remarked. "You come to my castle with a shipwrecked sailor and a Spanish stallion, only to steal them away from me again. I know few men who would be so brave—or so foolish. I can only hope that you are as loyal to your kinsmen as you are to this boy and this horse." He paused and glanced appreciatively at Lir, who was standing with his ears pricked forward, staring into the shadows. "I'd pay a good price for a horse such as this, but would I be right in thinking he's not for sale?"

Nora shook her head firmly, relief making her bold. "No, he's not," she said, running her hand the length of Lir's damp neck.

Murray ne Doe's face creased into a smile. "Then I'll trust him to take good care of you on the journey back to Errislannan. You'll be going alone, yes?" His gaze slid sideways to where the Spanish men were holding a shallow boat steady in the waves and climbing in one by one.

Nora felt her heart clench with pain as she saw José looking hopefully toward the boat. "Yes, I'll be going home alone," she said.

"Godspeed," Murray ne Doe said to the boy, lifting his axe in farewell. "Believe me, I am glad to see you leave."

José nodded. Nora wondered if he guessed tonight's attack was the chieftain's way of making amends for surrendering the Spanish sailors four days earlier.

The old man turned his horse and trotted over to where his men were gathering, some limping or cradling their arms, their fingers sticky with blood, but none lying still and lifeless on the stones. Nora saw Con Foyle helping another kern onto a pony. There was blood on Con's jacket, but he lifted the other man easily onto the horse's back before leading it away into the shadows. Nora tried not to look at the two English bodies slumped on the ground.

There was a shout from the boat, "José Medovar, are you coming or not?" and José's face lit up.

"Pedro Velásquez!" he cried. "I thought you were lost with the ship!"

A stout, hook-nosed man came up and slapped his hand against José's thigh. "Me? Never! I floated ashore like a barrel where a priest in peasant's clothes found me. He took me and these others to a drafty little hut in the middle of nowhere, and brought us food until he heard this ship was coming."

Following the rapid Spanish with difficultly, Nora realized that Father Francis hadn't been the only priest trying to help their Catholic allies return home.

"Is there anyone else here from our ship?" José asked eagerly, and Nora saw his eyes darken with grief as Pedro shook his head.

"None that I have seen," he said solemnly. "It looks as if you and I were the lucky ones, my friend." Then his face cleared and he said, "Who is this you've brought with you, eh?"

José smiled. "This is Nora," he said, and she was warmed by the pride that shone in his eyes. "She risked her life for me many times—and for this horse, too."

Pedro frowned and opened his mouth to speak, but he was interrupted by a shout from the boat.

"Hurry up, you two! We don't want to be here if those

English pigs decide to come back."

"All right, we're coming," Pedro called back. He ran down the beach and waded into the sea toward the boat.

José swung his leg over Dunlin's withers and jumped to the ground. "Good-bye, little horse, and thank you," he murmured, pressing his face briefly against her neck. He glanced up at Nora, his eyes full of emotion, then turned and started to walk over the stones, favoring his injured leg once more so that his footsteps crunched unevenly.

"Wait!" Nora called, kicking Lir forward until he was standing next to the boy. "I—You—It won't do your leg any good to get wet again. Climb up behind me and Lir can take you to the boat." She knew she was talking nonsense, but she didn't want to let José go so quickly, not yet. A smile flickered across his face and he reached up to grasp her hand, then heaved himself up behind her. He sat very still without saying a word, and Nora knew with a strange flash of certainty that nothing they could say would ever be enough.

The men in the boat cheered loudly as they rode down to the edge of the water, but Nora ignored them and urged Lir into the waves. The stallion hesitated before stepping into the sea with his neck arched, blowing at the foam that surged around his knees. They splashed through the shallow water and eager hands reached out to help José into the boat. Lir stumbled sideways as the weight was lifted from his back and

Nora closed her legs against him to keep him still. There was a painful lump in her throat, and her eyes were suddenly blurred with tears.

José knelt down in the bottom of the boat and hung over the side toward her. His eyes were wide and pleading, and Nora felt something heavy lurch like a falling stone in her chest.

"I don't want to leave you, Nonita," José whispered. "Please, come with me."

30

───◦◦◦◦◦───

A PICTURE FLASHED INTO NORA'S mind of white-walled houses under a scorching blue sky, and round, sun-colored fruit hanging from a tree with glossy, green leaves. She saw herself and José riding tall, gray horses just like Lir, seafoam tails streaming behind them as they cantered across the dusty brown sand. The shipwreck had already changed her life forever. Would her family even notice if she didn't go back? she wondered.

Then Lir snorted and stamped his foreleg against a breaking wave, and Nora was jolted back to the mountains of Connemara and the sound of the cold sea washing against the rocks. "José, I can't come with you," she said, and it felt as if her heart was overflowing with sadness. "This is where I belong. I'm sorry."

José's eyes were soft with understanding as he reached out and cupped her face between his hands. "I know, Nonita," he murmured. He leaned forward and kissed her very gently on the cheek. "I will never forget you, never. I will tell my children, and my children's children, about the beautiful girl who risked her life for me, and who rode the wildest horses"—there was a jolt as the men dug long oars into the sea and the boat started to pull away from the shore—"and everyone in Cádiz will know that you have the bravest and kindest heart I have ever met . . ."

His voice faded against the splash of the oars, and Nora found herself laughing in spite of the tears that ran down her face and soaked into her hair. "Good-bye, José Medovar!" she cried into the darkness.

There was no reply. The sound of the oars was swallowed up by the waves, and the shadows gave no sign of the ship that was waiting silently in the bay to take the sailors home. There was nothing more that Nora could do to help José; she had risked everything to bring him here, but now she could only pray for a swift voyage back to Spain, where his father would be watching every day for his son's return.

Nora thought of the sea god riding his horse beneath the waves and her eyes narrowed defiantly. Any one of the Spanish prisoners at Aughnanure would have been payment enough for José's soul. Whatever debt she had brought upon herself by dragging José out of the sea had been more than repaid. *I know you wanted him, Manannan mac Lir,* she murmured, not even sure if she was speaking out loud, *but he is mine now. Look after him for me, please.*

Then she turned Lir back toward the shore where Dunlin

was watching them with her ears pricked forward, a light brown shape against the gray stones.

THE NIGHT SEEMED TO GROW colder and blacker as the horses headed back into the mountains. Nora pulled her brat around her and let Lir find his own way across the scree slopes. He walked steadily with his head low, placing each hoof confidently on the narrow path and not even flinching when a shower of stones rattled away down the side of the mountain. She thought back to the first time she had ridden him and could hardly believe that she had ever been unbalanced by his long, smooth stride. Ahead of them, Dunlin walked with quick, surefooted steps, breaking into a trot when the path flattened out into the grassy valley at the head of Lough Inagh.

Nora pictured José standing on the deck of the ship, his peat-dark hair lifted by the breeze as he stared across the endless waves for the first glimpse of his home. Without him, the mountains seemed emptier than before, and when a pair of slanted, yellow eyes gleamed at her from the shadows, Nora gasped out loud before telling herself crossly that it was only a hare. Lir snorted and the eyes vanished at once, with only the faintest whisper of paws over the grass to show where the creature had been.

Lough Inagh stretched out in front of them, silver-gray and still, cleanly dividing the Maam Tuircs from the mountains of

Connemara. Dunlin bucked and cantered for a few strides as if she knew she was nearly home before slowing down to trot beside Lir again. Nora knew that she could walk from here and still be back in Sraith Salach before sunrise; with luck, Mainie wouldn't notice that she had been away all night, and she might even be able to sleep for a while before the children awoke. She would go back to Errislannan soon, she decided. If she was stronger-willed than before, more ready to talk to strangers and go to the feasts at Aughnanure, her brothers and sisters would think only that she was growing up at last. Rescuing José and helping him to escape had been the bravest, most dangerous, and most foolhardy thing Nora had ever done, but she had succeeded. No one could ever tell her again that she lacked courage or wits.

She looked down at the stallion's broad, gray neck and knew that the hardest part was yet to come. For a heartbeat, she wildly considered taking Lir back to Errislannan and persuading her parents to keep him as a work-pony, ready to take over when Ballach grew too old for long journeys to Sraith Salach and Aughnanure. But he was too long-legged to pull their cart, and needed much more grazing than their scrubby square of pasture could provide. And more than that, Dan Devlin would find him at once, and take him away to sell to a chieftain or a merchant in return for keeping quiet about Nora's visit to Galway. Lir only stood a chance of being safe if he stayed out here, deep in the mountains where people rarely came—except the kerns with Murray ne Doe's herds of cattle and Father Francis when he traveled between villages, fearless of the fairies and bog-wraiths who hid in the valleys. None of them would pay any attention to a wild pony that stood several hands taller than the others, whose coat was the color of clouds, and whose tail swept past his hocks to the ground.

And if Dan Devlin carried out his threat and told Nora's parents out of spite because she would not lead him to the Spanish horse, then she would just have to face whatever punishment they saw fit to bring upon her. They need never know exactly why she had gone, and perhaps the very fact that she had come home safely would make them relieved enough not to be too hard on her. She could promise quite truthfully never to go to the city again, that was for sure.

A cold breeze swept across the surface of the lake and Lir danced sideways, his long mane streaming out beside him. Nora squeezed her legs against him and smiled with delight as the stallion broke into a slow, measured canter with his neck arched and his nose tucked close to his chest. She leaned forward and urged him on until his hooves drummed like rain on the springy grass and she saw his forelegs stretching out in front, snatched quickly up as soon as they touched the ground.

Faster and faster they galloped, overtaking Dunlin until they were running alone beside the lake, with the water a silvery blur beside them and the sky paling to the gray of a heron's wing above the mountains. Nora sat up straight with her fingers knotted in Lir's mane and laughed out loud. She felt as if, with a touch of her heels, the stallion would jump over the lake, over the mountains, and soar up through the sky.

They passed the end of the lake and the ground began to slope up toward the end of the valley. Any further, and they would be too close to Sraith Salach and the road that led from Errislannan to Galway. If Nora was going to set the stallion free, it had to be here, out of sight from curious travelers.

Lir slowed to a trot, shaking his head and flicking out his front hooves so that they made a tiny shushing sound against the wet grass. Nora halted him with the lightest pressure on his mane and slid to the ground. Her cheeks were already wet with tears at the thought of what she had to do, and the stallion lowered his head to sniff at the saltwater trails running down her face.

"You are the most precious, beautiful horse I have ever known," Nora whispered into his mane, hugging him so hard that his sweat soaked into her shirt. "This is for your own good, I promise."

She stepped back, brushing angrily at the tears that were dripping off her chin. "Go on, Lir, go," she whispered, gesturing at the empty mountains beyond the lake. "I can't keep you. This is where you belong now."

The stallion turned and blew down his nostrils at her, then tossed his head so that his forelock fell over one eye.

"Shoo!" Nora said desperately, flapping her arms like she did when the cow refused to go into the cottage at night. She somehow had to make Lir understand that he no longer needed people to look after him and find him food. Whatever his life had been like far away in Spain, fate and Manannan mac Lir had brought him here, to these mountains and these gray skies.

"I can't be your friend anymore. No one can. You're a wild horse now." She was crying so hard she could hardly speak, and Lir looked at her curiously, his ears flicking back and forth.

"Please go," Nora sobbed, and she felt a piece of her heart break because she had to send the stallion away like this, believing that she didn't want him anymore. It was the only way she could be sure he didn't befriend the next person who came along, because it might be Dan Devlin, and Nora would rather lose Lir to the mountain ponies than let him be sold as a merchant's riding pony or a chieftain's war horse.

She ran toward the stallion with her arms flailing, stumbling over the grass, her breath coming in noisy gasps. Lir shied away, then stopped and gazed back at her with his ears pricked forward as if he couldn't understand what she was doing. Nora sank to her knees in despair, convinced that she was going to fail.

There was a quiet whinny from behind the stallion, and she

looked up to see Dunlin standing at the head of the lake. The mare whinnied again, and this time Lir wheeled around to face her, his head held high so that Nora had never seen him look more beautiful, or more like a wild, fairy horse. Maybe she couldn't persuade him to leave her and live in the mountains, but Dunlin might. She had been spending less and less time with her herd recently, so perhaps she was willing to break away and be with Lir. Nora felt a smile spread across her face as her imagination raced on: Fiach would not be strong enough to chase Lir away forever, and maybe next year the Spanish horse would take over the herd to begin a long line of foals the color of seafoam with long legs and broad chests.

"Go with her," she murmured, and Lir glanced back at her as if he wanted to be sure that he was really free. Nora stayed very still and watched through a blur of tears as the stallion let out a piercing call that echoed from hill to hill. Then he reared up, carving the air with his front hooves, before galloping away toward Dunlin.

The mare waited until he had nearly reached the shore before trotting up to meet him, holding her tail high and blowing down her nostrils. The two horses sniffed at each other with their necks stretched out as though they had never met before, then wheeled around to canter side by side up the grassy slope, and vanished in the shadows at the foot of the mountain.

Nora stared after them until they were nothing more than the palest smudges, gray and dun, in the half-light. There would be other mountain ponies that she would befriend, starting with Dunlin's foal, Dubh, who was old enough to live without his dam and already well used to Nora visiting his herd. But she would have to leave these two horses alone, to live in the heart of the mountains where people wouldn't find them and where the Spanish stallion could forget that he had ever been tamed and stabled by lords and chieftains.

"Good-bye, Lir," she whispered, feeling the wind whip her hair around her face as it dried the tears on her cheeks. "Be safe, forever."